REVELATIONS

HALLY WILLMOTT

REVELATIONS

Limitless Publishing, LLC
Kailua, HI 96734
www.limitlesspublishing.com

Formatting: Limitless Publishing

ISBN-13: 978-1495496028
ISBN-10: 1495496023

DEDICATION

To my family. Your unwavering support and encouragement has allowed me to 'Dream Big!"

Jerry, Jacob and Jordan; your love and understanding are my pillars of strength when I doubt...me.

Thank you for loving me as you do.

"Let us think of education as the means of developing our greatest abilities, because in each of us there is a private hope and dream which, fulfilled, can be translated into benefit for everyone and greater strength for our nation."

John F. Kennedy *(1917-1963), Thirty-fifth President of the USA*

"Education is the kindling of a flame, not the filling of a vessel."

Socrates, Ancient Greek Philosopher 470 BC-399 BC

"Educating the mind without educating the heart is no education at all."

Aristotle, Ancient Greek Philosopher, Scientist and Physician, 384 BC-322 BC

CHAPTER ONE

Waiting for direction
Hoping to find your way
Unexpected prophecies bring unexpected guests
Nemele
Welcome to the first day of the rest of your life.

As we left the Inception Chamber and headed to the inner sanctum of St. Nemele, my attention was caught up in thoughts of things to come. What was I expected to do with all of the information about my life and the lives of my parents which I'd learned today? What was everyone else expecting from me because of the revelations from today? My mind played on as my body moved on auto-pilot with everyone else who was walking with Herecerti.

I wasn't paying attention while we ventured down corridor after corridor. It wasn't until Herecerti spoke up that I finally left my own thoughts to join everyone else.

"Grace, since you, Hudson, and Jen will be staying, I have arranged for you to stay in the dorm you shared with your sister. I have also arranged for Jen and Jacey to stay with you."

"Yes, Herecerti, thank you," Aunt Grace replied.

I noticed then I wasn't the only one lost within my own thoughts. Aunt Grace was obviously in some state of shock and rightfully so. Who wouldn't be after finding out the husband and daughter you believed to be dead for fourteen years were possibly still alive and had been waiting for family or others to come and rescue them all that time?

"Aunt Grace...?"

"Yes, Jacey?"

"Thanks for staying with me."

"There's no need for you to thank me, Jacey." She stopped and put both hands on my shoulders. She then turned to me so I was facing her. "You're my family, Jacey. I love you and I'll always be here for you and Hudson. There's no other place I'd rather be right now, in this world or any other, than right here with you." She finished and gave me her mom smile, then hugged me.

We didn't say another word as we continued on to our dorm rooms. I began to take in my surroundings. The hallways of Nemele were amazing. They were covered with hand painted murals, each one distinct and separate from the previous. Reoccurring through each were events and beings who'd attended St. Nemele. The paintings appeared to be so life-like, I expected the subjects within them to try and reach out and touch me—I was surprised when not one did.

"They are remembrances of times which have passed. The canvases depict times and events Nemelites have taken part in," Herecerti said while we started up a huge set of stone stairs.

"They include all of the beings within Nemele. They recall our own Origins," Herecerti said as we came to a stop on a large landing. The wall to our immediate right had an engraving directly in the center of it. It looked like a happy face with two dashes at each end of the mouth.

"What does it mean?" I asked Herecerti as we all stood in front of it.

"These are the Primary dorms for males of all species who are Nemelite. This is where Hudson will be staying." As he finished and held his hand up to the symbol, it began to glow.

"When and where are we going to meet in the morning?" Hudson asked, turning to Herecerti.

"You don't have to wait until the morning to see one another. Once I get Jen, Grace, and Jacey settled, you're all welcome to go about the grounds and get acquainted with all there is to offer here. However—" Herecerti paused and looked directly at Hudson. "There are absolutely no males allowed in the Primary wing for females and vice versa." He took a long hard look at Jen.

"Once we've all settled in, I'll show you girls and Hudson around," Aunt Grace offered as she gave Hudson a quick hug.

"I'll be waiting," Hudson replied.

The wall where the symbol had been disappeared and in its place appeared a huge entryway. Hudson turned to it, and right before he entered, he paused and then turned to me.

"We're all going to be okay, you know. You completely blew me away today, Jace, with how together you were in the Inception chamber. Like I've always said, you really are more like your brother than you think." He gave me a wink and a quick half hug. Before he could pull away, I whispered in his ear.

"I'm actually scared to death! Thanks for staying with me."

"No other place in this entire Universe I'd rather be," he whispered back, then turned away and entered the corridor to where he'd be staying.

Before the opening closed, I was able to catch a quick glimpse. Slightly inside and to the right of the entrance stood a massive looking male who appeared to be waiting for Hudson. They greeted one another in traditional Nemelite fashion and continued on their way further into the dorm. Before I could focus enough to make anything else out in the corridor, the entryway shut.

"Let's move on this way." Herecerti said.

While we made our way deeper into the castle's frame, I paid more attention this time. The windows along each passageway were as large as the main entryway'. The main difference between the two was that these were completely formed of stained glass. The colors reflecting from them were brilliant, almost blinding. Within each pane was an illustrative landscape of beings and scenes from origins which I was completely clueless about. I watched in awe as we passed picture after picture. Each one made me realize just how diminutive the human race really was when taking in the entire realm of things.

We came upon an indoor pond surrounded by eight white marble columns. Each one was covered in swirling patterns of intricately carved symbols. Swaddling the columns from top to bottom was green leafy foliage. It encircled the pillars without covering any areas where the carvings existed.

"This is the inner sanctum of Nemele. This pond is called the Infinite Waters and is reflective of all who have been and all who are to be," Herecerti pointed out.

I went over to the pond and peered into its stilled waters. There peering back at me was a reflection of myself. I guess because we were in Nemele, I expected to see some kind of mystical phenomenon when I looked into the pool of water, but there was nothing. The only thing staring back at me was me. As I stood up to follow the others out of the sanctum, I heard Jen gasp.

I turned to my right. Floating over the center of the pool was Mom. This version of her was much younger; like the girl in the albums I'd gone through in Aunt Grace's attic back home. She looked to be about eighteen years old and was wearing a long flowing dress which swayed back and forth as though there was a slight breeze in the room—which, by the way, there wasn't.

"Mom!" I called out as I walked back over to the pool.

She responded but not to me. "Gracie! How cool is this!"

Aunt Grace had followed me back to the pool and was now leaning up against one of the marble pillars. Just above her were two markings which began to glow when she leaned the back of her head against them. They looked like the number three facing each other. Both glowed brilliant yellow and white. As Aunt Grace watched Mom, a single tear travelled down her right cheek. I reached over to her as she silently swept the lone tear from her cheek with the back of her left hand.

"We created this on one of the first nights we came here. We knew we were supposed to wait for instruction on how to prepare a message, but you knew Ria. There was no stopping her when she put her mind to something. She was so excited to have been invited to come here and learn about her powers. There was no way anyone could have stopped her from doing what she wanted to do when she wanted to do it." Aunt Grace looked towards Herecerti.

"I find it quite interesting that we have not come across this transfer before," Herecerti offered, appearing to be somewhat intrigued by the existence of this message.

"Ria did some kind of blinding spell on it so the only beings able to see it would be herself, me, or some generation of her family. I guess you could say we broke more than a few rules that night." Aunt Grace walked over to the hologram of my mom as she finished. She leaned over the pool and attempted to touch the hologram's hand.

A gust of wind, this time one all of us could feel swept through the room. A smile broke across my face. Mom! I knew she wouldn't have missed *everything* from today.

Mom's essence took over the form hovering above the pool. To everyone else looking at the hologram, it didn't change appearance, but to me, as soon as Mom became more materialized, I saw the Mom I knew appear before my eyes.

"Mom!"

"Jacey, your Dad and I tried everything to be there with you in the Inception Chamber, but we couldn't get in. There was an exclusion spell cast upon it," Mom said, turning from me to see Jen, Aunt Grace, and Herecerti all open mouthed, staring at her.

"I guess you now know I tried to put a message in before I was supposed to," Mom sheepishly admitted to Herecerti.

"I have to say the message is nothing compared to the fact *we* are having this conversation right now," Herecerti retorted. "How is this possible?"

"Mom's been appearing to me since her funeral. I don't know how it happens, but I'm more than grateful it's been happening at all," I said.

"Ria!" Aunt Grace exclaimed. She was no longer attempting to hold onto Mom's hand. Mom had completely encompassed her within an embrace as they both hovered over the Infinite Waters.

"Wow," was the only thing Jen was able to say.

"This is... this is...not possible," Herecerti whispered under his breath, barely loud enough for us to hear.

7

"I miss you. Thank you for taking Jacey and Hudson. I love you," Mom said to Aunt Grace.

"I miss you, Ri. I miss you so much. There's so much you need to know." She paused only for a second to catch her breath. "Ri, Faith's alive."

"How? Where?" Mom asked.

"She's in the Shenuy Quarter past the Charta Zone. She appeared in the Inception Chamber, Ri. She looks just like Jacey. She said there are others of *our* kind with her there—maybe I haven't lost everything. Gideon may be with her." Aunt Grace rambled until Mom put her hand on Aunt Grace's shoulder.

"Be wary. I know you remember what we learned after the last battle. You do remember the consequences of all being brought together? I can only hope Gideon is with her now and has been since she was taken from us. I know if they are together, and if there is a possibility of them being rescued and returned to us, there will be much all of us have to prepare for." Mom turned her attention from Aunt Grace and looked at me.

"Jacey, I know a lot was revealed to you in the chamber, but I also know the truth of this revelation and its effects were not discussed. It will bring both good and bad. Herecerti, you have to ensure Jacey is safe. No one is to gain access to her. Hearte and I will go to the Quarter and see what has transpired there. We will report back to you within a day's time. While I'm gone, you must be vigilant in your training and in your protection of one another." Mom paused for only a second, then continued.

"It appears I have the ability to converse with others in this form. I'll return here to continue to communicate in this way. I'll be back here tomorrow night at dusk once I figure out what's going on."

"We have Heathe and others from the Sentry watching Jacey as we speak. They are to stand guard and assist in training over the next week," Herecerti stated.

"Where are they now? How come they have not come forward as I stand here?" Mom asked.

"Some are escorting the elders to their homelands and others have gone with Vincent and Daichi to the Shenuy Quarter. They were instructed to come and stand guard later this evening," Herecerti offered.

"Vincent's gone to the Shenuy Quarter? With who?" Mom asked.

"Daichi. She's the Seeker who followed us from Hewfawe to Nevaeh. The one Jacey met in the rest stop washroom," Jen spoke up.

"She's a Shenuy—a Seeker—and Vincent is with her?" Mom asked.

"Yes, Vincent and a few others returned her to the truce line so her Elders wouldn't know she'd been sent here by Faith. If her Elders found she had come here, they would never allow her to leave the Charta Zone again, which means she wouldn't be able to come back and guide us to the Zone so we could find Faith and Gideon," Aunt Grace said.

"I hadn't realized so much happened in the Chamber. I'm more than a little surprised the Elders allowed our people to escort a *Seeker* to the truce lines. Much has changed. I believe now more than ever, Jacey needs to be protected. Since the Seeker knows where Jacey is, then all will know she's here—Necroseek will know she's here. You can't wait for this evening or sometime later for the Sentry to be here, they must be here now!" Mom urged.

"Grace, I of all people want nothing more than to rejoice with you in finding Faith, but…" she paused for a minute as Aunt Grace backed out of the pool to stand beside me. "But I think we know what this means. It means the prophecy of the Nephilim is upon us—" Before Mom could finish, Jen spoke up.

"One will be virtuous while the other shall—bear a resemblance in an attempt to deceive, but with sureness ought to befall the core of depravity—" Jen stopped. It looked as though all of the blood had drained from her face.

"We will see you at the hour requested," Herecerti cut in. He then pulled Jen and I out of the inner sanctum of Nemele towards another long stone hallway which ended in a large stone wall with a symbol carved into it. It looked like a cross with two markings in the upper left side. The marks looked like two elongated quote marks. Aunt Grace silently followed without any prompting from Herecerti.

"This is the Primary dorm for females where you, Jen, and Grace will be staying. There is a guide inside waiting to escort you." Herecerti put his hand up to the symbol. It glowed and the wall dissolved into itself. It revealed a large cavern of marble and stone. Herecerti turned to leave.

"You aren't going to stay with us?" I asked, feeling very unsure of myself for some reason.

"I have much to follow up on since the visit from your mother. You are in safe hands here. The Sentry are here and I'm certain you are well guarded. I will return for you in the morning. Your schedule and lessons have already been set for the next week's training." Herecerti turned to leave again.

"But when will I know what's happened to Vincent? Or when he returns or where he is now?" I was now definitely feeling the stress of today's events. My proverbial blanket of calmness Vincent had tucked me into earlier was slipping.

"We will be fine, Herecerti. I know you have much to look into. I'll make sure all is okay here," Aunt Grace said, placing her hands on my shoulders.

"In the morning, then," Herecerti said. He disappeared from view and the wall reappeared before me.

"We'll be fine. Now let's go and see who has been chosen to show us around," Aunt Grace said, ushering both Jen and I into the cavern.

As I started to feel a little more at ease, a flash of red turned my calm into a moment of déjà vu. Standing at the end of the hallway was none other than Chanary.

"Great—" I mumbled to myself.

Instinctively, Jen grabbed onto my hand.

"Just breathe. Don't let her get to you," she whispered.

"Well, well. Here we are again. Hi, I'm Chanary," she said as she held her hand out to my aunt.

Aunt Grace must have felt the tension radiating off me. She looked my way with one eyebrow raised while she greeted Chanary in the traditional Nemele.

"I've been chosen to show you around," Chanary chimed in, flashing me her most annoying Cheshire cat grin yet.

"Welcome to Nemele and the first day of the rest of your life," she finished. I turned back to look at the reformed wall behind us, thinking *great...no escape route there*.

CHAPTER TWO

Signs, signs everywhere there's signs....
Which ones do you follow?
Which ones do you avoid?
The ones which tell all...
They never lie

Great, of all things I needed at this particular moment in my life—Chanary. She definitely wasn't one of my top ten. Heck she didn't even crest the top one thousand of my need now list. How was I supposed to 'follow' someone I could barely stand to look at? As my mind wound in a million different directions, Aunt Grace's hand gently tapped my shoulder.

"Patience; all is as it should be. Know Chanary was chosen for a reason. Don't let your feelings of anger and frustration cloud your better judgement," she said with a slight squeeze to my shoulder.

I had to keep my feelings bottled up—at least for now. Within these walls I truly was at Chanary's mercy.

"Since I'm a Junior here and Heathe's sister, the Elders thought it best I show you around. I know Grace has been here before, but the Elders still thought a guide would be helpful."

"Thank you. I'm sure you'll do a fine job," Aunt Grace replied.

We followed Chanary down an oversized hallway. Jen had pretty much attached herself to my arm, watching my every move.

As I trudged on, I made it a point to look anywhere except in the direction of Chanary. The hall was decorated with scenes from beings which had once attended here. As it came to an end, a scene captured within a remembrance caught not only my attention, but Aunt Grace's as well.

It was one of her with Mom, Dad, and a man I now knew as Uncle Gideon. They were standing in front of a garden maze which resembled the one in Nevaeh.

"Where was this taken?" I asked Aunt Grace.

"At the same Bulwark you entered today. It was the first day we came here to Nemele. The Nemele you entered through the maze in the center of town didn't exist when this picture was taken. The maze used to bring us directly here until the battle of Lythea—the battle where Gideon was lost. Lythea's the small village on the truce line between Yietimpi and Nemele, where the battle ended and the treaty was signed," Aunt Grace said.

I was filled with more questions but knew Aunt Grace had gone through enough today. I would save them for another time. We left the hall and came to a landing which overlooked a huge cylindrical chasm. Lining the walls were a number of entrances to different hallways.

"Each level contains different beings at different intervals of training here. Since you *aren't* a training member here, you and Jen will be staying in the lower level. Since Grace is a graduate member, Herecerti made arrangements for her to stay in the room she and Ria shared," Chanary stated.

"Herecerti said Jen and Jacey would be staying with me. They will not be staying in the lower level," Aunt Grace asserted. Chanary's face turned the same crimson color of her hair. It was obvious Aunt Grace had left no room for question. I had to admit, it made me smile inside.

"If that's what Herecerti said, then I'll show you the way to your dorm and leave you to reacquaint yourself with the level," Chanary replied, composing herself rather quickly.

There were engravings to the right of Chanary on the wall behind us. They were the same symbols which were embroidered on the seats and carved above the murals the Elders had in the Inception Chamber.

"There are nineteen levels in each of the dorm areas. Each level is representative of all of our Nations," Chanary answered, as though I had spoken my thoughts out loud.

"Each of the levels has a number of outcroppings which coincide with the training rank each being holds," Chanary said, lifting her hand to the engraving which had adorned the back of Bronson's seat.

Instantly, a stairwell formed, spiralling through the chasm. It led to a chamber with a large ‫ת‬ engraved overhead.

"For now, since Herecerti told Grace you are all staying together, you'll all be here on the fifth elements level. This is the level where *graduating* or graduated—members stay." Chanary turned to glare my way with one of her many faces. Not surprisingly, she was able to flash a completely innocent look towards my aunt at the same time.

"Thank you, Chanary. I know the way to the room where we'll be staying. If we need anything else, I'm sure we'll be able to locate you on the *first* level of this section," Aunt Grace said, completely straight-faced and doe-eyed.

"I won't be on the *first* level, I'm on the third. Heathe is going to be standing guard at the entrance with a Sentry detail of ten. *If* you need me, all you have to do is channel it and I'll show up wherever you are in the building. May the elements be with you." She held her hands to her chest, then turned on the balls of her feet, and *poof* she was gone in a flash of red and green light.

"Well, I think that went well," I said with a giggle.

"We need not worry about her. Let's get to our room," Aunt Grace said, leading us down the hallway adjacent to the stairwell.

We passed a number of people as we ventured towards our room. Each one looked—normal. They all appeared human.

"We're part of the Genapiene clan, one of the nineteen which make up Nemele. In Earth terms, human beings."

"Let me get this straight. There are nineteen Nations of Nemele," I said.

"Yes," Aunt Grace answered.

"One of them is humans?"

"Yes," she answered again.

"Who makes up the other nineteen?" I questioned as we stopped in front of a door with what looked like the letter 'C' engraved in it.

"You'll learn who and what make them up over the next week while you attend classes here. Remember the Inception Chamber? There were nineteen Elders represented there. Each one of those Elders represents the Nations which make up Nemele," Aunt Grace replied as she held her hand up to the symbol.

Another hallway appeared as the door faded. We entered through a stone archway which led to an enormous opening. There were people everywhere. The opening had a number of hallways and stairwells running from it in a hundred different directions.

"Wow," was all I could say.

"The center concourse leads to all of the dormitories. At any given time, there may be hundreds of people milling about here," Aunt Grace said, ushering Jen and I towards our room. I took a look up and was blown away. The ceiling was a prism of Visionaries. Each of them had a different landscape within. They all looked like places on Earth, places you'd expect to see humans.

17

"Humans are not solely within 'Earth's realms, Jacey. They reside throughout the Universes. Each of the eight Visionaries above depict eight different worlds—all Earth-like, but not all of Earth," Aunt Grace said.

"There's so much I don't know," I admitted.

"But there's so much you are going to learn," Aunt Grace said, leading Jen and I off to a hallway in the far right of the concourse.

We came upon a room which had the number 707 carved into the door. Aunt Grace held her hand up to it and it faded away. We entered the room where we'd be staying for the next while.

The room was nothing like you'd expect to see in a dorm. It was more like a mini apartment. There was a living space as soon as you walked in. One of the walls was a visionary, ceiling to floor. There was furniture scattered around it. Off in the far right was a kitchen area with a four chair dinette in the center of it. In the middle and back left of the room were three doors.

"There are three bedrooms back there. I'll take the one closest to the kitchen and you girls can pick from the other two," Aunt Grace said, heading towards her room.

I went to the middle room and Jen headed to the far left one. I entered my room. In it was a simple bed, dresser, and nightstand. I sat on the edge of the bed to take in my surroundings. Looking at the ceiling, I expected to see the same wood which made up the walls of the room. I was astonished to see a visionary staring down at me.

I jumped up off the bed and went out into the living room.

"Aunt Grace—" I called out, knocking on her door.

"Jacey, is there something wrong?" she asked.

"No, sorry...I noticed there's a visionary on my ceiling."

"There's one in every dorm room," she answered.

"How do you use it?"

"Come on, I'll show you," she said, heading towards my room.

Inside the entrance to the right was a clear glass panel. It was the size of my hand.

"All you need to do is put your hand up to it and visualize what you want to see," Aunt Grace said as she put her hand up to the glass.

Instantly, the ceiling in my room changed from black to Aunt Grace's home back in Nevaeh.

"Wow, how cool is that! How did you do that?" I asked.

"All you need to do is visualize what you want to see and it appears within the visionary. There are a few rules though," Aunt Grace said, escorting me over to sit on the edge of my bed.

"These Visionaries will only allow you to view what is acceptable within public realms. That means no trying to sneak any peeks into places you shouldn't be. If you happen to try and go into an area which would be restricted, it automatically sends the attempt to the headmaster—Herecerti— and that's a conversation you don't want to have," she said with a hint she'd had one of them in the past.

"I won't go where I'm not supposed to. But does this mean I can visualize Vincent and see where he is?" I asked, full of hope.

"No, dear. The place has to be a structure or a location. These Visionaries would never allow for the intrusion upon a person. The only way you could see Vincent was if you knew where he was going to be."

"Thanks…"

"One other thing," she said, getting up to go over to the door. "These wall enhancers are only there for those who are unsure of their powers—those who have not been able to assume their natural forms. Once you can assume your form, all you do is float up to the visionary and touch it directly."

"What's with the one in the living room?" I asked.

"It's for all of us to use, but it's also the main communication device for those here in Nemele. When you need a question answered or a map to show where you need to be, it appears within it."

"So, that's what Chanary meant when she said you could contact her anywhere here."

"Yes. Not to say we couldn't get some television shows on it—we could seriously attempt it," Aunt Grace said as she left the room.

What did I want to see? I already knew who I wanted to see—Vincent—that was a no-brainer. If I had to limit myself to structures or locations, only one made sense to me.

I walked over to the panel and placed my hand upon it. I returned to my bed and flopped down on it.

Looking up, I was comforted by memories and a sense of home —flashing down upon me was the ceiling from my old house in Hewfawe. There floating above me were Ria, Hearte, Rife, Tawer, Nidw and Kawanening.

Being able to bring a bit of my old life here helped me settle—a little. I knew I was going to need something to help remind me where I truly was now... and what better way than to have the signs which had been my anchor to reality in my previous life...

CHAPTER THREE

Travelling along a path
Waiting for the answers
Not hearing what you want

"Jacey, do you and Jen want to go meet up with Hudson now?" Aunt Grace asked from behind my closed door.

"Yeah, sounds good. Just give me a minute," I replied. I got up and went over to the dresser in the far corner of the room. The mirror affixed to it reflected the same image of the girl who had looked into one this morning—I was wearing the same black Aero Capris and beige short sleeved Hollister hoodie.

"I might look the same, but I sure as heck don't feel the same," I mumbled to myself. I pulled open one of the dresser drawers and folded within were my clothes from Aunt Grace's. "What the…" I went over to the closet and hanging within were the rest of my clothes and shoes.

"Yeah, like I should be surprised..." I changed into a pair of dark blue jeans and a long sleeved purple shirt with thumb holes. It nicely covered the Seeker brand Daichi had branded me with in our not so pleasant washroom episode days ago. I had to admit, having it covered made me feel less self-conscious about it.

I exited my room and found Aunt Grace and Jen in the living room.

"Ready to go?" I asked.

"Let's sit for a minute," Aunt Grace said.

"Sure, what's up?"

"Grace and I want to know how you're feeling," Jen asked.

"How I'm feeling? Right now, numb...I knew there was going to be a lot to take in today but—I never expected so much."

"There was no other way to reveal everything to you. Time obviously wasn't on our side and all of us knew it needed to be done. If not for you and your safety, for everyone else's," Aunt Grace said. "In revealing everything to you today, I was so wrapped up in it, I forgot about the Nephilim Prophecy and in turn, forgot about the dangers until Ria reminded us."

"At least we're aware of it so we can prepare. Heathe and the others are waiting for us outside... So, we know we're protected within Nemele. I'm more worried about everyone outside of here," Jen said.

"Like Vincent." My heart jumped as I said his name.

"Yeah, like Vincent and all of the others who went with him," Aunt Grace said.

"Are the Elders aware of the prophecy?" I was sure they were, but were they as worried as Mom had seemed to be about it?

"They're aware. They, like most of us, were not as concerned about it. Our priority, as I said earlier, was to reveal everything to you and find out why Daichi was here and what her motives were," Aunt Grace said.

"Well, we now know *why* she was here—her message was pretty clear. But now I'm second guessing her motives. Are you guys doing the same?" They were silent for a moment before Jen answered.

"I'm sure her message was real—Faith and Gideon are alive and in the Charta Zone. But I'm leaning more towards what your mom said, Jacey. We totally need to slow down and study the prophecy to ensure we all aren't running into a trap."

"Is that what you think I sent Vincent into?" I asked, choking on the last syllable.

"You didn't send Vincent into anything. He chose to go. I believe prophecies are subjective. They say what the person reading them wants them to. We need to slow down, take a deep breath, and take a serious look at what we need to do," Aunt Grace said.

"I think Hudson will be able to help us make a decision here. Can we go see him now? Please..." Jen pleaded.

"I think you're right. Let's go," I said, getting up from the couch and making my way to the doorway.

As I held my hand up, Jen placed her hand on my arm. "I'm with you no matter what," she stated without faltering.

"I know," I replied, squeezing her hand in a reassuring gesture.

As the doorway faded and I exited, a flash of green and red formed in front of me.

"Heathe…" I stated, rolling my eyes and chuckling a bit. I couldn't help but picture him flying across the Inception Chamber when he didn't listen when I warned him about Daichi.

"Jacey," he retorted.

"What can I possibly do for you now?" I asked, not hiding my irritation.

"It's not what you can do for me, it's what I can do for you," he said smugly.

"What you can do for me…is find Vincent, make Necroseek disappear, and quit trying to come across like I need you! " I replied before I could take three deep breaths.

"Seriously, you think I think you need me…That's a laugh. How's this for a suggestion, we learn to deal with one another because I'm not going anywhere and neither are you," he said through clenched teeth.

"That's pretty obvious. I know you'd rather be somewhere else and personally, I'd rather you be there too," I said through clenched teeth of my own.

"Time out! Back to your corners," Jen said, placing herself between the two of us. "Heathe, you must have shown yourself for some reason. What is it?" Jen asked.

"I only wanted to ask where you were going. I didn't want to just follow you," he replied.

"We're going to find Hudson and look around Nemele," Aunt Grace answered.

"Can't you channel him from your room? He could come…" Before he could finish I cut him off.

"Yeah, we could have but I'm not going to sit around and go nuts in that room waiting for things to be shown to me or for someone to come looking for me." Wow, I was being a bit more aggressive than usual. Why, I couldn't tell you, other than he was here and Vincent wasn't.

"I've been *assigned* to you. I didn't *ask* for it…and by the way, I didn't *want* it! So, let's try and make this as painless as possible. I'm not going anywhere, no matter how much it bothers you. From now on while you're here, I won't be forming in front of you, but I will be guarding you." A flash of green and red sparked in front of me and Heathe was gone.

"What was that?" I asked Jen and Aunt Grace.

"That was a pissed off Sentry guard," Jen replied, not hiding the chuckle in her voice.

"I for one am more than a little taken aback by that display. I'm grateful he won't be showing up in form anytime soon. Heathe, I know you can hear me, let's pull the drama back and not have a repeat of that," Aunt Grace said, obviously flustered by Heathe's outburst and disappearance.

"Alrighty then," I said, moving towards the exit into the main area of the concourse.

"What was that all about?" Jen asked.

"I didn't like the way he treated Daichi back in the Inception Chamber," I replied.

"Well, get used to him. He's going to be around us for as long as the Elders see fit," Aunt Grace replied. "And you may want to mind your words. You're being watched when we're out here."

"Are we watched in our rooms, too?" I asked, now feeling very intruded upon.

"No, not in our rooms. Only in open public places," Jen said.

We left the hallway of our level and entered the concourse. There were more than a hundred people milling about in the main area of the dormitory.

"How do you know we aren't watched?" I asked.

"When?" Jen asked.

"In our rooms? How do you know they don't watch us in our rooms?" I asked again.

"The Visionaries won't allow it. They aren't only mirrors into other worlds, they are intelligent beings in their own right," Aunt Grace said.

"They're alive?" I asked.

"They are in their own way. They were gifted to our race a long time ago. When they were, we were told they wouldn't allow anyone to peer in on any private moments. For all the eons I've been around, I've never witnessed them on anything other than public areas," Aunt Grace said.

"Eons? How old are you, Aunt Grace?" I asked.

"I'm quite old in human years. I would be forty in human years, so in Nemele years, I'd be closer to four hundred years old." She stopped as she revealed her true age to me.

"W-what! How—well, then how old were Mom and Dad?"

"Ria was younger than me, but not by much. She was two hundred and fifty when she left. She would have been 350 this year if she and Hearte would have stayed with us," Aunt Grace said.

"Time here and time on Earth pass differently. Earth is, well, its time is seeded to move along faster. Here, time is not measured on clocks by seconds and minutes or on a calendar. Here it is measured by moon eclipses. We still have night and day, but in one cycle you could have twenty nights and twenty days, but they would be equivalent to one Earth day," Jen said.

"I do have a lot left to learn. Does that mean that Vincent will be gone longer than I thought?" I asked.

"It may seem longer to you because you're not accustomed to our time yet. So, it will feel like he is gone longer," Aunt Grace said.

"Great…" I mumbled.

We passed through the concourse and headed to the main chasm of our dormitory wing. Walking along, I tried to calculate the time when Vincent would be returning. I never thought calculus was going to be important in my life, but I was wrong again. I gave up after the tenth attempt. By then we had re-entered Nemele's main corridors.

"The days will soon pass easier, Jacey. They may seem long at first, but I know Herecerti has much planned for your training. It will keep you occupied," Aunt Grace said as she led us back to Hudson's dorm area.

He was waiting in the hall outside when we arrived. Jen went to him and they embraced, then greeted each other in the traditional Nemelite way—hands intertwined, placed over Jen's heart.

Jen calmed instantly once they were together and their newfound mood spread out to both Aunt Grace and I.

"You okay, Jace?" Hudson asked.

"I'm fine. We need to figure some things out, though. Like this Nephilim Prophecy," I replied, not making eye contact.

"There's way more to it than that. What's going on, Jace? Talk to me," Hudson said.

"Can't right now. We have people listening in," was all I said.

"What are you talking about?"

"The Sentry and Heathe are here. They've been assigned to guard Jacey," Jen said.

"We need to get to the archives of Nemele. We have to research the prophecy and the Charta Zone," Aunt Grace said.

"Let's go," I said, leading the way away from Hudson's dorm.

"I'm going to point out a few areas for you to acquaint yourself with as we move along to the archives," Aunt Grace said.

Jen and Hudson straggled on behind Aunt Grace and I. I knew I was being a tad bit cranky at this point, but my mind was totally consumed with worry about Vincent. Where was he now? Who was he with? Was he safe?

"How long will he be gone?" I asked Aunt Grace.

"I don't know, Jacey. Originally I thought he'd be gone for less than one cycle. But with the prophecy coming back to us, I think he may be gone longer than anticipated."

"What's that mean?"

"Jacey, I don't know if he's heading into a trap or not. I don't know what's going to happen to Vincent," Aunt Grace said, stopping and facing me.

"But, but why can't we warn him? Why can't we go for him? Why can't..."

"Stop. Breathe," Jen said, coming up to me and encompassing me in an embrace.

"Why would we let him leave if we knew it was a trap? Why would they do that?" I asked, sobbing into Jen's shoulder.

"Because we didn't know," Heathe said, appearing before me.

CHAPTER FOUR

Looking for answers
Not finding what you need
Comfort from unexpected places

"What do you mean you didn't know?" I yelled at Heathe, like this was all his fault.

"We didn't pay as much attention to the prophecy like your mother said we should have. We need to be calm and try to connect with Vincent and warn him," Heathe said.

"And how am I supposed to do that? Can you tell me? If I could warn him, don't you think I would have already?" I screeched.

A crowd had started to gather around us and I began to feel hot and anxious. My mind was racing. I was envisioning all these terrible things happening to Vincent, all because of me…yet again…

My breathing quickened and my hands started to glow white hot.

"What—wh—what's happening? Why am I feeling like this?" Before I could get out what I wanted to say, Heathe grabbed me before I hit the floor. My knees gave out and my eyes started dilating, giving me tunnel vision.

"Shhh, it's okay, I'll take care of you. I promised him I would and I won't let anything happen to you—ever," Heathe said over and over again as consciousness ran from me. What was with me passing out and having hot guys hold onto me telling me everything was going to be okay? Heathe grabbed onto my hand, and for reasons I can't explain, our hands intertwined in a traditional greeting. As they did, a shot of adrenalin burst through my body. I grabbed onto him—my life jacket analogy ran through my mind—hold on like your life depends on it. As I did, a hot, pleasant, electric feeling shocked the hand Heathe held and our eyes connected right before darkness engulfed me.

A pleasant warm breeze caressed my cheek. I was curled up on a hard, concrete floor. I sat up and a rush of my dream colors came at me. I was blinded for a second or two and when my eyes refocused, I stood and knew I was still unconscious.

I was standing in my new room back at Aunt Grace's house, only the room was fitted the way it had been in my dream, which I now knew was about Faith and me when we were babies.

"Hello…" I called out, hoping, wanting someone, anyone to answer me.

There was a long moment of silence and then finally a voice answered. "Jacey." It was Faith's voice. "Turn around," she said.

I did, and standing under the frame of the door between my room and Jen's was Faith. She was tracing the engravings on the doorway with her fingers. The symbols were glowing red hot.

"Forever family, neither time nor distance shall break the ties that bind," Faith chanted as she traced the symbols one more time, then focused her attention on me. The symbols' colors subdued, but still moved as though alive with her touch. They reflected off the doors and encompassed Faith as she stood there. Encircling the symbols and Faith was the infinity symbol, flowing a deep rusted brown color—seemingly holding everything together.

"It's the saying our parents grew up reading every day of their lives. It became their motto. Family..." Faith said, now staring wordlessly at me.

I approached her with my hand out. "Stop. I will only be able to hold you here for a small amount of time and if you interrupt the portal, I don't know will happen."

"The portal? What's the portal?" I asked.

"The niche this doorway frames when its symbols are connected. You have to trace them and chant its saying in a few different dialects. It took me some time to figure it out, but here I am."

"Where are you? Where's Vincent and Daichi?" I asked, stopping directly in front of her. Our resemblance was astounding. She was me but blonder and blue-eyed.

"I thought they were with you. They haven't returned yet. I had hoped it would have only taken a quarter of a cycle for me to hear from them but I appear to be wrong."

"Returned to you...Vincent was only bringing Daichi to the truce line. He wasn't going to travel to see you. The Elders hadn't figured out how we were going to rescue you and Gideon yet," I said.

"I only meant Daichi would have been able to communicate with me at the truce lines and that was where she would have returned. They may be held up at one of the Bulwarks. The fundamental Seekers I warned you about in the Inception Chamber were not easily swayed when I said Daichi had gone to retrieve some information for them. They may have intercepted Daichi and Vincent before they got to the truce line, but—"

"Intercepted? Why? What would they do with them?" I interrupted, my voice rising.

"But," she prolonged the 't', "I would have heard something by now if they had been detained. I think they are being extra vigilant not to leave traces behind and that's why they haven't arrived yet."

"You think? How and when will we know?" I asked, louder than I meant. As I did, my palms began to itch and burn. I looked down to them. They had started to glow white again.

"Breathe, Jacey. That's how I was able to communicate with you," she said, pointing to my hands.

"What?"

"Because I was able to connect with you in the Inception Chamber through Daichi, I was able to re-establish the bond we had as children. I was able to link our signatures. In doing so, I can feel what you feel. So tonight as I was sitting waiting for Daichi, I felt your anxiety. I thought something terrible happened. There was only one way I believed I could get to you to make sure you were okay— through this portal. I had been trying to get it to work for years but it never would—until tonight."

"You can *feel* me?" I asked, suddenly very uneasy

"I can. I can only feel intense emotion right now. When we're reunited, I'm sure we'll be able to feel more. But right now, with the distance and the fact your parents hadn't raised you in our ways, I'm the only one in this pairing who can summon you."

"Summon me?" I was starting to feel like Hudson here. Not actually saying more than one or two words, but still having a conversation nonetheless.

"I felt your emotion, I chanted the aphorism, and suddenly I appeared here," she said, obviously proud of herself. "I didn't know how it was going to work, but it brought you here."

"It didn't bring me here. It made me pass out and only brought my essence here. See the room?" I asked.

She turned within the door's arch and the symbols boundary, taking in the two rooms.

"Yes," she answered, now looking back at me, confused.

"The rooms don't look this way now. This is how they looked when we were babies. So, here," I said, sweeping my arms out, indicating both rooms, "isn't in the *now*."

She was quiet for a moment, obviously contemplating what I'd said. "How did you get here then?" she asked.

"I passed out. I started to panic a bit and my hands got all white and burning and then *poof*! I was here," I said, looking down at my hands, which had stopped itching and glowing.

"*Poof*...really?" she said a little too sarcastically.

"Yeah, *poof*. I woke here, but I'm—the physical me—isn't here. It's back in Nemele."

"Well, I guess there's a few more secrets to this portal that I need to uncover. I thought bringing you here would have helped you...saved you from the pain you were feeling. I didn't know it was going to cause you to pass out," Faith answered.

"The pain is gone, but my confusion is at an all time high. How do I get back and where are Vincent and the others?" I asked.

"The getting back part is easy. I can close the portal and you'll return to Nemele. Vincent and the others..." She paused. "They should have Daichi here by half a cycle. For you it will feel more like ten days."

"Ten days. No one told me that. I thought he'd be back by night fall," I murmured.

"Night fall within the cycle, Jacey. Not night fall in the terms you grew up in," she answered.

The colors around her started to shimmer bright and the infinity symbol began to glow a deep black.

"What's going on?" I asked.

"The drawing back at home must be fading. It means this portal is closing and I'll be returning to the Charta Zone."

"Wait! Before you go, how are we going to be able to talk—how are we going to know if Daichi and Vincent are all right?" I asked, reaching out to her.

"I'll re-open the portal and summon you again. Next time I'll try to give you some warning so it doesn't cause you to pass out. Until then, I can still visit in your dreams." She was starting to dim.

"Faith, I didn't get to ask you about the Nep—" As I was saying it, she disappeared and the doorway between the rooms slammed shut. I jumped back, tripping over the corner of the bed in the middle of the room.

Not only had the portal shut, but the room changed back to present day. I lay back on the bed and stared up to the ceiling. Summon me...This encounter compared to the one in the Inception Chamber was quite different. Within the Chamber, Faith looked all prim and proper. She played the role of long lost daughter trying to get home. Here, she looked and sounded more, in charge. Strange, I know, but very true...who did she think she was?

I looked up to the ceiling, raised my hand and began to air trace its symbols. They began to move. As they did, the Bulwark in the middle of town appeared above me. Kawanening was moving as it had the first day I entered it. I reached up and was sucked into the Bulwark.

It felt the same as when I travelled through it earlier today, but the elemental symbols were brighter and moving at a quicker pace. It smelled like cinnamon and saffron—the odors Vincent said he smelled as he went through the Bulwark.

I didn't exit the Bulwark as I had this morning. I stayed suspended within it. I reached out, running my fingers through the symbols and feeling all of their textures.

"Jacey..." It was Vincent's voice.

I turned, and floating beside me was Vincent's pure form—blue eyes and all. I reached out to hold him but my hands went through him instead.

"Are you okay?" I asked, bringing my hands back down to my sides.

"We're fine. The need to conceal our travels has taken more time than we originally thought. But we should be home within half a cycle," he said, bringing what would have been his hand up towards my face and brushing a wayward strand of hair behind my ear.

The instant he touched me, my blanket of calm from earlier was replaced and of course my heart rate increased as it felt a tugging from him.

"Can you come home now?" I pleaded. "Things have changed and I'm so worried about you."

"We're too far gone to return now. But there's no need to worry. I will return to you, soon."

As we were talking, Vincent began to take his human shape.

"I need to warn you. You and all of the others are in—" As I was talking, his body shifted back to his elemental form and began to disappear.

"No, no, no! Come back!" I yelled.

"Jacey, I need to finish our mission and I will return to you."

"Please, come back," I called out.

The symbols within the Bulwark glowed a bright white before fading. I was back in Nemele, laying on a hard surface. I tried to sit up, but Aunt Grace reached over and placed her hands on my shoulders, holding me down.

"Jacey, thank Nemele. You're in the infirmary. We're all here. Lay back," she said, brushing her hand across my forehead sweeping my bangs away from my eyes.

"Hudson, Jen! She's awake," Aunt Grace called out.

"I'm okay. I saw Vincent," I said, causing the commotion in the room to halt.

"What happened? Where did you go?" Hudson asked, coming up on my other side.

"Faith called me. Better yet, as she put it...I was *summoned*." I said, pulling myself up into a seated position on the bed.

"Faith?" Aunt Grace asked.

"Yeah. She said we re-connected in the Inception Chamber and she can now feel what I feel." I was now sitting upright and taking in my surroundings.

We were in a room painted bright white with pot light fixtures. There were some machines over in the far right corner and a door directly in front of me. The door was closed. I heard a commotion outside which drew my attention away from the room.

"Well, I'm going to talk to her now!" It was a male's voice but I couldn't make it out—it was muffled by the doorway.

As I strained to hear who it was, the doorway disappeared and standing in the frame, more like, filling the frame, was Heathe. I was surprised by my reaction. I wanted to yell at him to get lost, but with his presence, a tingling sensation found a place deep in my stomach. I wasn't so sure why, but I think it had something to do with when we 'connected' earlier.

He entered the room, all full of himself, and came to stand at the foot of my bed.

"So, you're up," he said.

"Yeah, I am," I replied.

His face softened a little at the abrasiveness of my reply. He smirked. "What happened?"

"Wouldn't we all like to know," Jen said, coming up from behind him and over to Hudson's side. She encompassed me in a tight embrace and then stood beside him. Everyone was staring down at me, wordless, waiting for me to talk.

"I don't know where I was. I only know Vincent hasn't returned Daichi to the Charta Zone yet, Faith has an ability to knock me out from wherever she is in the universe, and your old room with Mom is a portal," I said to everyone in the room. My gaze lingered on Heathe for a second longer than the rest. *And I know there's something going on with you and me—what it is, I haven't a clue…yet.* I thought as I wound my hands together in my lap.

CHAPTER FIVE

Realities set in
Becoming aware
Time has changed

"Faith said she expected it to take a least half a cycle for Vincent to return. That means ten days, right?" I asked.

"It does. So, we have half a cycle to review the prophecy and then act. If Vincent isn't back by then, we move," Heathe said, backing up and taking a place at the end of the bed.

"It means we have half a cycle to review more than the prophecy," Herecerti said as he entered the room. "I take it you are feeling better?" he asked, coming to stand beside Aunt Grace.

"Yeah, I am. Faith summoned me to the room Aunt Grace and Mom shared as children. But it wasn't in the present. The room was set up like it would have been when she and I were in it as babies. She looked surprised when I pointed it out to her." I paused for a second, thinking about how

41

to approach what I was going to say next. "Faith didn't seem like she was in the chamber. It was more like she was in charge—like she was put off when I told her we weren't in the here and now. She said she'd been working on getting the portal to work for a long time and it wasn't until she and I reconnected in the Inception Chamber that she was able to do it at all. Aunt Grace, did you know the doorway was a portal?" I asked.

"We did. We also sealed it when Faith was kidnapped. Our family had used it to visit our relatives throughout the galaxies. It was one of the only ways we were able to visit our parents while they were away with other family," Aunt Grace answered.

"I have grandparents?" I asked.

"You did, I mean you do, but we haven't been able to communicate with them since we had to seal the portal. They closed it from their side and we secured it from ours. With Faith being able to open it, this may mean we'll be able to communicate with them again," Aunt Grace said.

"No one has lost hope in connecting with Joseph and Violet," Herecerti said. "But we have to take into account Jacey's rendition of the portal being opened within another time. The portal is not as much a priority as the prophecy and keeping Jacey safe. I have arranged for a Hinderer to attend the infirmary and place a block on her. It will impede Faith's summoning to an extent," Herecerti said as he headed for the exit.

"Hold up, we're doing what? I can't stop Faith from contacting me. If I do, then I won't be able to know what's going on with Vincent," I said, starting to freak out a little. My abrasiveness slowed Herecerti's departure and caused Jen to pinch me.

"The Hinderer will only place a block upon you so you can regulate who and what communicates with you. If you completely block her, it will be by your choice. This will prevent another episode of Heathe bowling over beings in an attempt to get you to an infirmary when you black out," Herecerti said, looking at a very flushed Heathe.

"We didn't know what had happened to her and I knew transporting her here through the corridors would be faster than waiting for the infirmary staff," Heathe mumbled defensively.

"From now on you will utilize the emergency corridors you were shown—correct Heathe?" Herecerti stated.

"Yes."

"No need to dwell upon it, considering the Hinderer's help should ensure there are no reoccurrences," Herecerti said as he continued to the doorway. He turned to me. "I'm pleased to see you are fine. We'll meet within the archives when you're dismissed from here." He nodded and left. The door reformed upon his departure.

"So, you knocked some people out?" I asked with a slight chuckle.

"No, he merely flashed through them as you knocked them over," Aunt Grace said.

"What?" I asked, very confused.

"We had no idea what happened and the instant you passed out, Heathe flashed into Sentry form and flew you through the corridors. He went *through*

43

beings—*you* knocked them over," Jen said, looking back and forth between Heathe and I.

"It's dealt with now, so let's move on," Heathe said, looking uncomfortable.

"Okay, when can I leave?" I asked.

"The Hinderer should be here soon. We can leave when they're done," Aunt Grace said.

"What's he going to do to me?" I asked.

"They'll give you a medallion to wear. It will have some elements within it which they've specifically chosen to keep you blocked. They're going to give you an axiom—that's their word for saying or motto—to chant when you feel a presence you don't want to communicate with," Aunt Grace said.

"Hudson, did you know we had grandparents?" I asked.

"Not until recently," he said, eying Aunt Grace and Heathe.

"When?" I asked.

"About two minutes before you found out," he said as Jen placed her arm around his waist and pulled him into her side.

"Are there any other relatives we should know about?" I asked Aunt Grace.

"No. Your grandparents have been gone a long time and all of us believed they fell to Necroseek's fundamentalist followers. I know my parents, and if they could have returned to us, we would have heard or seen them by now," Aunt Grace said.

"But you thought the same about Faith and Gideon. Now we know they're alive and waiting for us. Could that mean my grandparents are doing the same?" I asked.

"I did believe Gideon was lost to me, but I never gave up hope of finding Faith. I knew they wouldn't harm her. She's too valuable to them. I believe anything is possible—it may mean a trip home to see if I can reconnect with my parents. We never tried after the attack on you and Faith because we closed it for everyone's safety."

A rustling from the doorway caught our attention and stopped the conversation. The doorway dissolved and a girl about twenty appeared within the frame.

"Verbeyna, what are you doing here?" Heathe asked.

"I'm the hinderer Herecerti asked to help with Jacey," she replied. I watched as she passed Heathe and glanced at him. He looked away and fixed his stare on the opposite side of the room.

Verbeyna was absolutely beautiful. When she entered the room, an intense floral, jasmine-like smell followed her. She was petite and had porcelain-like features. Her long braided white-blonde hair touched her waist. Throughout the braid were small purple and green flowers. She glowed a hue of blue green as she approached.

"Hello, Jacey, Herecerti asked me to prepare a block for you. He insisted it be a most powerful one. He wanted me to be the one to deliver it and train you in its use." She smiled and extended her hand out to me. I took her hand and we greeted in the traditional Nemelite fashion.

"May the five elements keep you eternal," she said as she held my hand over the center of her chest.

"And you," I replied.

I didn't get any kind of feeling from her other than one of patience. I had been told when we 'connect' like this, we're supposed to know the intentions of the person greeting us. With Verbeyna, I didn't get a feeling either way.

"I have blocks of my own," was all she replied as we both took our hands back. She had a bag with her and started rifling through it. She looked at Heathe again. He hadn't moved his stare from the wall. She pulled out a small wooden box and placed it on the bedside table. Aunt Grace had moved, allowing Verbeyna to stand at the head of the bed.

"I don't mind commencing with everyone in the room as long as it's okay with you," she said.

"No, I'm fine with it. Go ahead," I responded.

She opened the box and lying within it was a silver chain with a crystal pendant. It was shaped like the letter 'J' affixed to a backwards three with a loop on the bottom portion of the three. The design was like one of the numbers I'd seen engraved on one of the pillars at the Infinite Waters.

Underneath the crystal flowed colors. They ranged in clarity and brightness. There were reds, blues, greens, pinks, and whites. She placed the locket in her hand and turned to me.

"Are you ready?" she asked.

"Yeah," I replied. I was feeling a little nervous.

"You need to repeat after me." She paused, waiting for a response. I nodded.

She closed her eyes and began.

"Through the elements I am alive."

"Through the elements I am alive," I repeated.

"I shall choose my mind's eye."

"I shall choose my mind's eye," I said. The locket glowed bright blue.

"I will not be summoned."

"I will not be summoned," I repeated, it glowed bright white.

"I am the portal for Kawaneing." Verbeyna began to glow a bright, swirly pink.

"I am the portal for Kawaneing." The pendant went clear and reflected my image.

"None shall be present unless I allow it." Her aura began to diminish in color.

"None shall be present unless I allow it." The pendant turned red and blue.

"I am the vessel." She stopped and looked directly at me. Her eyes had turned from honey yellow to deep black.

I paused for a second, taken aback by her eyes. "I-I am the vessel." The pendant turned gold in color and started to steam in her hand.

"You must not take it off. It will protect your thoughts, your being, and your vessel. None other can touch it. It will only be for Jacey," she chanted as she placed it around my neck. I watched as she drew back.

"Are you okay?" I asked, reaching out for her hand.

"We as Hinderers always give a piece of ourselves to those we have aided in placing blocks. It doesn't hurt us, it strengthens our abilities," she replied, looking at me through golden yellow eyes. She took the box off the bedside and peered at Heathe once more. He had been watching as she performed the block, but as soon as she turned to look at him, he went back to staring at the wall.

"It's not burning me," I said, holding it in my hand. The chain was long enough so the pendant hung above my heart.

"It won't, because it's meant for you. If another tries to touch or take it, it will burn them. It won't work for them," she said, placing the box within her bag.

"How do I use it?" I asked. The locket had returned to its original state.

"The pendant will glow when someone or something is trying to communicate with you. It will turn the colors of the elements. Once you decide you want the communication, you must chant, 'I am the vessel through Kawaneing.' Once you speak the words, you will be able to adjust your body and mind to how much you are willing to share with or communicate with the being attempting to contact you," she said.

"I don't know how to adjust my mind and body. How do I do that?" I asked, feeling my anxiety rise. As it did, a flash of blue and red came into the room. No one other than Verbeyna moved to allow the essence to enter. They were all oblivious to it. I knew who it was immediately—Mom. My pendant began to spin and glow bright green and yellow. That caught everyone else's attention.

"It's okay, it's Mom," I said. When I did, nothing happened. I was confused because I would normally go into my Mom and me zone once I acknowledged Mom.

"You need to use the chant," Verbeyna said as her eyes followed Mom's essence around the room. Mom was flying around crazily—like she couldn't see or feel me.

"I am the vessel through Kawaneing," I said out loud, sounding more like a question than a statement. The second it was said, I was able to be with Mom. She rushed over and wound me in her essence colors. When she decided I was okay, she turned into her corporeal being.

"What's going on? I couldn't see you! I couldn't hear you! Are you okay?" she asked, ruffling the bangs on my forehead.

"Everything's okay now. Faith summoned me through the portal in your old room," I said, trying to make it sound like no big deal.

"You were what? That's impossible. We sealed it when we left," she said.

"Since Faith and I reconnected in the Inception Chamber, she's now able to reopen it," I revealed.

"What are we doing about it?"

"A Hinderer was called in. That's why you couldn't see me. I had to *allow* you to."

"Did Herecerti call it?"

"Call it? What do you mean?" I asked.

"Anytime a Hinderer is called in, it means they're granted more powers and someone loses a power in return. If Herecerti felt the need to call one in, we're in more trouble than I originally thought," Mom said.

"We were already in trouble, Mom. When Faith *summoned* me…by the way…not so happy about that! I don't like being *summoned* by anyone—it knocked me completely out. That's why Herecerti brought in Verbeyna."

"Knocked you out?"

"Mom, I'm fine. Heathe caught me."

"At least he's around to protect you. That calms me a little. Verbeyna does come from a very powerful line. I'm glad to see Herecerti took the initiative to implement her. It usually takes an Elder council agreement for one to happen—legally—that is. There are always others who break the rules. Have we heard from Vincent or anyone else yet?"

With the mention of his name my heart squeezed. "He's not back and he won't be right away. I got to talk to him before I came to in the infirmary. He said they were trying to cover their trail…but he'd return as soon as he could." I choked up a little on the last syllable. Worrying about Vincent was something I knew I'd be doing for the rest of my life. Right now, I needed to ask Mom some questions about someone else.

"I need to talk to you about some stuff I wasn't too comfortable talking to Aunt Grace about."

"Go ahead."

"Faith's different. She said Vincent didn't get to her yet. Mom, he was never supposed to go to her. She gives me a bad feeling. I don't know why and I can't put my finger on it, but I can't talk to Aunt Grace about any of it, because, well, you know. Faith's not the same Faith I saw in the Inception Chamber. She seems more—not lost. I don't know if that makes sense but she didn't seem like someone who was looking to be 'rescued' anytime soon."

"She is lost to us, Jacey. She was the minute Christine stole her from us. Grace knows this and she's holding on to the hope Gideon has been with Faith all this time. If he has been, there may still be good left in her. If he hasn't, then Faith may well be lost to Necroseek and his followers. We won't know until the two of you are reunited, which won't happen until we're prepared. Time is on our side. When is Vincent expected back?"

"In half a cycle," I answered.

"Half a cycle, you're becoming acquainted with Nemele's teachings," she said, smiling.

"I've also been acquainted with the knowledge my mom was over 250 when she left and I have grandparents, too," I replied.

"Closer to 260 actually, and who told you about Mom and Dad?" she asked.

"When Aunt Grace heard the portal was reopened, she said it was how you and your family communicated before. She thinks because Gideon is still alive, Joseph and Violet may be, too," I said.

"My parents still alive, what a wonderful thought. Grace experimenting with the family portal is not a safe thing to be doing. We need to focus on the prophecy and keeping you safe. What are the plans of everyone involved?" Mom asked.

"Now that I'm blocked, we're going to meet Herecerti in the archives to study the prophecy. Heathe's not going anywhere anytime soon. So, I guess being safe is covered, too." My stomach did a little flip when I mentioned Heathe. It reminded me of the 'embrace' we were in before I passed out. How our hands intertwined and the surge of heat which went through my body.

"Are you okay? You look flushed all of a sudden," Mom asked.

"No, no, I'm fine. I need to get back so we can get on to the archives. Are you and Dad still looking at things?"

"We are. We'll be back at the Infinite Waters later and talk about it. I love you, Jacey."

"I love you, Mom."

I was back in the hospital bed with five sets of eyes staring at me. I had the pendant around my neck, clutched in my hand.

"Was it Ria?" Aunt Grace asked.

"Yeah...how did you guys know?"

"With the block you won't be in another time— time passes wherever you will be the same as it passes here," Verbeyna said.

"How long was I gone?"

"About an hour," Heathe said, looking very bothered.

"I need to return home. If you need me, Herecerti can channel me through the Visionaries. May the elements keep you all safe," Verbeyna said as she placed her hand to her chest and disappeared with her aura of pink and aroma of jasmine.

"Can we leave now?" I asked.

"Yeah. But first can I talk to Jacey alone?" Hudson asked.

Everyone other than Hudson left.

"What's wrong?" It wasn't like him to clear a room to ask me anything.

"You sure everything's good with you?" he asked.

"Yeah...why?"

"Because I'm not leaving you alone with Heathe or Aunt Grace again."

CHAPTER SIX

True intentions are questioned
More beings are revealed
Archives become a place of revelations

"What are you talking about?" I said, totally stunned. "As if I won't be alone with Aunt Grace again. Where is all this coming from?"

"You happened to be unconscious, Jace...Aunt Grace has too much invested in this other than us now. She now has her entire family, one she thought she'd never be part of again within her reach. Remember her daughter—Faith?" Hudson asked.

"You've got to be kidding. She's always been there for us, Hudson! How can you question her?" I was blown away by his newfound mistrust of Aunt Grace.

"Jacey, she tried to stop Heathe from bringing you to the infirmary. It took both Jen and I to hold her back," he said, shaking his head, looking down at the floor.

"W-what do you mean she tried to stop Heathe?"

"Right before you passed out, you said 'Faith.' Aunt Grace thought you had connected with her, so she tried to stop Heathe from taking you. But he didn't hesitate. He was gone with you before I could even say a thing."

"I'm sure she wasn't trying to stop Heathe from *helping* me. She probably only wanted to see if I was going to say anything else. Hudson, she loves us...she'd never do anything to hurt me or you. You know that."

"I did. I don't so much anymore. I know she loves us, Jacey, but her daughter's back in the picture and I for one am nervous about it. She knew about the portal, she knew about our grandparents, and she knew about the connection you had with Faith even before you woke up and told us about it. How do you explain her not telling us about any of it? Or better yet, warning us."

"Hudson, she'd never do anything to hurt us. I'm sure there's an explanation for everything. Once we're done at the archives, we'll ask her, okay?"

"Jacey, I'm not letting anything happen to you. You and Jen are all I have left," he said, showing a side I'd rarely seen.

"Hudson, I'm not going anywhere, other than out of here." I went to get up, wavering a little as I tried to stand. I sat on the corner of the bed and took a few deep breaths.

"What's got you so worried about Heathe now? It's not like I have a choice to be around him. Believe me, if I had a say in it, I'd vote not to have him or anyone else following my every move," I said, while deep down my stomach squeezed.

"I don't like the way he looks at you. I think he's getting too close," Hudson said.

"Okay, seriously. We're talking about the same Heathe here. Vincent's best friend, the Sentry Guard who was zapped across a room by Daichi…Hello, Chanary's brother! Oh yeah, and not to mention, someone who has the attention of one very powerful Hinderer."

"What?" Hudson asked, confused.

"You can't tell me you didn't see the way he acted when Verbeyna came in. Or the way she acted around him. So, trust me, brother, there's nothing to worry about when it comes to him and me," I said, sounding more sure than I felt.

"I still don't trust him. I get we don't have a choice and he'll be around until Vincent comes back, but I want you to be careful around him." He paused, waiting for me to respond.

"O-o-okay. I promise to be careful. Can we go now?"

"Not yet. When I'm not with you, Jen's going to be. She feels the same way I do about Aunt Grace and Heathe, Jace."

"I think you're way off with the whole Aunt Grace/Heathe thing. I promise to be careful and I promise to stay with Jen when you're not around, but—I want us to talk things over with Aunt Grace after the archives. I really don't think she'd do anything to put me or you in any kind of danger. Agreed?"

"Agreed." He hugged me and helped me stand. I took a few more deep breaths and headed to the doorway.

The door faded in front of us and we walked out into a stone corridor where Jen, Aunt Grace, and Heathe were all waiting.

"Are we all ready to go?" Aunt Grace asked.

"Yeah, I hope so. We're going to meet Herecerti, right?" I asked.

"Of course. We need to get to the archives and try to understand more of this prophecy," Jen said, taking Hudson's hand in hers.

Heathe hung out against the wall, watching all of us. Aunt Grace wound her arm through mine.

"How are you feeling? Are you up for this? Or would you rather take a break?" she asked.

"Aunt Grace, I'm really okay. We need to get to Herecerti and see what we can find out," I answered.

"I only want to be sure you're all right. I love you, Jacey, and I don't want you burning yourself out," she said, smiling at me.

"I love you too, Aunt Grace. I'll let you know if I'm feeling tired," I replied, watching Hudson as I spoke, raising an eyebrow at him in an 'I told you so' gesture.

"I'll be around if you need me," Heathe said, turning into his pure essence and vanishing before us.

"Subtle as always," Hudson mumbled sarcastically.

"This way," Aunt Grace said, leading the three of us down the dimly lit corridor. We walked for a few minutes, passing other doors with symbols engraved in them. I assumed they were other infirmary rooms. The hallway ended in a half wall of stone. Standing behind it was a man and woman engaged in conversation. She was holding a tablet in one hand and bottles in the other. Their discussion ended as we approached.

"Jacey, I see the Hinderer has aided you. I'm John. I was your caregiver when Heathe brought you to us." He was at least eight feet tall and had long, braided black hair. He had a warm full smile and kind eyes. He was wearing a white button down shirt and had a tablet of his own in hand.

"I'm feeling much better, thank you." I reached up to my neck and swirled the amulet Verbeyna gave to me through my fingers.

"We'll be keeping a close eye on you. Since Heathe was able to catch you before you fell to the ground, our concerns are focused mainly on your conscious states. When one is incapacitated like you were, by being drawn through an unexpected summons, there are always side effects such as headaches and light-headedness which can last for a few days," John said.

"I have a few people keeping me under wraps for the next while. So, if I am feeling bad, I'm sure they'll be bringing me back," I said, looking at Jen, Hudson, and Aunt Grace.

"I have no doubt they'll return you if they fear something is amiss," John said, coming around from behind the half wall.

As he came into full view, I had to physically gauge my reaction. John wasn't an eight foot tall human looking being, he was a centaur. One which was trotting right out in front of me. You'd think I'd be prepared to see all of the mythical creatures I'd been reading about since I was a child, considering everything I'd witnessed over the last month. I can tell you I wasn't.

Most centaurs from the readings I'd done weren't very nice. They weren't the social types—especially when it came to humans. From everything I'd read about them, they were pretty unpredictable and super violent, qualities John wasn't showing whatsoever.

"Here's a potion in case you start having any type of headaches." He grabbed a bottle from the woman behind the counter and handed it to me.

"T-thank you," I stuttered—way to go Jacey—subtle...I was still feeling pretty overwhelmed with everything, and everyone.

"I'll be checking in on you every now and then myself," John said, walking past us. The woman behind the wall accompanied him towards the medical ward we'd just left. She appeared to be human, but I wasn't sure.

The wall in front of us dissolved and we exited into the main concourse. We had returned to the main entrance of Nemele. There were still Sentry guards standing point guard on either side of the main doors. Instead of going off to the right where the Inception Chamber was, we took the hallway directly in front of the doors this time.

I had a million questions running through my mind about Doctor John. I waited until I believed we were completely out of John's earshot before I asked any of them.

"He was a centaur, right?" I asked Jen, Hudson, and Aunt Grace.

"He *is*," Aunt Grace corrected me.

"How could he—how could a centaur be—" I was having a hard time forming my thoughts into questions. I stopped. "Aren't they supposed to be really dangerous? How could he be a doctor?"

"He is a direct descendant of Kheiron, a centaur who cared for others and wasn't the typical centaur as most were depicted." Aunt Grace paused for a second. "Jacey, you'll find a lot of the teachings you've had are based loosely in truth. Staying here, you'll see a number of the writings, folklores, fairy tales and myths of Earth have minimal facts based in truth to them."

"I'll make sure to try and hide my reactions better next time," I said, embarrassed, remembering the comment made by Mr. Willows in 'Origins' class—'humans were so predictable, so self-opinionated and so utterly closed minded they assumed they were the only 'intelligent' species within their universe...way to represent yet again, Jacey, I thought.

"You did fine. We should move to the archives," Aunt Grace said, reassuringly squeezing my arm.

We walked on for fifteen minutes and stopped in front of another hovering door engraved with what looked like an upright infinity symbol with a calligraphy 'K' on its right and an upside down version on the left of it.

"We're here," Aunt Grace said.

We entered an enormous room. It went on forever in all directions, up, down, and side to side. The space within the Archives would have made Glyth—the Goliath from the Inception Chamber—feel small in comparison. The area was cylindrical and had more stairwells than I could count going off in all directions.

"We need to go to the main level and check in. I'm sure Herecerti will be waiting for us there," Aunt Grace said, leading us over to the left. As we stepped out onto a stairwell landing, it began to shift and move. Suddenly, we were floating out into the center of the room and then descending.

As we dropped further into the belly of the room, I watched as we passed by a number of levels.

"Are each of the levels part of the archive?" I asked.

"Each level is linked to one of the nineteen Nations of Nemele. There are sub-sections which have combined Nations' information. Every being, be it Nemelite or Yietimpi, is documented here. Their origins, their affiliations, and any other writing or saying that's associated with any of us," Aunt Grace said as we slowed in our descent.

I looked over the edge of the landing and it appeared we were on the main level of the Archives.

"This is where we must check in with the Keepers. They're the guardians of the Archives and all it holds," Aunt Grace said.

I looked down as the ground approached us. In the center of the room was a hemisphere of electric blue light. Reflected all over it were a number of symbols. Coming up directly from the center was a yellow beam of light. It shot up the landing and continued on above it.

"Wow. It's beautiful," I said.

"This is the Keepers' Gate. It's where we check in and get direction from the Keepers. They know where all the writings are within this chamber," Jen said, stepping from the landing with Hudson.

Aunt Grace and I followed Jen and Hudson to the entrance. It was governed by two arched access points. I stood within them, staring spellbound at the arch of lights and colors emanating and reflected within them.

"Herecerti should be inside waiting for us," Hudson said as he entered with Jen.

"This place is amazing," I said to Aunt Grace.

"It is, and you haven't even been to any of the Archives yet." She smiled, pulling me in through the entrance with her.

Standing in the center of the room was Herecerti. There was nothing else in the room. From the inside you could make out the symbols reflected on the outside, but to my surprise the only other thing in the chamber was the beam of yellow light. It came up through the floor and exited through the ceiling. Herecerti was standing off to the right.

"I see you've made it. It's time we begin researching the Prophecy." Herecerti turned to the beam of light and announced, "We are present for the Nephilim Prophecy, can one assist?" Once he asked, the light flashed from yellow to green and a figure appeared. The beam returned to its original yellow as the being came to stand beside Herecerti.

I couldn't tell whether it was a man or woman. It bore no gender identifying traits. Its skin was an opaque white and there was no hair on its head. It was wearing a black toga-like robe which was fitted at the waist by a blood red tie.

"I am Lore, I will be your guide. Who is asking for the Prophecy?" Lore asked.

"I am," Herecerti replied.

"Yet come with five?" Lore asked.

"Four," I corrected before I could stop myself.

This drew Lore's attention to me. "I will guide you and you alone," Lore said to Herecerti as it floated towards me.

Lore stopped half a foot in front of me and cocked its head to the side. Its eyes were a deep grey with splashes of purple throughout.

"You bear no essence. How are you here?" It went to place its hand on my arm and a flash of blue intercepted its touch. Heathe formed in front of me.

Herecerti came to stand beside me and spoke. Lore retracted its hand and folded it within the other.

"No need to over react, Heathe. I was merely curious—as our kind is," Lore stated.

"You don't need to touch her to know why she's here. You can ask." Heathe said, looking between the two of us. "He will not touch you, Jacey."

"She is half of the Anomaly, Lore. I'm more than sure the Elders have made the Keepers aware of recent events. Jacey and her family will accompany me to the level of Nephilim to assist in researching the prophecy. It has all been sanctified by the

Guild," Herecerti said, stopping on the other side of me.

I was starting to feel uncomfortable. Aunt Grace had me covered on one side, Herecerti on the other, Jen and Hudson were behind me and Heathe had taken a stance in front of me.

Lore floated over to the beam of light in the center of the room. He placed his hand in it and peered up to the roof of the Gate. The symbols above moved and formed into new ones.

The beam turned from yellow to crystal blue.

"The channel is ready," Lore stated.

We moved in unison. Heathe did not turn back into his essence. He stayed solid in front of me. Once we reached Lore, Herecerti offered his hand to the center beam. His other hand touched my shoulder. As he did, a landing appeared within the Gate and all of us, including Lore, stepped onto it. My family hadn't moved and Lore hadn't stopped staring at me through his purple grey eyes. The hair on the back of my neck stood on end and Aunt Grace reassuringly squeezed my arm.

The landing travelled parallel to the beam up towards the roof. As we approached the top of the sphere, it split, allowing us to exit the gate. The Archive had changed. Now, there were a number of others on landings of their own floating throughout the chasm. Each level was lit and had beings moving about in them as we passed one after the other. The areas I initially thought were stairwells were travel ways for the landings.

My family, along with Heathe and Herecerti, didn't budge as we moved along. Lore continued to make me feel completely uncomfortable and it was taking everything I had not to tell him off. What was with this guy and hadn't anyone ever told him staring at someone was just not okay? I was about to educate him myself when the landing veered right and came to a stop in front of a section which didn't appear to have any others in it.

"Here are the Nephilims. There are a number of other sections which join into it. You are looking for the Origin level within this section. Follow me," Lore said, stepping off of the landing.

I stayed back with Aunt Grace as Jen, Hudson, Herecerti and Heathe followed directly behind Lore.

"What's with this guy? Why is he staring at me? And what's up with Heathe?" I whispered.

"He's a Keeper. They are curious by nature and he's never seen anyone like you before. For him that's a big deal. They also don't socialize much outside of their own kind. Their lives are encompassed by their duty to safe keep Nemelite records. He doesn't mean to make you feel uncomfortable; he doesn't understand other beings' social cues," Aunt Grace whispered back.

"Okay, what about the Heathe thing?" I asked, watching closely to make sure Lore couldn't over hear us.

"A Keeper isn't only the guardian of knowledge. They can also be the hoarders of it. Some are known to 'steal' the memories of those they touch. Not all of them have the ability, but none of us were willing to take that chance."

"So, Heathe was protecting me from losing my memories."

"Not only from losing them but also from being violated. Some of the stories told by those who have been touched by Keepers with the ability have said the intrusion can be painful and is not easily forgotten," Aunt Grace said.

Heathe turned as though he had heard our conversation and our eyes met. He nodded his head once and then turned his attention back on Lore. My heart jumped and my palms got all sweaty. I knew I needed to thank him for what he'd done and I was surprisingly nervous about doing it.

"Here is the section you are looking for," Lore announced as we entered a niche with books and scrolls from ceiling to floor.

"I am unsure what exactly you are looking for, but I can guide you to the earliest of our chronicles." He went over to the far back wall. "This is the section I would recommend you spend your time on. I will be within the walls of this section, waiting to escort you out once you are finished here," Lore said, turning and walking away from the wall and towards me.

Herecerti stood in front of me this time and I was flanked by the rest of my family and Heathe.

"I would like for us to speak when you are comfortable, Jacey. I have been a Keeper for eight centuries and I have never met one like you," Lore asked, realizing he would not have the chance to talk to me now or touch me.

"We are centering our energies on this Prophecy. We will call when we are done," Herecerti stated, cutting Lore off and guiding us all towards the back of the room.

"Until then," Lore answered, disappearing.

"Seriously…creepy," I said as Jen came up to me from behind and patted my back in support.

"We won't be leaving you alone with him. There's nothing to worry about. However, now we need to focus on the works here," Aunt Grace said, going over and taking a number of scrolls from a shelf, sitting down at one of the tables in the room, and starting to read through them.

"Yeah, focus…" I said, walking over to the wall and staring at the never ending rows of scrolls and books.

"Here, try this." My breath caught as Heathe brushed my arm reaching over top of me.

"Am I going to be able to read any of these?" I asked, thinking if these books had been written by the Nephilim, I highly doubted they'd be in English.

"I'll help," he said, taking a number of books and going over to a table in the far back corner of the room.

I paused for a second, looking over at Hudson. He was watching me closely. Jen looked up and put her hand on Hudson's arm, drawing his attention towards the papers they had in front of them.

I took a deep breath and turned back towards Heathe. "Like swimming…" I mumbled to myself, and jumped in.

CHAPTER SEVEN

Prophecies
Unique methods of communicating
Deciphering...books and things

I took a seat on the opposite side of the table. Heathe looked up at me and smirked.

"Unless you can read upside down, it may be a better idea for you to sit here," he said, pulling the chair out beside him.

My ears felt a sudden rush of heat. I tried thinking of a smart one liner but ultimately decided he was right. I got up, went over, and took the seat beside him.

"Who were the Nephilim?" I asked, fully aware the only information I'd had on them I'd read about on Earth. From everything I'd seen so far, I knew that info was probably a very small portion of the truth.

"When the Elders decided to create Earth and humankind, they sent a species of beings to be their guides. The Nephilim were chosen. They were the sons and daughters from the most ancient race within Nemelite society. "

"Why did the Elders choose them?"

"Because they were the most honorable of all species within our world. Not to mention they were all gifted with different elements and talents," Heathe said, unravelling the scrolls in front of us.

"Their writings are easily read. Here," Heathe said, rolling one out in front of me and pointing to the writings scribed upon the parchments.

As he rolled them out, I placed my hand on the corner to hold them down. They began to glow a dull blue.

"They can be read as long as the two of us are here together. The scrolls make themselves readable to anyone they choose, once the Keepers allow the being to be present," he said.

I looked down at the scroll and found I could read its writings.

The Nephilim world is ruled within five Societies.

The Amazarak, Armers, Barkayals, Akibeels and the Asaradels.

The Amazaraks shall educate and rule all those who are enchanted.

The Amazaraks' talents may put forth betterment into a society as well as their downfall.

The Armers shall classify each of the talents bequeathed upon each Nephilim.

The Armers shall keep watch upon the Amazarak.

Barkayal shall be the third ruling society.

They will birth and delimit all cosmic structures.

Constellations shall be their title.

They will constitute the travelled portions between all universes.

They are the atlas to all within Nemele.

The Barkayals will govern the utilization of all charts.

They will train all in their use.

Akibeel shall be the fourth nation within Nephilim.

The Akibeel shall interpret all markings.

They will educate all within the scriptures of pure and united markings.

The Asaradels shall complete Nephilim.

They will oversee all six universal fundamentals: earth, wind, air, fire, water, kawaneing.

They shall classify the means of enlightenment within Awakening."

"That's amazing," I said, taking my hand away from the parchment. As I did, the glow emanating from it dimmed then disappeared. "Can I read everything in the Archives?"

"You can only read the ones the Keepers allow you entry to. We'll be able to read whatever is in the Nephilim section but, if you tried to go off into another area, you wouldn't be able to. It's their way of keeping everyone in line. Control freaks..." Heathe said, looking over at me. As we made eye contact, a slight smile formed in the corners of his mouth. It was the first time I'd actually seen him smile. My stomach fluttered and I placed both my arms around my mid-section thinking, I was going to be sick.

"Are you okay?" he asked, his eyes now filled with concern.

I took a few deep breaths and steadied myself. I wasn't nauseous and I wasn't light-headed, I had no idea why my body was reacting the way it was.

I was first to look away, turning my attention back to the scripture in front of us.

"I'm fine. Just a little tired. I can understand some of it, but I think we need to focus our attention on the five ruling societies."

"The breakdown of the Prophecy is in one of these somewhere. Let's start with the Amazarak. Do you want to ask everyone else who they're looking through?" Heathe asked, getting up from the table.

He headed back to the wall to get another armful of scriptures.

I looked around the room to see where everyone else was. Herecerti was seated and engrossed in his scriptures at the same table as Aunt Grace. They were oblivious to anyone else in the room. Hudson was in the far corner rifling through a number of loose papers. I turned in my seat looking for Jen and nearly jumped out of skin when I came nose to nose with her. She had taken Heathe's seat and was sitting there staring at me.

"Jen...holy flip! Seriously, do not sneak up on me like that."

"I didn't. So, where are you guys in the scriptures?" she asked.

"Heathe thinks we should start with the Amazaraks. How are we supposed to find what the prophecy means in all of this? It'll take years just to get through one of the Nephilim's five societies," I said, placing my elbows on the table and my head in my hands. "Vincent doesn't have years..." I mumbled, frustrated.

Jen placed her hand on my back. "He's going to be okay, Jacey. We'll find what we need and by then Vincent will be back."

"I don't think so. There's something about how Faith *summoned* me that's got me on edge. Vincent told me half a cycle, and I'll stick by that, but if he isn't back by then, Elders, prophecy, or whatever else won't hold me back from going to look for him," I said with more emotion than I meant to let out.

"Jacey, we have to trust in the writings and in our Elders. They know more about our worlds and how to travel within them than any of us. We can't go running off without a plan."

"I won't go without a plan, but I won't sit around doing nothing, either," I replied.

"And you won't be going anywhere on your own," Heathe said, making both Jen and I jump.

"We aren't going anywhere. Jacey's obviously upset about Vincent and we were only talking about how important it is we find out about the prophecy and how we're going to deal with it," Jen said, getting up from Heathe's seat.

"We're all upset, but running off without any kind of knowledge of what you're running into isn't smart. It only puts the rest of us at risk," Heathe said, obviously irritated.

"Which area are you and Hudson focusing on?" he asked Jen.

"We're trying to stay within the last five hundred years. Finding the prophecy writing isn't the issue—It's finding who wrote it and what they meant," Jen said.

"Can I see it? Maybe just reading it we may be able to find some clues," I suggested.

"It's in a different section within these archives. Here," Heathe said, laying down the arm full of scrolls he'd taken from the shelves behind us and putting them on the table in front of me.

"We'll go over to the area it's in so I can show her the writing itself. Do you and Hudson want to take these?" He pointed to the scrolls he'd put down.

"Sure, why not," Jen said, looking over at Hudson, who was now watching the three of us.

He made his way over to our table.

"Heathe's going to show Jacey the prophecy," Jen said, placing her hand on Hudson's forearm.

"We can all go," he replied, looking directly at me. I hadn't forgotten his talk about not wanting me to be alone with Heathe. It was ridiculous.

Before I could say something in return or even roll my eyes at him, Heathe responded. "I think having you and Jen reading these while I show Jacey the prophecy would be a better use of all of our time."

"I think—" Hudson started, but I interrupted, knowing full well as he took a step forward that he was going to tell Heathe off.

"Isn't it just around the corner?" I asked.

"Yeah, it is," Jen said.

"We'll be gone for like five minutes, Hudson," I said, emphasizing the *we* part of it. He knew it meant only Heathe and I.

"I really—" Hudson started again, this time only to be cut off by Herecerti.

"I do believe that Heathe is right in this case. Jen and Hudson, your time would be better spent here. Heathe and Jacey, be quick about it. I'm certain Lore will want to guide you to the area in question." He left no room for argument.

Hudson was obviously not impressed but he didn't push it. He and Jen sat at the table. He looked up at me and mouthed "five minutes" as he pointed to his watch.

Heathe and I walked out of the room and went around the corner. Lore was standing off to the right of the entrance.

"We need to go to the area where the prophecies are held," Heathe said as he placed himself between Lore and I.

"This way," Lore responded as he took the lead.

We walked for a couple of minutes and turned into a cave-like area. It looked like the room we had left but was a lot smaller.

Lore went over to a shelf and took a parchment from it. He returned to us and held it out to me. Heathe stepped in again, taking it.

"Thanks. We'll just be a minute."

Lore tilted his head to the side, appearing slightly confused.

"We don't need you to interpret it. I'll help her with it," Heathe said.

"I'm sure you will be able to read it well, Heathe, but would it not be to your advantage if I assisted?" Lore asked.

"If you're needed, I'll let you know," Heathe said, moving us over to a table in the corner of the room.

"Very well," Lore said, leaving the room.

"Why don't you want his help? Wouldn't it be better if we had him read it with us? He's supposed to be the expert…isn't he?"

"He is, but I'm not comfortable with him. Once a Keeper does you a 'favor,' they expect something in return. I'm not willing to find out what he wants. Plus, we have prophecy classes from the first day we attend St. Nemele. This one is taught from day one. So, I've seen it, studied it, and know it," Heathe said.

"Okay, then, let's get to it." I reached out to unroll the scroll Lore had given us.

Heathe reached out at the same time and our hands touched. He didn't budge—I, on the other hand—acted as though I'd touched a live wire. The instant our hands came into contact, I felt a tingling like you'd feel if you held your hand too close to an electric fence. It traveled from my hand right to the pit of my gut.

Heathe looked unaffected and didn't seem to notice I had pulled away.

"Here, put your hand in the upper corner so you can read it," he said as he pulled himself further away from me and positioned himself just in reach of the parchment.

I placed my hand on it and it began to glow as the other scrolls had.

Wherefore two destroyed as one flooded
Two are none to own
Yet millennia pass
Kin of origin
Progeny bore
Under the shadow of the dark moons
Dio borne unto either
The veil of lineage dispersed thou line
Guise shall be its veil
One immersed in virtue
whilst its shadow—bore resemblance
To deceive with sureness

ought befall the core of depravity
lineage within from one to five
Will dictate the tribe within the Anomalies
To unite once more
Shall bond the lines of Barkayal

"Seriously, that's it?" I asked.

"Yeah."

"I don't understand it. Are you sure we don't need Lore to interpret it for us?"

"Yeah, I'm sure we don't need him and we don't want to owe him anything."

"Should we go over it now or do we take it with us to the other enclave?" I asked, knowing Hudson was probably ready to come looking for us.

"Wait here a second," Heathe said. Not waiting for my response, he got up and went over to the entrance of the room. He exited, and within seconds was back with Lore.

"We're ready to join the others. Are we able to take this scroll with us?" Heathe asked.

"They cannot leave the area where they are stored. I can create a double of it if you like," Lore offered.

"We would," Heathe said.

Lore took the scroll and exited the room. He was back within seconds with a rolled up piece of parchment. He looked at me and raised the scroll to me. Heathe interceded, taking the scroll and pointing to the exit in a gesture of 'time to go.'

Lore tilted his head again, looking at me through his deep grey eyes. The purple patterns within them were swirling around. I chose not to break eye contact this time and watched as he stood there looking at me.

"I think it's time to go," I said, sounding way more confident than I felt. I stayed behind Heathe and even backed up a bit before Lore could move any closer.

"Indeed," he replied, losing the staring competition we'd been locked in. He turned and we followed him out of the room.

"Seriously...creepy," I whispered to Heathe.

He looked at me and smiled, a genuine one which reached his eyes. The tingling in my hand started again and wandered into my belly. I looked away, blushing. *What the hell is that? Why am I having this weird reaction to him? I need some sleep...maybe I'm just really tired. Jen and I need to chat.*

We were back in the room with everyone else within minutes.

"I was coming to look for you," Hudson said, coming up beside me.

"Okay, seriously, I was gone for like ten minutes," I shot back at him with a little more attitude than I planned.

"How did things go?" Jen asked in an obvious attempt to break the tension.

"We have a copy of the original prophecy. All of us have to go through it. I read it, and to tell you the truth, I didn't get too much from it," I said, coming out from behind Heathe. He handed it to me and I made sure not to have any kind of contact with him whatsoever.

Aunt Grace and Herecerti came up to us. Lore stayed within the entrance.

"Jacey, you must be exhausted. It's been an extremely long day for everyone—but for you, I can only imagine," she said, giving me a one-arm hug me.

"Actually, I am pretty pooped. Can we take a break?" I asked.

"I believe having Jen, Hudson, and Heathe escorting you to your dormitory will suffice. I will stay and research what I can. If Grace isn't tired, she may stay with me," Herecerti said.

"Will you be okay?" Aunt Grace asked, smiling her mom smile at me.

"Yeah. What time are we supposed to meet Mom at the Infinity Waters?" I asked, realizing I'd almost completely forgotten about it.

"We have more than enough time, Jacey. I'll send for you when the meeting is to take place," Herecerti said, turning back to his table.

Lore came back into the room. "Mial will stay with you while I escort the others out," he said to Aunt Grace and Herecerti.

"I'll see you later," Aunt Grace said, placing a kiss on my forehead and turning back to the table.

Hudson, Jen and Heathe took up positions around me as Lore showed us the way out. We all stepped onto the platform and traveled to the doors we had entered a few hours ago. As the platform came to a stop, Lore stepped off first and waited for the rest of us to exit. As I passed him, he spoke up.

"Jacey, I am still quite curious about you. If you do find it in you to share your journey with me, I would be more than pleased to sit and document it."

"Thanks, I think, but I really don't see how my journey would be very interesting to you or anyone else."

"I can tell you there are many who'd be intrigued to learn of your…talents," Lore said. As he said the word 'talent,' he made the hair on the back of my neck stand on end.

I was unsure how to answer, so I just smiled and walked past him with everyone else. I turned as we got to the exit and saw that Lore hadn't moved. He stared at me through grey and purple eyes, which would make anyone feel the hair on the back of their neck stand on end.

"Someone needs to teach these guys about 'social norms,'" I said to Jen as we exited the archives.

"Been tried. Doesn't really have an effect on them. They're just…creepy," Jen said, smiling and grabbing onto my forearm as we followed Heathe and Hudson.

"We're dropping Hudson off at his dorm then going to ours," Jen said.

"Okay, sounds good. Is anyone else hungry? Can we get something and bring it back to our room or is there a place we have to go to get food?" I said in unison with the growling of my stomach.

"We can get something in our dorm wing," Jen said.

Hudson had been listening in on our conversation. I could tell from his body language that he wasn't comfortable with Heathe. He didn't protest about going to his dorm.

"I'm going to read up on some things in my room. When Herecerti comes to get you to go meet Mom, I'll be with him," he said, turning back and walking on in front of us.

We got to Hudson's dorm faster than I thought. He approached the symbol on the entrance and turned to me.

"I'll be just a call away if you need me. Jen, you're staying with Jacey, right?"

"I'll be with her the whole time," Jen said, going up on her tip-toes to kiss Hudson on the lips.

"I'll call if I need you," I said.

Hudson hugged me and whispered in my ear. "I'm only looking out for you. I don't want to see anyone take advantage of you. Love you, Jace." He backed away and held his hand up to the symbol.

"Love you too, Hudson. I'll be fine. All grown up now," I said, smiling at him.

The symbol glowed and he entered the dorm. He turned before the door reformed and looked right at me. "All grown up but still my little sister." He winked and the door formed in front of him.

"Now, time to get you two back to your dorm," Heathe said, walking off in the direction of our room.

Jen and I didn't talk while we walked. Once there, Heathe turned to us and stated, "I'll be right outside your dorm room. If you need me, just call." He turned into his origin self and disappeared.

"I don't know if I'll ever get use to people turning into swirling colors and disappearing," I said as I held my hand up to the main entrance.

The door disappeared and we entered and made our way to our room.

"I'm sure in time, Jacey, you'll be more comfortable with it," Jen said, giving my back a reassuring pat.

"The disappearing thing isn't what's really bothering me. It's the knowing he's watching and I can't see where he is," I said as a flash of red caught my eye.

Great...Chanary. I really didn't feel like having a Chanary moment right now. I turned to our door and held my hand to it, willing it to open faster than it was.

"Jen, Jacey," Chanary said as the door finally disappeared.

I tried to look as unbothered as I could, but I knew it was plastered all over my face. Thankfully, Jen answered her so I didn't have to.

"Yes, Chanary?"

"I was wondering...have you heard anything about Vincent yet?" she asked, looking concerned.

Jen grabbed onto my hand before I could reply. "We haven't heard a word yet, Chanary."

"Nothing at all?" she asked, moving closer to Jen and I.

"No, nothing," Jen stated, turning herself so she was face to face with Chanary.

"I know he should have been back by now. And I also know he was already supposed to contact you guys to let you know he was on his way back," Chanary said without flinching.

"Seriously… I really haven't got the patience to deal with you or anyone else right now. He hasn't contacted us and when he does, I can guarantee I won't be letting you in on it," I stated to Chanary as I walked through the door to our room.

"Chanary, right now isn't the best time to be asking Jacey anything. I think you need to wait for us to come to you and let you in on things," Jen said diplomatically.

"I only wanted to know what was going on. If I can help in any way, I want to. I've known Vincent all my life and he and Heathe are best friends. I only want to help."

The last words out of her mouth made me hesitate for a second, I knew Vincent wouldn't liked it if I was miserable to his friends…and I was pretty sure Chanary was one of them.

I seriously wanted to kick myself right now. My head and emotions were at war—for what I was sure wouldn't be the last time.

"I spoke to him in a trance…He won't be back for half a cycle," I said as I turned and watched my door close in Chanary's face. Right before it reformed, I saw the relief in her eyes and it actually relieved me a little.

"That was pretty decent of you," Jen said, tapping my back as we moved into the living room.

"I honestly didn't want to say anything to her, but for some unknown reason I knew Vincent would have wanted her to know what was up with everything."

"I'm sure he'd be pretty proud of you right now," Jen said, hugging me.

"At first all I wanted to do was punch her…Not the most cordial thing to do, but I figured with Heathe watching and all, I didn't want to have to deal with the two of them," I said, letting myself relax in Jen's embrace.

"I think we need to eat, relax, and sleep a little."

"I agree. What kind of food can I get here?"

"Anything you want."

"Salad and wings?" I asked.

"Sure, as long as you promise to try and sleep afterwards," Jen said, all mother-like.

"Cross my heart," I replied, making the sign with my hand over my heart while at the same time knowing sleep was the last thing on my mind. If I had read some of the signs right, I should be able to summon Vincent when everyone finally left me alone, and that was exactly what I planned on doing.

CHAPTER EIGHT

Summons in reverse
Enemies become allies
Life gets even more complicated

We ordered dinner through the visionary in the living room. At first I thought I wouldn't be able to eat until I got a whiff of the wings once they were delivered. It took the two of us about five minutes to polish off dinner.

"I can't eat another bite," I said to Jen as I laid back on the couch rubbing my now very protruding belly.

"Ditto. I didn't think I was as hungry as I was. Now I definitely need to get some sleep. How about you?" Jen asked, rubbing her own full belly.

"Sleep? I think I could try it," I said, getting up and stretching.

"Me too. Do you want me to bunk in with you?"

"No, no. I'm good. Thanks, anyway. I'll probably pass out the second my head hits my pillow."

"You sure?"

"Yeah, I'm sure. Night, Jen," I said, going over to hug her and then turned to my room.

"Night…" she replied, looking at me curiously.

The door opened as I put my hand to it. I walked slowly to my bed, willing the door to form quicker behind me. Once it did, I sat on my bed and grabbed the amulet around my neck. I hadn't a clue how to summon anyone but I was willing to try almost anything to try to talk to Vincent, even if it was for only a second.

I sat cross-legged in the middle of my bed, thinking about him. Nothing. I tried concentrating harder on visualizing him and still… nothing. I wasn't going to give up that easily. Maybe I had to be more comfortable. I went over to the closet and grabbed a pair of cut off shorts and a tank top and changed into it. I crawled back onto the bed and curled up under the comforter.

I lay there for what seemed like forever with nothing happening. I seriously needed to find a way for this to work…What had Verbeyna told me about blocking? Then it hit me, I needed to chant. I figured I didn't need to take up the pinched fingers crossed leg sitting position. So, I laid back, closed my eyes, visualized Vincent and started to call out to him.

At first I felt seriously silly and was only whispering his name, "Vincent, Vincent, Vincent." I stopped and looked down at my amulet. Still nothing.

I took in three deep breaths and started again.

86

"Vincent, please come to me. Vincent I need to see you. I'm…I'm—" I stopped, feeling even more silly. I rolled over to my side with my amulet still in hand. What was it Verbeyna told me to chant to keep from being summoned? It came back to me.

"Through the elements I am alive,

I shall choose my mind's eye.

I will not be summoned.

I am the portal for Kawaneing.

None shall be present unless I allow it.

I am the vessel."

So, if that kept people away, how about this to bring people to me…

"Through the elements I am alive,

I shall choose my mind's eye—Vincent,

I shall summon Vincent." My amulet began to glow pink.

"I am the portal for Kawaneing, I want to see Vincent." My amulet began to float and spin blues and reds.

"I want him present, now." A bright flash of white encompassed my room.

"I am his vessel." My room dulled in brightness.

I sat up and looked around, hoping to see Vincent, but there was nothing.

As I began to believe I'd failed at trying to summon him, my vision went blurry and started to recede like I was looking down a long black tunnel with a pinpoint of light at the end. I started to freak out a little. I knew I was about to lose consciousness. My breathing increased. As I turned my head to try and gain some perspective, I noticed not only had my vision been affected, but my body was as well…I was floating about two feet off my bed and I had no control over my limbs. I tried screaming but my mouth and vocal cords were not cooperating.

Then all went black. I floated in a sensory deprived bubble for a while. I still had my mind but nothing else. What was I thinking? What did I get myself into now? I burrowed deep in my mind, trying to figure a way out of this when I heard a voice.

"Jacey, I can't believe you made it."

My vision flowed back slowly, and I watched myself walking out into a large open field towards Vincent.

I didn't understand how I was seeing myself walking in the field but still being present in my body floating over my bed. It was super confusing, but at the same time I was overjoyed to see Vincent. I tried calling out but again my voice wouldn't cooperate—I was merely an observer.

"Vincent, I'm so worried about you. Have you led Daichi to the Shenuy Quarter? Are you coming home soon?" the me in the field asked.

"We've come upon a number of adversaries along the way and have had to alter our course a number of times. I can't say when we'll be home. But I can say I will try my hardest to make it home to you," Vincent said, embracing the me in the field.

As he did, I watched and felt a twinge of anger, something I thought was completely misplaced—until the me in the field turned around and looked directly into my eyes.

It was me, but a version with lighter hair and blue eyes. The girl Vincent was embracing wasn't me, it was Faith.

I tried calling out, I tried moving, I tried praying to move. Nothing. I watched helplessly as Faith reached up to Vincent's face and slowly traced her fingers down either side of cheeks. She raised up on her tip-toes and leaned into him. He reacted as I thought he would with me; he bent his head down so Faith wouldn't have to be on her tip-toes. He encircled her with his arms and pulled her close. I could hear their breathing deep and ragged. I could almost hear their heartbeats increasing with every inch they moved closer and every touch they exchanged. At the moment their faces came together, my vision filled with a pink aura. I felt a hardness on my back and I heard Heathe.

"Is she going to be okay?"

"She will. But I need to talk with her and outline the dangers of using magic she has no idea how to control. She could have opened a Bulwark right here. Right here in Nemele in the middle of our origin. How is that even possible?" a female voice asked.

"She has no idea about her powers and obviously we don't, either," Jen said.

"I—I was only…" My voice was back. "I was only trying to see Vincent," I said.

I opened my eyes. Standing around my bed were Jen, Heathe, and Verbeyna.

"I take it I screwed up," I said, sitting up in bed.

"You could have done a whole lot more than just screwed up," Verbeyna said as she came over and took a seat on the edge of my bed.

"What were you thinking?" Jen asked, obviously upset.

"I thought I'd be able to talk with Vincent. I thought I'd be able to find out what's going on."

"You put us all in danger. The only reason we don't have a full Sentry guard on top of us right now is because Heathe was able to hold in your signal while Jen channeled me," Verbeyna said.

Heathe moved back to the doorway. He stood there staring down at me. At first I thought he was looking at me through anger-filled eyes, like he had when I first entered Nemele, but when I looked closer, I saw concern reflected there instead.

"I'm sorry. I had no idea."

"I get that you're sorry, Jacey. I get that you want to see Vincent. But I also *get* that you almost opened a Bulwark here—right here in your dorm room! I have no idea how you were even able to use a summons on an amulet I powered for repulsion."

"I don't know how, either. I only thought..." I said but Verbeyna cut me off.

"That's just it. You didn't think." Her words were filled with annoyance.

"Take it easy. She didn't know what she was doing and she's had a pretty long day. No one outside of here knows what happened and we can keep it that way. Can't you sit with her for a while and explain the powers of the amulet a little better?" Heathe asked, moving from the doorway and coming to stand beside Jen.

Verbeyna shot him a look which could have frozen water. Heathe didn't flinch.

"I can. But she's got to understand I won't keep another one of these episodes to myself. She's a threat, a danger to everyone else in here, and I won't be a part of her bringing a Yietimpi faction into the heart of Nemele," Verbeyna stated without so much as blinking.

"I won't do it again, I promise. I'm soooo sorry I caused all this trouble. I really, really didn't mean to." I looked directly into her eyes

"Fine." Verbeyna looked at Heathe. "Last time, Heathe. Jacey, the amulet's powers were meant to keep you from being summoned against your will. To work it in reverse would…well, I think we saw what almost happened here tonight—"

"I don't know what I saw…other than Vincent. He was in a field. I tried to move, to talk, to go to him, but I couldn't. But then I saw me—but it really wasn't me. It was Faith and she was pretending to be me. He said their adversaries were more in number than they expected and he wasn't sure now when he would be coming home. Was any of it real?"

"It was and wasn't. You opened a channel for beings who can propel their thoughts through a summons. We all know Faith has the ability because of what she did to you. I can't tell you if what you saw was real or not. It may be your imagination playing games with you or…it may be a vision you were able to intercept and see. I can't tell you which is true. What I can tell you is I have empowered the amulet now to never become a beacon to another. In other words, it won't let you try and summon anyone ever again." She was obviously irritated with me; I could hear it in her sharp tone.

"I truly never meant to endanger anyone. I am sorry I put you, Heathe, and Jen in the position I did. Thank you for not including anyone else in it," I said as Verbeyna got up from my bed and headed to the door. She passed Heathe and their eyes connected. There was a tangible vibe in the room. They had a definite history together. She placed her hand on his arm and said, "I'll see you later for... you know." She turned to me, nodded once, then disappeared through the doorway.

"Wow, I screwed up, didn't I?" I said to both Jen and Heathe.

"I get why you tried. I really do, but from now on you have to promise me you'll keep me in the loop when you want to try something like this ever again," Jen said, coming over and sitting beside me.

"I will, I promise," I said, crossing my heart.

Heathe hadn't moved. He stood there staring at me. I looked into his eyes, and for a brief second, a tinge of guilt attacked my stomach.

"I can't cover it again. Your powers are way too strong," he said, not losing eye contact.

"You won't have to cover it again, I promise. And I'm sorry." I knew he was going against every rule right now keeping what happened here to the confines of the room and the people who involved.

"I know. How did Vincent look?" he asked, catching me a little off guard.

"He looked…good. Faith was the only other person with him. I still don't know if it was real or not."

"I think it's partially real. You and Vincent have a connection. Whether it was him in the flesh you saw or the projection of him through someone else, at least we all know that he's alive and trying to come home," Heathe said.

"Do you want me to stay in here with you?" Jen asked. "We all still have to get some rest."

"No, I really am okay and I swear I won't try anything again."

"Jen, can I talk to Jacey alone for a second?" Heathe asked.

"Yeah, sure, if Jacey's all right with it."

"Yeah, it's okay."

"I'll be right next door if you need me and Grace should be returning really soon," Jen said, squeezing my hand and getting up from the bed.

The door reformed as Jen left. My room suddenly felt very small with just the two of us in it. Heathe hadn't moved from the door.

"Jacey, I promised Vincent I'd take care of you…no matter what. But I don't ever want to have to break into a room again to make sure you're not getting killed or something. I get that you don't know me that well yet, but I need you to start coming to me when you have an idea or a compulsion to do something you're unsure of." He paused long enough for me to cut in.

"I—I will. I really didn't mean to cause anything. I had no idea it would turn out like this."

"That's the reason why I've asked you to come and talk to me if or when you ever get another idea like this one." His eyes drifted for a second to my chest and then back up to my face. It was then I realized I was in nothing but my tank top and cut offs. I crossed my arms over my chest, attempting to cover up a bit.

"How'd you get in here?" I asked as a slow tingling heat rose from my chest into my face.

"I can get in wherever I need to be. I wouldn't have come into your room but I felt your pain." He stopped quickly, as though he'd said something he hadn't meant to.

"My pain? How?" I was now curious as to what he meant.

He moved closer to my bed and took a seat on the chair beside it. "When we—when we..." He paused, looking slightly uncomfortable for a second, then cleared his throat and sat up straight and continued all Sentry-like. "The moment we connected in our traditional way, there was a bond formed between the two of us. I'm unsure if you're able to feel as I am, but there was a link, and with it comes my ability to sense your feelings." He stopped and looked directly into my eyes.

"You mean when our hands intertwined it created a connection between the two of us?"

"Yes. I don't know if it's because I told Vincent I'd watch out for you or if there are other reasons behind it."

His last couple of words stuck in my mind: 'other reasons behind it.' What did that even mean?

I was unsure on how to proceed with our conversation.

"Jacey, I needed to tell you because I…I promised Verbeyna I'd meet with her tonight, and that means I have to leave you alone for a while. So, I'm trusting you to not get into anything—because if you do, I won't be here. I'm not supposed to leave an assignment—ever—but because of calling her in earlier, I now have to go and hold up my end of the deal." He stopped and looked at me like I should know what he was talking about.

"Heathe, if you have to go see your *girlfriend*, I get it. Really, I do. Don't worry about me. I can totally take care of myself and trust me, I won't be doing anything but sleeping anyway," I said with way more emotion than I meant to.

"She's not my girl."

"Listen, you don't need to explain. We can talk about all the other stuff later. I'm starting to get tired, so if you want to get going, now would be a good time." I smiled but it didn't reach my eyes, and I could tell he wasn't buying into my cheeriness, either.

"Fine. I only wanted to make you aware that I can feel your emotions because when I'm gone, it won't matter where I am, I'll still be able to feel you." He got up from the chair and started towards my door. "I'll be back soon." He flashed into his natural essence and disappeared.

What the hell was wrong with me? Why was I giving him attitude about going to see another girl? I was Vincent's Wirposh—wasn't I? So why was I feeling like someone had punched me in the gut when Heathe said he was going over to see Verbeyna? Serious confusion was not a place I needed to be visiting right now.

I needed to ask Jen about all of this, but more important right now was for me to try and get some sleep. I was exhausted and I knew without some rest I'd be of no use to anyone.

I curled up under my covers and closed my eyes. I tried turning my mind off of the conversation I'd had with Heathe and tried focusing in on the visual I'd had of Vincent in the field with Faith.

A buzzing sound from the entrance to my dorm woke me. I sat up, shocked I'd been asleep at all. I hadn't dreamed at all and my dream colors hadn't visited. I grabbed my neck and felt the weight of the amulet still present. With the comfort of it, a new discomfort came to mind, I wondered if Heathe was still with Verbeyna.

The buzzing persisted and I grabbed a sweat top, threw it on, and went out to answer the door. Jen met me in the living room area and we both answered the door.

A flash of red entered our dorm and stopped just inside the doorway.

"What kind of crap have you got my brother into now?" Chanary demanded as she stood there with her foot tapping and arms crossed over her chest.

"What are you talking about?" Jen asked.

"I know Heathe had to go meet with Verbeyna tonight, something he's been avoiding since they broke up like a year ago, so I know it had to have something to do with the two of you."

"Why would you think we had anything to do with him going out with Verbeyna?" I asked, getting really irritated with her brassiness. At least that's what I thought the nagging gut feeling I was experiencing was from.

"Uh, hello. He's my brother and I know when there's something going on with him. Not to mention Verbeyna's been trying to get back together with him since they broke up, and now, for some crazy reason, he's over at her dorm…which, by the way, is in the same area as mine."

"Crap," Jen said as she went over to the couch and took a seat.

"Crap what?" both Chanary and I asked simultaneously.

"Heathe didn't want anyone to know," Jen said, grabbing her hair up into a pony tail and placing an elastic in it, pulling it halfway through. She pulled her knees up to her chest and placed her head on top of them.

"Spill it," I said, now very confused as to why Jen was having this kind of reaction.

"Jen, I know we don't really like one another, but when it comes to my brother, I would do absolutely anything to make sure he's safe. It took him forever to finally get rid of Verbeyna—it must have been something pretty big for him to go and see her," Chanary said, looking between both Jen and I.

Jen looked at me as though the decision was mine to let Chanary in on things. At first I had assumed Heathe went to see Verbeyna because there was some kind of romantic thing between the two of them, now I was feeling guilty knowing he only went to see her because of me.

"Chanary, when a Hinderer is called in to help out with a situation, what is their payment?" I asked, knowing they got something from the being that was asking for their services, but not knowing exactly what the payment was.

"It depends on what they do, but they are very much an eye for an eye society. What did my brother do for you?"

Jen looked over at me as I took up a seat beside her. "It's yours to tell, Jacey," Jen said.

"How do we know if we can even trust her?" I asked, acting like Chanary wasn't in the room.

"Seriously…You don't have a choice. If you don't tell me what's going on, I'm heading to the Archives to see Herecerti."

I didn't know where to begin. I took in two deep breaths and steadied myself. "I almost opened a Bulwark in my room."

"I want the truth. Quit wasting my time," Chanary said through clenched teeth.

"I am telling you the truth. I swear."

Chanary held out her hand to me. She wasn't going to trust my word; she wanted to 'connect' in our traditional Nemelite way.

I hesitated for a second, looking at Jen for some kind of direction. All she did was nod and I knew it was the only way we were going to be able to gain Chanary's silence.

I held out my hand and she grasped it, holding it to her chest. "May the elements keep you eternal," we said in unison.

The feeling I received from Chanary at first was pure loathing. It was obvious even before we'd connected that she couldn't stand me. I had no idea what she was feeling from me, but within a few seconds, her feelings changed slightly.

She began to radiate tolerance and trust…as though something she felt from me had changed her perspective. She let go of my hand and stood there silent for a minute.

"So, you're telling the truth. What else happened?" she asked, uncrossing her arms.

"I tried to summon Vincent and it completely backfired. Heathe must have called Verbeyna in when he sensed I was in pain, and from there I have no idea what went on between the two of them," I said.

Jen looked at me, confused. "He felt your pain?" she asked.

"Yeah, that's what he said before he told me he had to go see Verbeyna. I thought he was going there because, well, because they were a couple," I replied, feeling completely dense. "I had no idea he was going there to pay off a debt, especially one for me."

"They haven't been a couple for a long time. Heathe had his reasons for ending the relationship. He never told me why, but Verbeyna wasn't easy to get rid of. Now she's found another way into his life." Chanary paused for a second then looked at me. "You said you tried to summon Vincent. What happened?"

I figured since I totally screwed up her brother, I owed Chanary at least an explanation of everything that happened here tonight. I told her everything. When I finished, we all sat in silence for a moment.

"It seems like you guys are going to need my help," Chanary said, leaving no room for anyone to deny her offer.

The door to the dorm faded and Aunt Grace walked in.

"Chanary," she said, walking past her and tossing an inquisitive look at Jen and I.

"I asked her to come over. Since she's Heathe's sister and has known Vincent forever, I figured we could use as much help as possible," I said, hoping Aunt Grace wouldn't question Chanary's presence any further.

"All right, then. We have a little while before we have to go to the Infinity Waters to meet Ria. Did you two get any rest?"

"Yeah, a little," I answered.

"Herecerti and I made a little headway with the prophecy. It appears that the Armers are the society within the Nephilim which wrote the original divination."

"Great! At least we have a start point now," Jen said.

"Not really," Chanary chimed in. We all looked over at the newest and most out of place addition to our group. "The Armers were the Sentry of sorts for the Nephilim, they were also the most secretive. It's going to be next to impossible to find any of their writings. They were destroyed along with the Armers when their world was vanquished."

"How would you know all of that?" Aunt Grace asked.

"Because, our originating world was destroyed along with the Nephilim's," Heathe said, forming beside Chanary.

"Now I'm totally confused. What world are you from? I thought you were from Nemele…" I said, feeling a slight twinge in my gut as we made eye contact…*great.*

CHAPTER NINE

Worlds of Nemele revealed
Connections are questioned
Promises—made just to be broken

"Heathe, now I'm more confused," Aunt Grace said.

"There are nineteen Nations in Nemele…now. Originally there were twenty-one. Are you saying that the two of you are descendants of the Nephilim?" Jen asked.

"No, I'm saying we're from another race of beings who were closely related to the Nephilim. We were a race the Armers created to ensure all followed the set of laws laid out by the Elders," Heathe said, not looking away from me.

"So, what you're saying is there were twenty-one Nations within Nemele at some point?" Aunt Grace asked.

"Yeah, that's what I'm saying. I didn't want to reveal anything about our race here at this time, but with the developments of late, I really don't have a choice," Heathe said.

The buzz of the visionary interrupted our conversation. Aunt Grace walked over to it, raised her hand to the switch on the wall, and instantly the visionary was filled with Herecerti and Hudson.

"Are you ready?" Herecerti asked.

"We are. However, there are some developments we need to discuss. Would the Infinity Waters be the best place to discuss them?" Aunt Grace asked.

"I have restricted the area. We will have complete seclusion while we're there," Herecerti replied.

"We're on our way," Aunt Grace said, turning the visionary off.

"Are you comfortable enough talking to all of us at the Infinity Waters?" Aunt Grace asked Heathe and Chanary.

"We're fine. It's time all knew, and with the return of Jacey, now is the only time I believe I won't be punished for sharing the information," Heathe said, moving over to Chanary's side.

"To the Infinity Waters then," Aunt Grace said.

"Ummm. Can I have a minute to change? I'm still in my pajamas; I'd like to put something else on," I said, looking over at Jen, hoping she'd come with me.

"Yeah, I need to change, too. We'll be out in a minute," Jen said, following my lead. We both went into my room. I waited for the door to reform and then turned to Jen.

"What the hell is going on? Heathe and Chanary aren't from here?" I asked Jen before she could say a word.

"Hold up. What's up with Heathe feeling your pain? Why didn't you say something to me?" Jen asked.

"Seriously, when was I supposed to do that? Before or after our new 'best friend' showed up?" I was being sarcastic, trying to deflect the question. Right now I really didn't want to have to talk about any kind of feelings I had or was having for Heathe. I already felt totally guilty over the fact they existed at all. I had no control over any of it and I didn't like *not* being in control of my emotions.

"Okay. I get it. Right now isn't the time to talk about any of this. We actually don't have time to. But you have to promise me we'll talk about the Heathe thing the second we're alone," Jen said, grabbing a pair of jeans and a t-shirt from my closet.

"I promise. I need to talk to you about it. I have no idea why any of this is happening to me. Sixteen years and no problems when it came to guys. Now, all of a sudden I have to watch who I touch because some kind of 'connection' can happen," I said, running my fingers through my hair as I placed it in a high pony tail. I grabbed a pair of jeans and a sweater and turned to Jen.

"Ready?" she asked.

"No, not really, but where else am I going to go? I can't hide in here."

She came over and hugged me. "Jacey, it'll all work out. I'll be here for you and we'll figure everything out. I promise," she said, letting me go and heading to the door. I followed her out to the living room. Once there, the conversation we'd walked into stopped.

"Let's get going. We have a lot to discuss," Aunt Grace said, opening the door to our room. "Heathe, it would be better if we met you there. I don't want to have to explain why you're here in our dorm."

"I'll see you there," he said, looking directly at me.

I nodded and he flashed into his origin form and disappeared. Damn my gut—whooshing again.

"Ready?" I said, following Aunt Grace, Jen and Chanary out of our dorm. Jen and Aunt Grace walked ahead.

"You know, the only reason I had issue with you initially is because I didn't think you belonged here," Chanary said.

"Well, thanks for making me feel so comfortable," I said.

"I'm trying to apologize."

"I'm not really in a forgiving mood right now, Chanary. For my whole life I've had to deal with people like you...or whatever you are. You think because you realized you were wrong in how you originally treated me that I'm just going to open up to you and say 'hey, let's be friends'? Don't hold your breath. It isn't going to happen. I know you want Vincent and that's not going to happen no matter how you try to weasel your way in."

Needless to say, the rest of the walk was done in silence. I didn't want to go off on Chanary but her trying to make excuses for her behavior up to this point and at this particular time was on my mind, not just her stepping over the line. She pretty much pole vaulted her way over it.

We arrived at the Infinity Waters at the same time Hudson and Herecerti did. Jen went over and hugged Hudson as Aunt Grace went and stood beside Herecerti. Chanary was still beside me, leaving me envisioning a thorn in my side with her head on the tip of it.

Heathe flashed in and stood leaning against one of the eight pillars of the waters.

With a gust, Mom appeared in the center of the waters. Everyone present could see her.

"How?" Chanary asked, moving from my side and going to stand beside Heathe.

"We're all here, now what are the revelations we need to discuss?" Herecerti interjected, leaving Chanary's half question still hanging in the air.

"Heathe," Aunt Grace said.

I moved closer to Jen and Hudson, who were standing close to the Waters and close to Mom.

"With the return of Jacey, there has been a new interest in the prophecies of the Nephilim. Along with that interest, it has stirred up ancient quarrels. The Armers were the sect of Nephilim who scribed the prophecy which spoke of Jacey and Faith. They were also the beings who created my race, the Draco. We were from the world of Ryu, a world filled with Songards. To translate to English—"

"You are of the Dragon world? How is it possible I have not been made aware of this?" Herecerti asked, looking more curious than mad.

"There are few who are aware we exist. We have not made it a point to advertise our existence because of the Armers. They, as well as the remaining other four societies of Nephilim, are spread throughout the nineteen remaining worlds. Most chose to survive within Earth's Realm. They've been there since the flooding," Heathe answered.

"The flooding?" Hudson asked.

"Yes, the flooding. The time in human history when the earth was flooded and Noah survived, as well as the creatures of Earth's domain. As Dracos, we were instructed by the Armers, Noah being one of them, to flood the Earth so they could take up position within the dimension to gain credibility in their existence," Heathe said, moving from Chanary to Herecerti.

"The five societies of the Nephilim were introduced to Earth's realm, upon their world's destruction. As guards or guides for the Nephilim, we have always stayed in the shadows. Until now. With the return of the anomaly—Jacey—it seems we can no longer stay within the periphery of Nemelite society," Heathe stated, taking Herecerti's hand.

They greeted in the traditional Nemelite way— "May the elements keep you eternal," both said as they embraced.

Herecerti tilted his head slightly to the right and completed the greeting with Heathe. "Shall I assume Chanary is of the Draco order as well?" he asked.

"I am. I don't have the same amount of powers as Heathe, but I am in training to become a guardian," she answered.

"What does all this mean for Jacey?" my mom interjected.

"It means she is the anomaly. There is no doubt of it and I can now explain her significance in our world," Heathe said, taking up a position in front of me. He extended his hand to me. I hesitated for a second, then took it. Instantly, there was a glow and a connection. My stomach felt the whoosh times a hundred and everyone around us witnessed it. I blushed from head to toe and tried to break the grip he had on my hand but was unsuccessful.

"Jacey, I have been chosen by the Armers to be your protector. That is the connection you are feeling as we come together. I pledge my life to keeping you safe and within Nemele's realm. I will not allow Necroseek's legions a chance to obtain you or your essence," Heathe revealed.

"Why you? Why me? Why is all of this is happening?" I asked.

"I have to recount the history of the Nephilim to explain how all of those events led us to today," he said, letting go of my hands and turning so everyone in the room could see him.

I took a seat on the ledge of the pool along with Jen, Hudson, and Chanary. Mom stayed quiet, hovering in the Waters behind me. Aunt Grace stood beside me with Herecerti by her side.

"It is through our journeys in history we all learn, Heathe. Please share yours with us," Herecerti asked.

"The Armers knew there was a sect of Nephilim who were choosing to go the way of the Yietimpi. Necroseek was an Amazarak. He was trusted with educating and mentoring our finest members. He believed he was not to be challenged. When the Elders of our twenty-one societies decided to rein in his teachings, he became more seditious. He sat in wait for eons, documenting the ways of the other tribes of Nephilim. His intent was to rule all of the societies within Nemele's domain. He nearly succeeded, however the Armers and the Draco intercepted his legions prior to their attack. During the battles, Ryu was destroyed and along with it, the Nephilim home world. Most were able to congregate on earth—causing the great flood. Necroseek swore vengeance and disappeared through the charts of the Barkayals who were faithful to him." He paused for a moment, choosing his next words carefully.

"When Necroseek disappeared, there was evidence a number of Nephilim loyal to him followed. Within the nineteen remaining worlds, the students of those Nephilim also chose to leave behind their worlds, their families, and their freedom to follow Necroseek. It was during this time the Nephilim true to Nemele destroyed the charts the Barkayals had created showing the portals throughout the universes. They knew Necroseek had acquired a number of them and had been utilizing them to spread his minions throughout the worlds to conquer and recruit. It was during this time the Armers wrote the prophecy of Kawaneing. They knew the time would come when

Necroseek's power would become a threat to all of the worlds within Nemele again. It may have taken him eons to gather the support for his first coup, but from their mistakes of the past they were preparing for the future." He paused only for a second to ensure there were no questions from anyone listening.

"The prophecy was written by the elders of Nephilim and placed within the archives in hopes to never have to deal with an anomaly born of their Awakening. They wrote it so it would be almost impossible for it to come true—to have two born of their Awakening is astonishing. The Elders didn't want to tilt the scales of the Fates in one direction or the other, so they prophesized one of virtue and one of wickedness. There were no indicators as to whom the children would be born or when they would arrive, but with the births of Jacey and Faith, it was believed the Fates had taken a hand in placing the two anomalies within Nemelite families filled with righteousness. The Nephilim Elders were pleased and believed they need not worry about the wickedness they had prophesized. They were cautious and they watched for the first two years. They were not within the Nemele realm when Faith's abduction occurred. They were aware of who had abducted her and where they had taken her, but still could not retrieve her. They believed because she'd been born within and witnessed morality within her developmental years, she would hold onto it as the legions of Necroseek attempted to corrupt her." Heathe paused as Aunt Grace sucked in a deep breath. It was obvious she was having a harder time than the rest of us listening to this. I placed my hand in Aunt Grace's and gave it a squeeze, hoping she would gain some strength from it. She looked down at me and squeezed my hand back. She smiled at me weakly.

"One probable outcome of the prophecy is if Jacey and Faith are brought together under Necroseek's rule, he will be able to open the gates the Barkayal had sealed. Jacey and Faith would be conduits to the paths of the ancients and would be able to forge new paths throughout each universe. Faith and Jacey are not blessed with one gift. They are, in true form, blessed with every gift imaginable. Together, there is no realm, world, or society that could reign in the power the two would have as one."

"'Have as one,' what does that mean?" Mom asked.

"If they are brought together under the right circumstances, one may be dominated by the other, not only in mind, but also in body. That is why they are doppelgangers of one another," Heathe said.

"So, does that mean Jacey may be over powered by Faith if they're reunited? As in Jacey may not exist as we know her if she and Faith are together?" Hudson asked.

"It means there is a possibility one may be possessed by the other, Faith to Jacey or vice versa. However, it's only a theory. It's unknown what will occur when they meet again."

"Well, they just won't meet again," Hudson said, standing up and coming over to stand in front of me. "It's way too much of a risk."

111

"Hold on. We don't know what will happen to me when I get to meet Faith. Who knows, maybe I'll be the one to possess her. Something I really have no desire to do. Or maybe, nothing will happen at all to either one of us. We both may be able to survive with each other and live happily ever after. None of us seriously has any idea what's going to happen. But I know one thing for sure, I wouldn't be able to live with myself if we didn't try to get Aunt Grace's family back to her. After everything she and Uncle Gideon have done to save us, it wouldn't be right to run and hide again." It came out before I could stop myself. I turned to Mom. She looked like someone had just punched her in the stomach.

"Mom, I didn't mean—" Before I could finish she cut me off.

"We did run, Jacey. We ran because we knew we couldn't keep the promise of staying and fighting when the risk of losing you was so great. I love my sister, niece, and Gideon for all they have sacrificed and I don't want to break any more promises I've made to them. I know we can't keep running. I believe it is time to stand up and fight. To unite our family again," Mom said.

"The battle will come, but not as soon as some hope for it to be. It's been reported Vincent made it to the truce line, but ventured over it with Daichi. It's not known how long it will take for us to fully understand where he is and how we're going to get him back. It appears for the time being, he is beyond our reach," Heathe said, coming over to stand before me as I wrapped my arms around my waist and hung my head.

"He promised. He promised to come back," I said over and over as I fell into Heathe's embrace when my legs gave out and a crushing grip of loss stilled in my heart.

CHAPTER TEN

Broken pieces come together
Creases upon one's heart
Leave chasms of grief
However, hope is not lost

Herecerti stepped forward, placing his hand on my shoulder. "He is not lost, Jacey. We will find him and return him home. Has anyone discussed this with Eve and Bronson? Are they aware of Vincent's status?"

"Not yet, but I do believe within the next while they shall be made aware," Heathe said, still holding me in an embrace.

"I believe the Elders need to reconvene within the Inception Chamber. Is it possible to have representatives of The Draco clans and members of the Nephilim rejoin us and take their rightful position within the Guild?" Herecerti asked.

"I can ask, but until I receive an answer, everyone here is to keep what I have revealed today within these walls. The Draco and the Nephilim as societies are still in the shadows of all remaining nineteen worlds. There are some who believe we should not yet reveal ourselves in an effort to keep an upper hand on Necroseek," Heathe said, pulling me to a standing position with him. He didn't let me go and I didn't try to get away from his embrace.

"I understand. Then all revealed here shall stay here. Ria, are you and Hearte able to venture through the realms and report back to us when you have some news?" Herecerti asked.

"We can. Grace," Mom said, waiting to ensure Aunt Grace was paying attention to her.

"Yes?"

"We will find her. We will find Gideon and we will all be reunited."

"I love you, Ri."

"I love you too, Gracie," Mom replied. "Jacey, Vincent will survive. He's strong and knows how to care for himself. I need you to be strong and train. Train with Heathe and the other Elders so we'll be able to rescue our family."

I straightened from Heathe's embrace and wiped away the tears that still clung to my lower eyelids.

"I can't believe he's gone. I need to know he's okay. Is there any way we can communicate with him?" I asked, playing with the amulet around my neck, hoping someone in the room would have an answer.

"I don't know, Jacey. I don't know how. I'm unsure of exactly where he and Daichi are," Herecerti said.

"We need to make sure when you do communicate with him, this time you're safe," Jen said, looking at Heathe and Chanary.

"What am I missing?" Hudson asked.

"Jacey," Jen said, placing her hand in Hudson's.

"I tried to do a reverse summons when I first got back to my room—it didn't go so well." I said, playing with the amulet around my neck. "I thought I'd be able to see Vincent and possibly get him back home. But the summons went wrong. He was with Faith and she was pretending to be me...and Vincent, well, he was falling for it. Verbeyna had to come and help us out." I let go of the amulet, and as I did, I realized I was still being held up by Heathe as I recounted the events. Hudson was obviously peeved.

"Seriously! Why am I only hearing about this now? What were you thinking, Jace? What if...what if I ended up losing you, too?" Hudson was so mad his voice cracked and you could see the pulse in his neck.

"You didn't and you won't. Verbeyna did something to the amulet to make it impossible for me to try a reverse summons again," I said, sounding like a five-year-old. I was pretty upset myself, but not for the same reasons. I had sent Vincent into a trap. How was I going to live with myself now? How was I going to get him back?

"Totally not the point, Jacey. You need to be a lot more careful when it comes to doing stuff like that because it doesn't only put you in danger. It puts all of us in danger!" Chanary chimed in. She wasn't going to let me get away with the '*I did it, it's over, let it go,'* attitude I tried to give off to everyone else.

"You need to start thinking about *everyone*…not only Vincent. Anyone who's going to be connected to you in any way is in danger. My brother is connected to you. I won't let anything happen to him no matter the circumstances." Chanary stopped talking and stared me down with blazing green eyes.

"I don't want anyone to get hurt." I cut back moving slightly to my right and away from Heathe's arms. "I only want to make sure Vincent gets home and we find a way to rescue Aunt Grace's family. I'm new to this and I won't ask for *anyone's* permission to think and feel the way I do. If something happens, I'll be the one in the forefront taking the brunt of whatever comes my way." I was now turning my own shade of color, red as my temper started to rear its ugly head in Chanary's direction.

"Jacey, Chanary's only pointing out the obvious. You may not want anything to happen to anyone around you, but that's just not the way things happen. We're all here because we have a vested interest in keeping you safe and in finding our loved ones. I love you and understand your desire to find Vincent, but we need to let the Elders take the lead in this one. Neither you nor I are prepared to take on the dark side of Nemele. We need to work together in sharing information about what is happening, both with Vincent and with you," Aunt Grace said, taking her time to make eye contact with Jen, Chanary, Heathe, and I.

"Are we comfortable with allowing Jacey to continue on in the dorm she's sharing with Jen and Grace?" Chanary asked Heathe as though I wasn't standing there.

"You are seriously starting to pis—" before I could speak any further, Heathe spoke up.

"I made arrangements with Verbeyna to place blockers on the dorm and I'll be there. I don't see a need in concerning anyone with moving Jacey from her family."

"Heathe, we'll talk later in regards to the price you've paid with Verbeyna. For now I must go to council. Hudson, I would appreciate you coming with me to represent your family in the Elders meeting," Herecerti said.

"Of course, but I want to be one of the guards assigned to my sister afterwards. I realize my training hasn't come close to a full guard, but I would appreciate being there," Hudson asked.

"I will see what I can do with your request. Jacey will have Jen, Heathe, your aunt and Chanary for protection, but I do understand why you feel the need to be there also. Jacey, it has been an extremely long and taxing day. I need for you to return to your dorm and get some rest. If you find it hard to get any, I can make arrangements for someone to come and assist you with sleep," Herecerti offered.

"I'll be okay, thank you. Jen, Aunt Grace, are you ready to go?" I asked, walking over to them.

"We are," Jen said, taking my arm in hers.

"Chanary and I will be along later. I need to make a report to our Elders of Nephilim and bring them your requests," Heathe said, coming closer to me. "If you need me, all you need to do is call out my name. I will ensure our connection is open at all times," he said with such conviction, my breath caught.

"I will. Can you look into where Vincent might be ?" I asked, staring into his deep chestnut eyes.

"He is my friend. I already have queries out. I promised him I'd keep you safe and I promise you now, we will find him." He gently brushed the top of my hand with his, then turned and left the room with Chanary.

"Herecerti and I will walk you back to the main entrance," Hudson said, walking up to me and taking my other arm.

Flanked by Jen and Hudson, Aunt Grace and Herecerti followed us out of the Infinity Waters' chamber.

"I'm still not comfortable with leaving you alone with Aunt Grace...but even more now with Heathe," Hudson grumbled in my ear.

"I'm with her, Hudson. She'll be okay," Jen whispered back.

"I know you're with her, but that doesn't mean I'm not going to worry. I'm actually more worried now about the *two* of you than just Jacey. Did anyone catch on to the question Herecerti had about what Heathe paid Verbeyna with?" Hudson asked.

"Yeah, we both did," I answered for Jen and I.

"Well, if he's indebted to a Hinderer—we have a lot more to worry about, and I won't be kept in the dark anymore about what's going on with you," Hudson stated.

"Maybe when we get back to our room, Jen, you and I can chat a little about some of the things going on. I'm not the most comfortable doing it while walking through the halls." As I said it, Jen and Hudson realized there was more than Aunt Grace and Herecerti around us. It was as though every Nemelite being had chosen that moment to be in the hallways of the Origin.

"Point taken," Jen said.

We walked on in silence until we made our way back to the main entrance.

"Hudson, will you accompany me?" Herecerti said.

"Of course." He hugged me close to him and whispered in my ear, "Sleep, but be careful. Listen to Jen."

"We'll meet up later," Hudson called back as he and Herecerti left in the direction of the Inception Chamber.

"Time for us to get some rest," Aunt Grace said, coming up beside me and taking the arm Hudson had let go of.

"I'm exhausted," I said, feeling an overwhelming rush of grief strike me in the center of my chest. It was as though someone had placed an enormous weight on it. I held it together as we made our way to the dorm.

Once inside, I took a deep breath, hoping it would alleviate the pressure within my chest. It didn't.

"I need to get some rest. I'll see you guys in the morning," I said, hugging Aunt Grace and making my way over to Jen.

"How about I stay with you until you fall asleep?" Jen offered.

"Sure, sounds good."

"Goodnight, Aunt Grace. Love you."

"I love you to, Jacey…never forget that," she said, walking past me, touching my cheek, and turning in to her room.

As we entered my room, the pain in my chest grew, migrating to my lungs, then to the back of my throat, and finally into my head. Behind my eyes the pressure was nearly unbearable.

"Jacey, let it out," Jen said, guiding me to my bed, then sitting with me on it and cradling me in her arms.

The second she said it, I allowed myself to let go. The tears flowed as I heaved, trying to gain breath after breath. I was in physical pain. The center of my being felt like someone had torn it apart. My head felt as though it were in a vice and with every wrenching sob, it tightened. Not since my parents' death had I cried the way I had tonight. My last memory was of Jen tucking me in and sitting by my bedside, wordlessly stroking my bangs and blotting my tear-streaked cheeks with a warm cloth.

My dream colors sluggishly edged into my consciousness. My colors were a lot of things but they were never timid in their appearances. They flashed in or flowed in, never edged in. I sat up and realized I was in the field I had seen Faith and Vincent in earlier. It seemed like everything was in slow motion. My movements were stalled but my consciousness was sharp. I sat looking for anyone else that may be in my dream. There was no one around. I lay back and stared up into a palette of color above me. There was no sky, only swirling colors. As I began to feel at ease, I felt a hand cushion into mine. I turned in slow motion over to my right, and lying beside me was Vincent. My heart skipped and joy exploded within me.

"I thought I'd never see you again," I said without moving my lips.

"I'll always be here," he said, moving his hand from mine and slowing tracing up along my arm to my neck, cheek, and finally resting on my temple. "I will never leave you." It was apparent we were not conversing in the normal sense of the word. We were speaking to one another through our minds.

"Are you safe?"

"I am. I won't be home as soon as I'd like. There are many things the Elders and others have kept from us," he said, turning onto his side in slow motion and pressing his side up against my arm. He was now positioned so he was staring directly down at me.

"Tell me what I can do to help get you home. We're all so worried..." Before I could finish my thought, Vincent leaned into me, bringing his right hand over to the left side of my body. He began tracing the outline of my cheek and traced the vein which was pulsing as though it were a kinked hose down my throat to the center at the base of my neck.

The look in his eyes was not one of someone waiting to be rescued. The look piercing though me was something I'd never seen before. It made the lower area of my stomach burn and my heart beat rapidly. It made me want to hold him and have him hold me. I was confused and trying to figure out how I went from desperately miserable to compliant and tingly.

"Wait, where are we?" I asked.

"We are where we can be together. Where I can feel you. Where I want to feel you," he replied. As he did, he moved his head down towards mine and our lips connected. He crushed me with his body weight and positioned himself directly above me. I kept my eyes open, slightly shocked by his brazenness. His eyes were closed as he slowly kissed me, at first gently and pensively. His lips were soft and full. He progressed to open mouth and kneading my mouth with his.

My pulse was in my ears and my belly was filled with a warm, tingly sensation. The second I thought I couldn't feel anymore, afraid of sensory overload, I experienced my first real kiss. Vincent slid his tongue into my mouth and claimed it as his own. My body reacted as though it had always been kissing him. At first he was gentle and I was overwhelmed with our connection. I closed my eyes and lost myself in his scent.

A burning smell invaded my senses and I opened my eyes. As I did, staring back at me in Vincent's face were onyx eyes filled with red sparks. As I stopped kissing him and tried to scream out, a coal black wing shot out from his back and encircled me, blacking out all light.

I could still feel the weight of his body on mine and my mind was still sharp. Everything else was muted. My heart rate increased and my breathing became rapid. I was starting to freak out. This was NOT Vincent. I had no idea who this was... The first thought to come to mind was to get to safety.

"HEATHE!" I yelled out in my mind.

There was nothing at first...I screamed again "HEATHE, I need you!"

The being holding onto me shuddered and convulsed. Two red piercing eyes stared at me in the darkness of the embrace I was imprisoned in.

"For now, Jacey...the Nephilim pet can't keep you safe forever," a low, sinister voice rumbled in my ear. The heat of its breath scorched the hair surrounding my ear and a long slow lick from the beast's mouth moved from below my ear lobe to the center of my ear.

"I will have you." In a burst of light, the beast was gone and I was sitting up in my bed with Jen sleeping soundly in the chair off to the right. I looked around for anyone else in the room and spotted Heathe's signature in the corner.

I grabbed my ear and felt wet behind it. My body instantly shivered in the memory of my nightmare. As I began to breathe in slowly, trying to regulate my heart rate, a long black feather drifted slowly but surely from the visionary in my room and landed on my lap. Heathe rushed forward in human form. I stopped him with a raised hand and grabbed onto the black feather. It was warm and soft.

"It's real?" I whispered, not wanting to wake Jen.

"Yes. He is."

"He who?"

"Necroseek."

124

CHAPTER ELEVEN

Secrets no more
Feathers bring revelations
Of information and history
Making connections…
the unwanted kind

"Necroseek?" I whispered back.

"Yes, it seems he's trying to connect with you."

"Oh, he connected all right. If I saw him, does that mean Vincent is l-lost?" I asked, my voice catching on the last word.

Heathe motioned for us to leave the room so we didn't wake Jen up. I followed him out into the living room.

We both took a seat on the couch—each at opposite ends.

"So, where is he then?" I asked, needing to know Vincent was okay.

"I truly don't know where he is. But I do know he's not lost. Necroseek attempting to connect with you means he's aware of your weaknesses. He's been alerted to the fact Vincent is your Wirposh. He'll use his image or any other information about him to get to you."

"So, how do I stop it? How do I know the difference between the two in my dreams?" I felt like a fool. I should've known from the beginning it wasn't Vincent.

"Jacey, Necroseek is one of the most, if not *the* most, powerful Yietimpi Nephilim in the known worlds. For him to come to you in your dreams tells us you're still a mystery to him. He knows you're here in the Origin but he'll not venture within these walls to claim you because he knows he can't risk it. There are too many powerful beings present and loyal to Nemele. He's going to try and draw you out. He knows Vincent is your lure."

"How do you know it was Necroseek?"

"I felt your pull when you called out to me. I witnessed through your eyes what you saw—I was his guard. I protected Necroseek when he was pure and righteous. I was the 'dog' that turned him in. He knew the second you thought my name you were under my protection. He knew to disappear when he did or I'd have been able to track him."

"You were... You are... How old are you, Heathe?"

"Older than time. Older than most here in this world and in others. My family were the reigning monarchs of Ryu before it was destroyed. We were all assigned to the elite Nephilim of the worlds. The stories and writings about the Nephilim within all the remaining worlds depicting them as the offspring of Fallen Angels and other beings isn't

126

correct. The Nephilim *are* the Akero, or what you've been taught to call Fallen Angels. The ones on Earth lived under sanctions of non-use of their magic, making them mortal, like your parents, after they chose not to use their powers."

"Seriously, older than time... what's that? Angels... Fallen Angels... And what's this..." I asked, holding up the black feather which had come through the visionary in my room.

"It means I am quite old. The Akero are the architectural guides to all universes within Nemele. They are formed by the four contingents I read to you in the Archives. As for the feather, it means we need to keep you away from Visionaries. I didn't foresee Necroseek using them as a conduit to reach you. But now I know he can. I will make arrangements for all of the Visionaries within your dorm to be removed, and—"

"Whoa, wait a second. Won't that annoy the beings that attend here? If you remove all of the Visionaries, they'll know it was because of me and I have enough of my own drama and problems to deal with right now without adding that to my list of 'to worry abouts.' I have a lot of training to do before I get the chance to rescue Vincent, and I'm going to need all of the help I can get. Being the reason they can't reach home or anywhere else really ...isn't a popular choice for me right now."

"Jacey, we can use the cover of training to remove the Visionaries. Most beings here realize training takes precedence over all else. I will ensure Herecerti knows what has gone on and he'll use that ruse to have the Visionaries de-activated."

"If you think that will work, I'm okay with it. Now... Fallen Angels... Are you talking about God and the Holy Spirit and stuff?" I asked, wishing I'd paid more attention in religion class.

"I am and I'm not. However, that's a conversation you need to have with someone other than me. As for right now, we need to get Herecerti." A knock at the door interrupted our conversation.

"Wait here." He left no room for argument. Heathe turned into his essence and disappeared through the ceiling. He was back within a second. I didn't move.

"It's Ms. Hullen," Heathe announced as he reformed in front of me.

"You aren't supposed to be in here. Disappear again. She'll freak if she finds you in here." I jumped up off the couch. It was then I noticed I'd been sitting in my pj's—shorts and a tank top. I needed to make sure to keep my monkey housecoat closer to my bed. I went off into my room and grabbed it out of the closet.

Wrapping myself in it, I answered the door.

"Jacey, are you all right?" Ms. Hullen asked, entering, not waiting for an invitation.

"I'm fine, why?"

The commotion woke Aunt Grace and Jen. They both came into the living area as Ms. Hullen took up a spot within the kitchenette area.

"What's going on?" Jen asked as she came up beside me.

"I could ask the same. Ms. Hullen, why are you here?" Aunt Grace asked.

"We detected a Yietimpi signature…from this room. I rushed here to ensure everyone was safe."

"What! Where's Heathe? What signature?" Jen turned to face Ms. Hullen and pulled me in behind her.

The signature was merely a blip on our radar. But from the events of late, I've been hyper vigilant since Daichi was able to breach our lands."

"Jacey," Aunt Grace asked, coming towards me, "what's going on?"

"There was, well, I tried, okay, the visionary—" Heathe appeared beside Jen and placed a hand on her shoulder.

"There was an issue, and now he's gone," Heathe announced.

"How did you get in here?" Ms. Hullen asked.

"I'm Jacey's guard. I wouldn't be very effective if I didn't have total access," he said, turning to Ms. Hullen. "We need to notify Herecerti and have him attend here so all can be notified. The threat is gone, for now. Jen, can you try to contact Hudson? He was supposed to be by as soon as the Elders meeting was completed. I haven't heard from him yet," Heathe asked.

"I'll do it now." Jen looked at me to see if I would be all right with her leaving.

"I'm fine," I said, prodding her to leave and find Hudson. She left without another word and went into her room.

"I'm not as *'delicate'* as everyone here seems to think," I mumbled to myself.

"I'll contact Herecerti," Aunt Grace offered, walking over to the visionary in the room. She swiped it and instantly Herecerti filled the wall.

"We need you here in the dorm. Are you available? Is Hudson with you?"

"I'll be there in a minute. He's heading towards you now, our meeting only just ended." The visionary went black and there was another knock on the door.

I answered it without waiting for someone to ensure it was safe to do so. Hudson was on the other side. He engulfed me in a bear hug as he came in.

"Are you okay?" he asked.

"Uh, yeah, are you? You're not allowed here."

"Herecerti told me to get here. He said you were in danger. That trumps any kind of girl in guy room or guy in girl room."

"I'm fine, Heathe was here."

"Here for what?" Herecerti asked as he came into my now very crowded dorm room.

"Are we able to speak freely?" Heathe asked, looking at Ms. Hullen.

"Yes. I have placed Ms. Hullen here within the Origin. She has inside knowledge of the inflections of Yietimpi strategies," Herecerti said.

"It looks like Necroseek made contact with Jacey." Before Heathe could continue, he was cut off by a number of whats, whens and hows by everyone in the room.

I wanted to yell, scream, and ask as many questions as everyone else, but I knew it wasn't going to get us anywhere. I knew if my family saw how really scared I was, it would set them off even more. I took in a couple of deep breaths to try and relax.

"Hold up, let me explain," I said, walking over to the couch and taking a seat, hoping my casual attitude would rub off a little on everyone in the room to calm them slightly. It didn't.

The looks in the room told me if I didn't speak up and do it quickly, there was going to be a full out explosion of attitudes coming my way.

"When we got back to our dorm, Jen stayed with me in my room. I fell asleep and started dreaming. I thought it was Vincent in my dream, but found out it wasn't. It was Necroseek."

"How do you know it was him?" Aunt Grace asked.

"Because of this," I said, taking the black feather out of the pocket of my robe.

"A feather? How does a feather tell you it's Necroseek?" Jen asked.

"It wasn't the feather or the dream which told Jacey Necroseek had visited her. It was me," Heathe said, coming over to stand behind the couch, and in turn, behind me.

"When Jacey and I connected, it opened a bond between the two of us. One which makes it possible for her to call out to me in times of need. While she was dreaming, she called out to me. I was able to see within her dream. I saw Necroseek."

"How would you know what he looks like?" Hudson asked.

"Because I used to be his protector."

"His what?" Ms. Hullen asked.

"His protector. Every Nephilim has one. Both Nemelite and Yietimpi. I was his protector when he was a Nemelite. When he turned to the Yietimpi side, I was the Draco who turned him in. He sensed me when Jacey called out for me. He knew I saw him and knew I'd be able to trace him if he stayed. He sent this," Heathe took the feather from me and held it up, "as a calling card. He sent it through the visionary."

The room was quiet for the first time since everyone arrived. We all sat there staring at one another in silence for what seemed a long time.

"We need to dismantle the Visionaries in this area," Herecerti said as he walked over towards the entrance to the room.

"We can make it appear to be part of training, so not to bring any suspicion or worry to any of the other beings here," Heathe offered.

"A good suggestion and one I will use," Herecerti said.

"Will that keep Necroseek away?" Aunt Grace asked.

"For the time being it will. He knows I've been appointed as Jacey's protector and he knows to cross over and attempt to try taking her would mean he would have to deal with me…again. He won't chance it for the time being," Heathe said, placing a warm hand on my shoulder.

"So, we remove the Visionaries and Jacey trains…then we go get Vincent?" Hudson asked.

"That's the plan of action for now," Herecerti said.

Hudson didn't seem too happy with Herecerti's response but didn't question him further.

"Can I stay with Jacey...until her training is complete and we go to the Charta Zone?" Hudson asked.

"You can be a member of Heathe's guard, but only if he considers it a good fit," Herecerti said.

"I will also be here," Ms. Hullen said without asking if it was okay with anyone.

"Of course," Heathe answered, looking at her and then at Hudson. "Hudson, do you believe you'll be able to guard your sister...at the expense of others?" he asked.

"Of course," Hudson replied without hesitation.

"Then I take you at your word. I have no issues with Hudson staying with me as we figure out a way to save Vincent and keep Jacey safe at the same time," Heathe announced.

My heart fluttered at his words. I wasn't sure if it was because of the mention of Vincent or the thought of Heathe keeping me safe.

"How did the events within the Inception Chamber go? How is Eve?" Aunt Grace asked, changing the subject slightly.

"She's doing as well as can be expected. She knows Vincent hasn't been lost to us. We will find him. We have every available Nemelite tracker out looking for him and those who traveled with him. The Elders were, of course, concerned for Vincent, but I have to say they were quite inquisitive about you, Heathe. They're pleased with the decision of the Nephilim to come forward and re-join the Guild.

They hope a member of the Draco will follow suit," Herecerti said.

"Nephilim, Draco, who are we talking about?" Ms. Hullen asked.

"You weren't present during our conversation within the Infinity Chambers. The Nephilim, better yet, the Aerco, are and have been with us, staying within the shadows of our worlds. The Draco are not extinct, they exist and are also within all our worlds," Herecerti said, looking at Heathe.

"I'm a Draco," Heathe admitted to Ms. Hullen.

"You are a ... a Dragon? We were all led to believe they were extinct. That they had all been terminated during the war of ages, the time of the Fallen Angels," Ms. Hullen said.

"We are a hardy breed, and at the end of the wars, we dispersed to all worlds within Nemele. Not to mention, the Nephilim of the Nemelite contingent kept the Draco lineage alive and well hidden. The Yietimpi, I'm sure, have their own body of Draco under their hold."

"This is... this is unheard of. Why have you been hiding? Have you not seen the loss and the corruption the Yietimpi have spread? Why haven't you helped?" Ms. Hullen asked, her voice for the first time ever showing anger.

"Have we not helped? Who do you think caused the truce when Faith and Jacey were lost to all of us? Who do you think has been guarding against Necroseek invading the Origin and taking over? Who do you think saved your life?" Heathe asked her. He had raised his voice and clenched his fists as he spoke. You could almost feel the heat emanating from him.

"Saved me...you saved me?" Ms. Hullen inquired.

"Your soul is pure. Your mind was fogged. It was the blood of the Draco that brought you to life and which brought you here," Heathe revealed.

As Ms. Hullen looked to the ground and to her hands, another knock at the door interrupted our conversation. No one moved at first.

"It's Chanary, she's worried," Heathe said over his shoulder as he went to answer the door.

She came into the room in a flurry. "Are you okay?" she asked Heathe as she grabbed onto his shoulders.

"I'm fine... merely tired. You didn't need to come," he said.

"Oh yes, I did. I could *feel* your fury. There was no way I wasn't coming," Chanary stated. She looked around the room at all of the beings present. Her eyes rested on Ms. Hullen and then returned to Heathe.

"They know not what they say," she said as she came over to the couch and took up a position beside Jen and behind me.

"I had no idea," Ms. Hullen said. "I have always wondered who and how I was brought back. The most prevalent has always been why?"

"As I indicated," Heathe said, walking over to Ms. Hullen and taking her clawed hands into his. "You have always been pure of soul. It was your judgement and actions which caused your demise. It was your repentance which allowed us to revive you. Your hands are reminders of what you do not want to return to."

A single tear flowed from Ms. Hullen's beautiful eyes. Heathe reached up and gently wiped it away. "You are now being entrusted with Jacey's life and the lives of millions of beings throughout the universes. If we didn't believe you were worthy, we wouldn't have allowed it."

"Thank you," Ms. Hullen replied, backing into the kitchen and crossing her arms upon her chest.

I didn't ask, even though the curiosity was almost killing me. How was Ms. Hullen before I met her? Why were her hands clawed? Who, or better yet, what was she before she began as an instructor at St. Nemele?

"Which Nephilim revealed themselves to you in the chambers?" Heathe asked Herecerti.

"Gabriel. He was brilliant. Magnificent in his appearance. I believe it was because of your trust in us he made the decision to reveal himself," Herecerti said.

"He is my elder. I have been his humble servant since Necroseek's treachery."

"Gabriel, as in the archangel Gabriel?" I asked.

"Yes, the archangels, the fallen angels, heaven, hell, purgatory… they all exist. Their stories are different within each and every realm you visit. Small pieces of the truth of their chronicles and their origins are within the writings in each world but their true origins and accurate histories are still held within the archives."

"The ones we were just at?" I asked.

"Yes. As I said when we were there, Jacey, the Archives have been around since the beginning. The Keepers are aware of and record all of the beings within Nemele. The information within each catacomb will only be shared with those who are supposed to have knowledge of them. That's why you're of such great interest to them. When your parents left, they had no way of tracing you or your progression."

"What progression? I haven't had any kind of powers. I didn't even know I belonged to this society."

"You forget you were here for the first two years of your life. There are writings about the unbelievable powers you and Faith possessed as children. Your parents told no one they planned on leaving Nemele, in effect because they were powerful Nemelites in their own right. It made it impossible for the Keepers of the Archives to follow you. They were only led back into your life when Hudson had his Awakening," Heathe said.

"So, they've known about me since I was fourteen?"

"They have known about you since the beginning of time... They were only able to reconnect with you when you were fourteen. Even so, there are lost times, your parents were very good at disappearing," Heathe revealed.

At the mention of my parents, I decided it was time for them to be here with me. I missed them. As everyone else continued on in their conversations, I began to chant the summoning ritual Verbeyna had taught me under my breath.

Within seconds, Mom came into my dorm. She flowed in with her colors as Dad followed behind. As they did, I was able to do as I always did with them and time stopped.

"Mom, Dad, do you know what's going on?" I asked as she and Dad materialized in front of me.

"Jacey, we were able to locate the Charta Zone. There are no signs of Vincent or anyone who traveled with him. We hoped you'd be able to make some contact through your dreams. Have you?" Dad asked.

"I have, but it hasn't been very successful. I've seen Vincent with Faith—who, by the way, was totally pretending to be me… and in another dream I was able to meet Necroseek. Now, that was pretty interesting," I said, again trying to come across all nonchalant.

"What!" they both said simultaneously.

"It was during my last dream. The one which brought everyone here tonight. At first it was pretty scary but, it's okay now. Heathe came in and was able to pull me from him."

"How are we going to keep her safe, Hearte?" Mom asked as though I wasn't standing right in front of them.

"Hello… Remember me? Still here! I have to have a say in what's going to happen. I can't run from this, Mom and Dad. He found me through the Visionaries. He isn't going to just go away now and I'm not running again! I have to help Vincent."

"No one wants you to run again, Jacey. Your Dad and I just want you to be safe."

"I am, with—" As I was about to say Heathe another signature came into our realm. My parents instantly went into color mode. I watched as the signature approached. It was slow and sleek. The colors flowed through each other in a symphony of dance and light. It was as though the signature were trying to not only get my attention but show how much brilliance there was to it.

I stood watching for only a moment before my hands started to burn. I looked down into them and within my palms there were thin sheets of purple and white light covering them. I held my hands up and straightened my arms out, palms up towards the signature when she appeared.

CHAPTER TWELVE

Unwanted visitor
Control
Plans of my own

"Verbeyna, what are you doing here?" I asked, sounding more irritated than I intended.

"Remember the amulet. If *anyone* tries to summons you, it causes the amulet to block the attempt… and guess what, coming here is like being summoned—wherever here is," she said, looking around.

"This is where I'm supposed to be able to talk with my parents in private. No one is supposed to be able to break into our conversations unless I allow it, and I definitely didn't want to be interrupted." Wow, I sounded like a total crank.

"Your amulet allowed me to bond with you. I am the Hinderer responsible for keeping you safe. A number of people have paid greatly to ensure your safety."

"Really, who?" I asked, being even more brash.

"That doesn't matter right now. What does is, you left a number of people in your dorm who are concerned about you. You zoned out and they freaked out. That's why they called me in."

"They called you in? How? I thought when I was here time froze for everyone else on the outside."

"Not anymore, Jacey. Your amulet doesn't allow for you to be anywhere other than in Nemele within real time. If you're called out—it illuminates and swings around until you return. A beckon of sorts to keep your corporeal self attached to real time. It's time to go back now." Verbeyna tried reaching out to me and was shocked, literally when she tried. My parents were still in protection mode and were flowing around me, in effect creating a protective barrier.

As Verbeyna brought her shocked hand up to her chest, she cried out "Owww, what the hell was that?"

"It would be a lot more polite and *safe* for you if the next time you want to touch me, you ask," I stated, not giving her any explanation as to what happened. I thought about my parents and thought about being safe and both of their signatures dulled in color and frequency. It was pretty obvious Verbeyna couldn't sense or see them. I told my parents I'd see them soon and not to worry, that all was okay. I did this though my mind, not uttering a word aloud. The second I did, they disappeared, but not before they both encircled me and gave me feathery kisses. The second they left, I willed myself back to my dorm.

As I took in everyone in the room, I realized all eyes were on me. I was standing with both Chanary and Heathe on either side of me, holding me under my arms as Verbeyna stood facing me with my amulet, which was still around my neck, in her hand, while Hudson was holding me up from behind.

I stood, taking my arms back and righting myself, then pulled my amulet from Verbeyna's hand.

"Where did you go?" Heathe asked, staring me down with more than concern in his eyes.

"I was talking with Mom and Dad. What happened here?" I asked, looking around the room and seeing Ms. Hullen still in the kitchen, Aunt Grace standing behind the couch, and Jen standing beside Hudson.

"I warned you. When you choose to leave this realm, the amulet will block all attempts or it will render you unconscious in the realm you are leaving," Verbeyna said as she took a step back and crossed her arms over her chest.

"So, I passed out?"

"Yeah, and scared the crap out of all of us," Hudson said, as Jen took his hand into hers.

"Well, it's not like I meant to. Mom and Dad showed up and I automatically went to see them. They said they'd been to the Charta Zone. They tried looking for Vincent, but there was no sign of him or anyone who traveled with him," I said, walking back towards the couch and taking a seat. Jen followed suit and sat beside me.

"I guess from now on I can't talk with my parents without passing out?" I accused Verbeyna.

"You can still talk with them, but I would suggest you do it in the Infinite Waters area instead of in the realm you went into. It's not as safe as you think and I'm afraid because you have the amulet now, it will always render you unconscious if you choose to leave. Any realm other than this one is completely unsafe... for you," Verbeyna answered.

"Then take it off. I'll watch out for myself. I don't need the amulet, anyway," I said, attempting to pull it off. There was no latch and it as too short to pull over my head. It wouldn't come off.

"It won't come off. It will stay with you until it is no longer needed," Herecerti said as he came over to me and placed his hands on mine.

"Why not? I want it off. I don't want to have to ask permission to speak with my parents! I shouldn't have to."

"No, you shouldn't, but you aren't like any of the others here. You, Jacey, are who we're all placing our hope in and not one person in this room is willing to take the chance of losing you like we lost Faith," Aunt Grace said as she came out from behind the couch and crouched in front of me. "I won't lose you like I lost her." A single tear traveled down her cheek. I gently wiped it away.

"I'll make arrangements for you to talk with your parents in private. I can ensure you'll still have some semblance of privacy at the Infinite Waters," Herecerti offered.

"Thank you," I said, knowing I would take him up on his offer, yet at the same time knowing I would find a way, some way to get the amulet off so I could control who I saw when I saw them. No one here needed to hear that… especially right now.

"Since Gabriel has decided to come back into the Elders' Guild, do you think Jordan will?" Chanary asked Heathe in an obvious attempt to change the subject, something I knew I was going to have to thank her for later.

"I think Jordan will choose when and who he reveals himself to," Heathe responded.

Who's Jordan?" Jen asked.

"He's my uncle. He took over the family throne when my father was killed during the war of ages," Heathe said.

"I'm hoping you and Chanary will be able to convince him we're in need of his assistance at this time," Herecerti replied.

"It won't be up to me to ask Jordan. Gabriel will speak with Michael and Uriel and see if they can communally convince Jordan to have the Dracos rejoin the Guild," Chanary spoke up.

"The meeting within the Chamber was productive. Gabriel indicated he would be speaking with the seven other leaders of Nephilim. He said they were spread out far and wide throughout Nemele and it would take some time to get all of them on board. I would assume they'll contact the Draco Nations while contacting the other Archangels. Do the Dracos still provide protection for the Nephilim?" Herecerti asked.

"We do. We have also evolved to be quite an independent nation. There are some who don't follow the original teachings and believe they can go throughout the universes without cause or question. We have lost a number of young Dracos to their own curiosity," Heathe said, not looking away from Chanary.

"In saying that, we are also aware that there are Dracos who have followed Necroseek for ages. They and their offspring must also serve the Yietimpi portion of the Fallen Angels. We have no intelligence on how many they are in number or who from the original bloodline still exists," Heathe said.

"We'll figure it out together," Herecerti said. "For now, we have to get the Visionaries disabled and it will be a large task. Heathe, Hudson, Jen, you'll be staying with Jacey. The day starts in a mere quad, therefore I would suggest you try to get some sleep. As soon as we left the Inception Chamber, I made arrangements for your classes here. You need to train and train hard so we can find the others," Herecerti said.

"What's a quad?" I asked

"It's time measurement here. Remember time here is much different than it is on Earth. A quad is about eight hours in Earth time," Jen answered.

"Ms. Hullen, you will continue to guard against Yietimpi signatures from the Sentry stations. Chanary, I do believe you also have a number of classes in the morning. Time for you to get some rest as well. Grace, if you wouldn't mind, I could use your assistance with the Visionaries," Herecerti asked.

"Of course. However, if it's okay with you, I'd like to go and see Eve as soon as we're done here."

"Yes, indeed. She and Bronson are staying in the instructors' chambers of the Origin. I believe she's waiting to see you," Herecerti said.

Aunt Grace came over to me and Hudson. "Will you be all right? I won't be gone long."

"We'll be fine. Please tell Eve and Bronson we'll do anything that needs to be done to get Vincent back," I said.

"Of course I will," she responded as she followed Herecerti to the door.

"Verbeyna, thank you for coming as quickly as you did," Heathe said.

"Will you be following me out?" she asked Heathe.

"Yes," he responded.

I didn't miss the look which was exchanged between Chanary and Verbeyna. Heathe, on the other hand, didn't make eye contact with any of us.

"I'll be back as soon as Verbeyna has left the Origin," Heathe announced. As quickly as he announced it, they left my dorm.

"I'll stay here on the couch," Hudson said, plopping himself down beside Jen, not asking if it was all right with anyone.

"I'll stay in your room with you, Jacey," Jen said, not moving as Hudson sat beside her.

"It's going to be a long day for you tomorrow, Jacey. We'll need to entrench you in classes which are set up for senior Nemelite graduates. These are beings who have been training in the use of their powers for years," Herecerti said.

"I'm up for the challenge. Anything to get Vincent back," I answered.

"Then so be it. Get some rest and Ms. Hullen will retrieve you and Jen to show you where your first set of training will take place," Herecerti said as he and Aunt Grace left my dorm.

Finally, everyone left. Hudson, Jen and I sat in silence for a few moments on the couch before I asked, "How did the meeting at the Inception Chamber really go?"

"It was pretty crazy at first. They were all questioning why I was there with Herecerti and when he began to explain what had been going on and the fact he'd contacted a Hinderer without consulting the Elders Guild first, they were all pretty upset. I didn't realize Hinderers were such a big deal. When Herecerti tried to explain his reasoning behind Verbeyna, the main thing they were all worried about was how Herecerti had paid her," Hudson said.

"Why is everyone so obsessed with how this girl is being paid?" I asked.

"Like who?" Jen asked.

"When I was talking with Verbeyna in the other realm, she told me a number of people had paid greatly to keep me safe... and then there was Chanary telling us about how upset she was that Heathe had to get together with Verbeyna again as payment for her helping me out."

"So, what kind of payment are we looking at?" Hudson asked.

"I haven't got a clue. But if it's got the Elders upset with Herecerti... then it's got to be huge," Jen said.

"I agree. I think we need to find out everything we can about who this Verbeyna is and how we can make it so she isn't getting paid from anyone here for anything." I said with more than just a passing interest in getting Herecerti out of crap... it was more like trying to get Jen and Hudson on my side to get this amulet off my neck. I also knew of a Draco that may want to help us when it came to stopping Verbeyna—Chanary.

"I think we also need to start paying attention to the fact that Archangels, fallen angels, and dragons exist. I knew about most of the other beings growing up here, but I can tell you there are going to be a whole lot of shocked Nations when they find out there are angels and dragons among us," Jen said.

"Why? It doesn't make much sense to me why other beings would be shocked at that fact. Aren't they myth and folklore just like the angels and the dragons?" I asked.

"They are, but they aren't from the Genesis. The angels and dragons we're talking about are from the time when there was only them... there were no other Nations within Nemele," Jen said.

"So, are there any writings about how everyone else was created?" I asked.

"I'm sure there are in the Archives, but I haven't seen any," she answered.

"I think once everyone sees that they're here to help, it won't be such a big deal," I offered. "Hudson, are you staying?" I asked.

"Of course. I'm not going anywhere. I still feel the same about Aunt Grace and Heathe. I still think there's something else going on."

"Seriously, I don't get what you mean when you say that. Aunt Grace wouldn't hurt us... ever! And Heathe, after the last couple of encounters I've had with him, I can tell you, he's not a risk to my safety... he's more of a safe guard for it," I said.

"And, like I've said before, I have no issue with Heathe being a safe guard for you, Jacey... if that's all he wanted. I can tell by the way he looks at you that there's way more. As for Aunt Grace, I love her, too. I wouldn't want to think there's anything else there but love, but Jace, I'm telling you, with the knowledge her daughter is alive and there's a possibility to exchange you for her... I just don't trust her," Hudson answered, staring me directly in the eye.

"I get why you feel that way, but at the same time I don't. I really don't think Aunt Grace would put us in danger," I said, and for the first time felt like I was saying it to protect my family, well, at least what was left of it.

"Jace, I love Aunt Grace, too... I've never questioned her loyalty before... well, before what I saw earlier when you lost consciousness and Heathe rushed you to the infirmary. I'm telling you... no, I'm warning you, if she steps out of line once, I won't wait to see what she has planned," Hudson asserted.

"Hudson, Jacey may be right. We have no idea what Grace is feeling right now, but she's never given any of us any indication she'd do something to threaten any of us," Jen said.

Neither Hudson nor I responded. We sat silently for some time. Neither one of us really wanted to think or believe our only living relative was going to put either one of us at risk.

For the first time since we arrived at the Origin, I had time to do nothing... just wait, rest, and gather my thoughts on how I was going to handle everything else that was going to be thrown my way over the next couple of days. Herecerti said ten days. I could handle that. I knew I could train and concentrate on it as long as no one tried to pull a fast one and not let me go along with the others to find Vincent.

I also knew I'd find a way or another being who would help me get this amulet off. As I twirled it round and round in my hand, I began to think of Heathe and everything he had revealed to us today.

What a life. One which I couldn't begin to understand. Over the last couple of days I had learned so much about Vincent's best friend. I wondered if Vincent knew as much about him as I did now.

I wondered if Vincent would approve of Heathe and I bonding. This place was definitely weird in some respects and absolutely amazing in others. From growing up where I did, on Earth, I had always believed when you met someone you were interested in as more than a friend, it would be just that person. The feelings I had for Vincent were irrefutable, but on the other hand, the feelings I was developing for Heathe were bordering on more than friendship. I was beginning to depend on him and I wasn't too sure I wanted to feel like that. But I also knew I really didn't have a choice in how I was feeling.

As I sat back lost in my thoughts over the last couple of days, Jen was lying with her head in Hudson's lap and her feet up on my lap. I watched them for a second, wondering if either one of them had feelings for others or if they were lucky enough to only have eyes for each other… How confusing.

"I think it's time to get some rest. We all have a pretty crazy day set for us tomorrow. Heathe's back and wants to talk," Hudson said.

"Heathe, it's not like you haven't been in here before; you can come in," I said out loud to the empty room. When I did, he appeared behind the couch.

"I didn't want to interfere with your time together. It seemed the three of you were finally able to relax without anyone bugging you," he said.

"You don't interfere. It's nice to know you're around," I said.

Both Jen and Hudson looked at me with questioning stares. Hudson more questioning and irritated than Jen's, of course.

"Thank you, Jacey," he said with a smile that actually reached his eyes this time.

My heart did a little somersault. My gut twisted with a twinge of guilt. I needed to stop these feelings. I needed to concentrate on Vincent.

"Do you know how long we have to wait before we can go looking for Vincent?" I asked, hoping the change in subject would cause Hudson to stop staring holes into the back of my head.

"I only know the Elders have chosen to wait and see if the Draco will join them on their quest," Heathe answered.

"How long is that going to be?" I asked.

"I'm not sure, Jacey. I know there are Dracos within each of the remaining nineteen worlds of Nemele, and if each of them are to be contacted, it may take some time," he responded.

"Herecerti originally said it was going to be half a cycle... ten days," I stated.

"We're all going to have to face the fact that we may have to wait longer than that. With the resurgence of the Nephilim and the Dracos, I'm pretty sure the game plan for us to go within the half cycle has changed," Jen said.

"We really need to concentrate on our training so they have no excuse to exclude us," Hudson said.

I wanted to scream. I was soooooo irritated with the thought of not going for the 'promised' ten day plan. I knew saying anything to Jen and Hudson would only worry them. I wasn't going to be waiting on anyone. If the Elders weren't going to be ready to go... I knew I would have a plan to go—with or without them.

CHAPTER THIRTEEN

Incantations…
Spells…
Beliefs…
All are tested

"We seriously need to get some rest. I think it's going to be a crazy day of training tomorrow," Jen said, lifting her head up and kissing Hudson goodnight.

"Uggggh, still not comfortable with that," I teased as I stood up and made my way to my room.

"Heathe and I will be hanging out here," Hudson said.

"See you guys in a few hours," Jen said, following me to my dorm room.

I waved over my shoulder to both of them as Heathe took a seat on the opposite end of the couch from Hudson. I took a chance and glanced back at them and found Hudson had *that* look on his face. The one he had when he'd confronted Vincent in the hallway at St. Nemele. I tried getting his attention but he was totally focused on Heathe. Jen nudged me with her elbow and we continued on to my room.

"You have to let him do what he thinks is best," Jen said.

"What's that supposed to mean?" I asked.

"He wants to ask Heathe what his intentions are. He knows they aren't only 'friendly,'" Jen said with a smile.

"What! Wait a second, I can't let him do that. Why would he do that?"

"Jacey, no matter what, your brother is always going to do what he thinks is best for you. If he thinks Heathe is overstepping, Dragon or not, your brother is going to take him on."

"But he's not overstepping. He hasn't done anything out of line!"

"Not yet he hasn't. It's totally obvious to anyone in a room with the two of you there's something going on."

"I haven't done anything!" I said, now completely shocked others might be noticing there was something between Heathe and I.

"Jacey, it's okay. The two of you bonded, right?"

"Yeah."

"Well, when bonding happens, sometimes our emotions get all screwed up. Hudson's only making sure Heathe gets that you're new to all of this. He doesn't want Heathe to take advantage of you."

"Why would Hudson even think that? Heathe wouldn't take advantage of me... and I wouldn't let him."

154

"He might be a Dragon, Jacey, but he's still a guy. I don't think he'd do it maliciously, but I do think he might not be able to control his own feelings when it comes to you."

"He doesn't have…" I stopped and remembered the look in his eyes when I came back from my talk with my parents. There was more than worry in his eyes. Could it be he had more than protective feelings for me? I shook my head, trying to shake out the thought.

"It would only seriously mess things up, Jen. You and Hudson have nothing to worry about. My main thought is training, getting Vincent back, and getting some sleep right now," I said while I put on my cut off joggers and a tank top for bed.

"Oka-y-y, let's try and get some sleep. But I'm not going to drop the Heathe subject. We'll talk more when we get up," Jen said, pulling out a pair of shorts and a t-shirt from my top drawer.

"Sure… when we get up," I said, sliding into bed. Jen slid in beside me and turned out the light.

"You know it's because we all love you… right?" she asked.

"I know… I'm just tired of people worrying about me… I'm tired of being the one everyone thinks they need to shelter. For once, I want people to trust in *my* judgment. To know I'm not like five anymore." I let out a breath I'd been holding in as I was talking. I was starting to get emotional. I knew it wasn't because of all of the events of late, I seriously was exhausted.

"No one thinks you can't handle yourself, Jacey. Everyone knows you have a good head on your shoulders. We're all worried about everyone else that's coming into your life."

"See you when we get up," I muttered, turning over on my side, effectively bringing the conversation to an end.

I knew they all wanted what was best for me. Hell, I wanted what was best for me, and I knew that was Vincent. Only ten days. If they couldn't get their crap together by then, I was gone—with or without *'everyone else.'*

I was a little apprehensive about falling asleep. My last 'dream' lingered and I totally didn't want a re-visit from Necroseek. I fought my heavy lids, but sleep soon took over. Thankfully, it was a dreamless one.

A knock on my door woke me. I reached up and turned on the overhead lights with the switch on the side of my bed. Jen stirred and woke.

"One minute," I called out, flinging my legs off the side of the bed, standing and stretching.

"How was your sleep?" Jen asked, getting out of bed and grabbing a housecoat.

"Dreamless," I said, grabbing my pink monkey housecoat and putting my hair up in a messy bun on the top of my head.

"Ready for today?" she asked.

I paused for second, realizing we were going to be 'training' with the best of the best today. I wasn't nervous. I was anxious.

"Yeah, I am," I replied, and for the first time in days my belly did a happy flip.

I made my way to the door and opened it. Ms. Hullen filled the entry.

"Ready for today? There are no Visionaries, therefore no food will be delivered to dorms, so we must make our way to the Great Hall. Here are your uniforms. Your first classes will be in defensive tactics." She handed me two bags and turned away. "I'll be waiting here for you. Hurry. We don't have much time."

"Do we have time to take a quick shower?"

"Yes." She turned and the door closed. I made my way to the bed. I handed Jen the bag with her name on it and poured out my bag on the bed.

"You're kiddin' me... right?" I asked as I held up two articles of clothing which looked to be blue spandex. "There's no way I'm wearing this out in public! And what's defensive tactics?"

"It's like phys. ed., Jacey. Put it on and you'll see, it's not as bad as you think," Jen said, giggling, as she started to take her own 'underwear' out of the bag.

"Seriously, Jen. This stuff is what I wore under my clothes when we lived in Hewfawe. This looks like thermal underwear—not clothing you'd wear out in public unless it was under a snowsuit or something." I felt my heart rate increase and my hands started to sweat. My normal outfits for phys. ed. were joggers and a sweatshirt.

"You need to put them on. It's a protective suit. It will keep you safe as long as you're wearing it. This 'phys. ed.' class is like no other you've ever been in. I'll go shower in my room and see you back in here in a couple of minutes," Jen said, taking her bag with her.

I held up the top portion and pulled at it. It looked like underwear. I went over to the closet, grabbed my underwear, socks, and a sports bra. I grabbed a pair of joggers and a t-shirt. I jumped in the shower off my bedroom and got ready.

I came out of my bathroom a couple of minutes later, dressed and ready to go. "Uhmmm. You have to wear this, Jacey. You need to train if you want to get Vincent. They won't let you if you wear those." She pointed at me and the clothes I was in.

I looked up as I was towel drying my hair at Jen. The suit looked see-through when it was off, but on—it took on the appearance of a wetsuit with padding in all the right places.

"You know, you could have told me it looked like that on."

She smiled at me and tossed me my top and bottoms.

I put them on and they formed to me. The suit was gel-like—it contoured to my body and had padding around the waist, elbows, knees and chest area. Jen tossed me the shoes and the gloves that were also in the bag.

"Ready?" she asked.

"Yep."

Once in the living room of the dorm, Hudson, Heathe, and Ms. Hullen's conversation stopped. All eyes were on us.

"Ready? Are Heathe and Hudson coming with us?" I asked, self-consciously pulling at the stomach area of my suit. Jen nudged me and I stopped pulling at myself and crossed my arms in front of me.

"They will be. Right now they need to go get their uniforms. I'll bring you to the Great Hall for food and they'll meet us in the center concourse, ready for class," Ms. Hullen answered as she ushered Jen and I out the door.

"See you guys in a while," I called over my shoulder as we left the dorm and headed out. I giggled to myself, thinking how Hudson was going to feel in one of these suits.

We walked in silence through the halls and up the stairwells to the main area of the Origin. As Jen and I followed Ms. Hullen, I realized I hadn't been to this portion of the Origin before.

"Are we near the main entrance?" I asked, trying to get my bearings as to where we were. "No. You'll become more acquainted with where everything is this afternoon. We've scheduled time for Hudson and Heathe to show you around to your classes," Ms. Hullen answered.

As we made our way down a number of hallways and stairwells, we came upon a foyer. It was massive. I looked around, trying to wrap my head around how this fit into the Origin. It was like two football stadiums in size. You couldn't see the ceiling unless you tilted your head all the way back and squinted.

"Wow," I whispered to Jen.

"I know..." she nodded back.

There were two arched entryways with enormous carvings in the wood doors. Ms. Hullen held her hand up to them, they glowed and opened into themselves. We entered and my breath caught for a second. There, laid out before me, was every mythical, imagined, written about, characters of every movie I'd ever seen, creatures and beings I'd been envisioning since I was a child.

We entered unnoticed. Jen nudged me and I moved along with her, but still found myself staring, mouth open, at everyone in the hall.

The hall wasn't like your normal cafeteria—it was much more formal. The tables were spread throughout the chamber and were made of stone and wood. Each differed in size and shape. Along the far back wall were large bay windows which facilitated the flow of natural light into the room.

We made our way to the back of the hall and took a seat at a table, which Jen and I fit into but was dwarfed by Ms. Hullen.

A small waif-looking girl came over to us and positioned herself at the end of our table.

"What is it you need?" she asked in a sing song voice which instantly put me at ease.

"We're in need of food for energy. We have defensive tactics training with the quarter," Ms. Hullen said.

"I'll be back," she sung as she left the table. I watched as she left. She didn't walk as she left, she floated. She wore a long skirt which flowed as she moved. She headed towards the visionary at the back of the hall. She approached it, raised her hand and stepped through.

"I thought the Visionaries had been removed," I said, feeling a bit nervous. The thought of Necroseek's black feather tickled my memory, causing goose bumps along my arms and neck.

"They've been removed from the living quarters. The ones within the public views will stay. They are of no threat. We've ensured the Travelers were made aware of Necroseek's attempts. They've programmed the Visionaries appropriately," Ms. Hullen said.

"The Travelers?" I asked.

"Yes, they're the beings who created the Visionaries and allow us to use them. They're the descendants of the Barkayal," Ms. Hullen said.

"As in the Nephilim Barkayal?" I asked.

"Yes, Jacey," she answered, as if I should know what she was talking about.

I shook my head and rubbed my neck as I thought of the time Heathe and I spent in the Archives learning about the four ruling classes of the Nephilim.

I hadn't been too sure of what my training was going to be over the next couple of days. I originally thought it was going to be a crash course on spells and chants. But wow, was I wrong. If I hadn't realized how much I needed to learn about Nemele before now, the reality of it was coming my way quickly and I only had a short time to learn it.

The waif-looking girl came back, holding a number of trays in her hands. I couldn't believe I hadn't noticed before, but she had two sets of hands... each one held a tray.

"I am Bella. I am Makara and Siren," she sang as she handed me a tray.

"I'm sorry, I didn't mean to—" I started to apologize but she cut me off with a sing song giggling noise.

"Jacey, it's all right. You're curious and I'm not insulted. There are few of us in existence." She handed Jen and Ms. Hullen their trays and left a fourth in the center of the table.

"We'll get to know one another through classes," she sang as she left the table.

"Okay, I feel like an ass. I didn't realize I was staring. Sorry, guys," I said, taking in the food in front of me.

"Jacey, it's all right. If she had been insulted, she would've said so. Bella was chosen to assist in meal times and training with us. She's a trusted senior here," Ms. Hullen said.

"She seemed really nice."

"She is. Now eat," Ms. Hullen said.

There were a couple of blueberry muffins and a bowl of granola with yogurt set in front of me. There was also some fresh fruit—at least I thought it was fruit. It looked like raspberries and blueberries with cantaloupe and watermelon slices in a large bowl in front of us. But when I took a spoon full of them and tasted it, they tasted nothing like the berries from home—they were juicier and the tastes were beyond description—they were d-e-l-i-c-i-o-u-s…

A flash of red caught my attention as I was finally relaxing; Chanary entered the Great Hall and had made her way over to us.

Bella appeared at the same time Chanary did.

"What can I get you, Chanary?" she sang, but not in the same tone she had with me… this one seemed more—annoyed.

"I'll have whatever they're eating," Chanary said as she took a seat beside Jen.

I noticed she was wearing a red outfit like the blue one I had on. Obviously she was also going to defensive tactics this morning.

"So, what time are we training?" Chanary asked as she reached over, grabbed an apple shaped fruit from the middle of the table, and took a large bite out of it.

"We'll be leaving soon," Ms. Hullen answered.

"Where are Heathe and Hudson?" Chanary asked as Bella re-appeared with a tray of food, dropped it in front of Chanary, then left without a word.

"Friends everywhere, eh?' I muttered under my breath.

"They're going to meet us in the center concourse as soon as we're done," Jen said as she popped a couple of berries in her mouth and gave me a wide-eyed 'stop it' look.

I gave Jen a smile and continued eating my breakfast. About ten minutes later we were all done and Bella returned. This time she was in a skin suit of her own, aqua blue.

"See you all out in the concourse." Bella sang as she passed all of us and headed out towards the main doors of the Great Hall.

"I'm guessing it's time for us to go, too?" I asked.

"It is, let's go." Ms. Hullen replied.

All four of us got up and left the hall. I watched as Chanary followed. I originally thought she would have had a number of friends here, considering the entourage she had following her at St. Nemele's.

She was alone. There wasn't anyone following her, she was following us. I felt a twinge of pity for her. It disappeared the second she opened her mouth.

"So, who do I need to talk to, to make sure I'm not partnered up with you?" she asked as if I were a plague she didn't want any part of.

"You'll be partnered with whomever the guide decides," Ms. Hullen said, not looking back at Chanary.

"Great…" she muttered.

We maneuvered through a number of hallways and stairwells. We stopped in front of a doorway engraved with a large symbol. It looked like two letters 'p s' back to back with asterisks above each. Ms. Hullen held her hand up and the door opened.

We stepped out of the hallway and into the outdoors. We were in the center concourse. The area stretched out before us was the size of at least four football fields. The grass covering it was the greenest grass I'd ever laid eyes on. Surrounding us on all sides in an octagonal shape was the 'Origin.' Its walls were made of large stone which reached at least 200 feet in height in some places and were covered in ivy. In some places along them were open windows which had groups of multi-colored flowers flowing from the open spaces.

We made our way over to a number of beings who were gathered in the center of the concourse. I figured this was our defensive tactics class because some were wearing the same outfit I was.

My exterior face and my interior emotions were polar opposites right now. I was pumped to be here with all of these beings—they ranged from humanoid looking to centaurs—but my stomach was flip flopping with every step I took. A large male came from the center of the group and stopped us before we joined the rest of the participants.

"Thor Odinson," Ms. Hullen said as she held her clawed hand out to him. He took her hand into his and held it to his chest for a moment.

"Hullen. How long has it been?" he replied in a booming voice while letting her hand go back down to her side.

"Too long," she replied, and I swear if I hadn't been watching as closely as I was I would have missed it. She actually blushed a little. Ms. Hullen and Thor…The Norse God of Thunder.

"And this must be Jacey," Thor said, turning his full attention on me. I could now see why Ms. Hullen blushed. Chris Hemsworth was a super hot guy who played Thor in the movies back home, but he had nothing on this Thor—the real one. He was… beautiful.

I stuttered at first, "H-h-h-i." I put my hand out to shake his but before I knew it, he was greeting me in the traditional Nemelite way.

"May the elements keep you eternal."

"And you," I replied as he held my hand to his chest.

The feeling I received was trust, strength, and friendship. I have to say I was relieved. I was afraid I would have 'bonded' with him like I had with Heathe and that would have thrown a huge curve ball into the mix of emotions I'd been feeling lately. I was instantly put at ease with his candor.

He released my hand and took a few steps back. I noticed then that Jen and Chanary had been standing beside me, looking like I had when we entered the Great Hall earlier—both wide-eyed and jaws dropped. It was my turn to return the favors of the 'nudge' to both of them. As I did, Heathe and Hudson came out onto the field.

Hudson had on a black suit like I wore and Heathe was wearing a deep blood red one. I watched as they made their way over to us.

"Jacey, you, Hudson, Jen, and Chanary will be sitting out for the first couple of run throughs. Ms. Hullen, would you care to join me in a hand to hand?"

"Of course," she answered without hesitation. "Jacey, you and the others will stay within this area and observe from the first level. Once we feel you're ready to participate, we'll call you in," Ms. Hullen said over her shoulder as she followed Thor out to the center of all of the other beings in the field.

"Didn't take her long to dump us," I said, chuckling a little.

"I soooooo would have chosen him over us too, if I was given the option," Chanary said.

Heathe and Hudson made their way over to us.

"I'll lead you to the first level," Heathe said, eyeing Chanary. He obviously heard what she'd said.

We went back into the doors we'd entered the concourse by. To the left was another set of doors. Heathe held his hand to them and they opened. Within the doorway was a landing like the ones in the Archives. All five of us stood on it and it moved upwards. Stone and mortar flashed by as we ascended. The landing stopped in front of another doorway and Heathe opened it. We entered a long hallway with windows overlooking the center concourse. We weren't the only ones observing the events on the concourse. There were a number of other beings here also.

There were benches/bleachers set up in front of the windows so you could peer out into the concourse. They weren't like normal windows, they were more like huge holes in the walls. I chose not to sit, but stand by one of the pillars which formed the frame to the window.

"I'll be down there. Watch, and when Thor says you're welcome to join, I'll come up and get you," Heathe said, turning away from me and walking back to the landing.

"You're quiet," I said as Hudson came up to me.

"I'm worried. I haven't been to one of these classes before and I'm not sure what goes on in them. I'm not sure you're ready for it."

"Time isn't on our side. I'm as ready now as I'll ever be," I replied, cutting him off.

"Have you seen Aunt Grace?" I asked, changing the topic.

"No, I think she's still with Eve. Once she helped with the Visionaries, she went over to stay with Eve and Bronson to see how she could help out," Hudson said.

"I'm glad she's not here. I'm pretty sure she'd have some issues with me participating today," I said, looking up to the bleachers where Jen and

Chanary had taken a seat next to some guys who looked to be as new to this as me. There were four of them sitting there with the same outfits on as Jen and I, but they were black like Hudson's. The looks on their faces mirrored the flip flopping my belly was doing.

"Why are the outfits in different colors?" I asked Hudson.

"They go by species, sex, and level of training. You and Jen, along with those guys," he looked over his shoulder indicating the guys beside Chanary and Jen, "are totally new to this, that's why you guys have the blue suits on—the black and blue ones carry most of the protective barriers for our kind. Blue for females from our species who are new to this, black for guys."

A loud whistle interrupted our talk. I looked down to the field. There were at least 20 species down there, not including Ms. Hullen, Thor and Heathe. They formed into a circle with Thor and Ms. Hullen in the middle.

"Two rows of five! Facing each other. You'll practice a basic energy spell, like this." Thor turned to Ms. Hullen and both took on a crouched stance.

Within seconds there were flashes of light being thrown back and forth between the two of them.

"At this point we're not using debilitating stuns. We're attempting to foster and control our energies. Now, you try." Ms. Hullen and Thor left the center of the circle and all of the students filed into place.

There was a long exchange of energies between all of the beings in the field.

168

The energy balls initiated the volley of practiced moves between everyone but it moved on to a number of other spells and manipulations of the elements. One was a freezing spell where each being tied up their partner with unseen ropes of air.

"Am I seriously going to be able to do any of that?" I asked Hudson.

"Uh, yeah, of course. Heathe's heading our way," Hudson said, lifting his chin and pointing towards the field, "Let's see what we can do," he winked. We turned from the window and headed over to the door to wait for him. Jen and Chanary joined us.

Heathe came onto the landing. "Are you ready?"

"It's now or never," I responded, trying to sound more sure than I felt.

Within a minute we were all in the middle of the field with all of the others. I watched as everyone paired off. I, of course, went over to Jen.

"No, Jacey, I want you to practice with one of the others," Thor instructed.

I looked around the crowd and hadn't a clue who I should try to 'friend.' A female humanoid came over to me. She was tall, lean, and wearing a blue suit with some white streaks through it.

"Hi, I'm Jacey," I said, raising my hand in a friendly wave.

"Yellesh," she responded, with no wave back.

"Pardon?"

"It's my name."

"Are you Genapiene?"

"Yeah."

This girl was starting to remind me of Hudson; I felt like I was pulling a conversation from her.

"From Earth?"

"No. There *are* other Nations with *intelligent* Genapiene life forms," she replied snottily.

"I didn't mean to, I didn't know there was…" Before I could finish, Thor's voice interrupted my attempt at an apology.

"You will start with a low level energy exchange and we will move to full on contact."

Yellesh crouched about fifteen feet from me and started to form her hands in a circular motions in front of her.

"I haven't done this before, I'm not sure how to…"

"Just catch it," she snarled at me.

Before I could register what she meant, a flash of light was flying at me. Within a second it had struck me in the stomach and I flew back on my butt. The wind had been knocked out of me and I placed my hand on my stomach. Thankfully, I was wearing the suit—nothing was bruised except my butt and my ego.

I jumped back up, feeling slightly peeved that she'd shot a bolt at me which knocked me down. No one came over to us, so I thought everyone else must be using the same intensity as Yellesh and I were. I wiped my butt off and went back to my spot.

Yellesh didn't let up. She threw another ten at me. Nine of them knocked me down but I got right back up and waited for the next.

"Yeah, you're really going to be helpful..." I heard Yellesh mumble under her breath. She set up for another barrage of energy flashes.

I couldn't believe this chick. She'd already made her mind up about me, obviously. I prepped myself this time for her 'assault,' but this time, I was irritated. If she wanted to see what kind of 'help' I was going to be, who was I not to show her. I envisioned grabbing the energy ball from her and tossing it back, nailing her in the gut like she'd already nailed me a number of times.

'It' happened extremely quickly. She threw the ball and I envisioned a white/blue light from my hands and stopped the ball of energy she threw mid-air, about five feet in front of me. The look on her face indicated this was something she wasn't use to seeing. I felt empowered. I envisioned throwing the energy back. The second I thought it, the energy ball was speeding back towards Yellesh and she was flying back through the air. She landed about ten feet back from where she'd been originally standing.

"Oh, bring it," she muttered as the look of shock on her face changed to annoyance.

We now had everyone else's full attention on us. Yellesh got up and crouched down low, placing both of her hands out in front of her. I mirrored her stance, waiting for the energy bolt to appear. Now knowing what to expect, I figured I could catch whatever she decided to throw this time.

She started to move her hands in a figure eight flow, a different configuration than what we'd been practising. I straightened a little and cocked my head to the side trying to figure out what she was doing. As I did, she volleyed herself at me, hands entwined in a red flow of fire which appeared out of thin air. My head snapped back as her hand came in contact with my nose. Her legs wrapped around my waist; she knocked me onto my back and straddled me.

All I could see were stars. My eyes were watering and I could taste blood in my mouth.

"Catching an energy signal won't keep you safe from getting your ass kicked. You Earth Genapienes make me sick," she whispered in my ear, then jumped off of me. She stood and brushed off my blood, which was on her hands, on the legs of her pants.

I sat up and saw Jen, Hudson, and Heathe heading my way. They got a good look at the blood flowing from nose and each one's expressions changed from mild curiosity to intense worry.

"What the hell?" Jen said, while helping me to my feet.

"It's nothing," I said, wiping my nose on the sleeve of my suit.

Being able to get up and brush off my bloody nose was a shock for me. I'd never been in a fight, never been hit, never had a bleeding nose before. I'd never had to worry about stuff like that growing up. My parents never supported physical violence—ever. Their beliefs were mine—violence only breeds more violence. That was, until now. My new belief: I was going to get the chance to kick Yellesh's butt—I didn't know when, how, or where, but I was going to and when I did, I was going to enjoy it.

CHAPTER FOURTEEN

Kicking butt
Thankful for Kung fu
Cynics all around

"I believe we may have to revisit teaching you more hand to hand along with your elemental training," Ms. Hullen said.

After Yellesh smacked me in the nose, Thor decided we all needed to take a break. He'd sent everyone off to the Great Hall to grab some refreshments. I stayed behind with Jen, Hudson, Ms. Hullen, and Heathe.

"Yeah, it's kind of obvious I need it," I said, sounding all stuffed up. I had a Kleenex stuck up my nose and my head was tilted back. My eyes finally stopped tearing up and the bleeding slowed.

"The class isn't over yet. Do you think you'll be able to participate?" Thor asked me.

"Yeah, I'll be fine."

"I'll partner up with her and go through the basics in open and closed hand techniques," Heathe said.

"I think at this point it may be the best option," Thor replied.

The others returned and everyone paired off again. Heathe didn't leave my side and Yellesh soon got the point. She threw me a look of disdain and paired off with a male centaur, the one Heathe had be sparring with earlier.

"I think she's pissed at me," I said as Heathe moved to stand in front of me.

"She overdid it and she knows she did. Yellesh isn't one of the nicest Genapienes from Rifeas. She's always had a nasty habit of being somewhat of a bully. Don't worry about her. Let's get to work on your self-defense skills instead," Heathe said, moving us both a little further away from the group than I had been before.

"Rifeas, as in the world where fairies, elves, leprechauns, nymphs and trolls are from?"

"Yes, that one."

"Are there Genapienes on all of the nineteen worlds within Nemele?" I asked.

"Not all of them. Some have environments which wouldn't allow for them to survive. But for now, we need to concentrate on your physical responses to attacks, Jacey. You'll learn more about all of the Nations in the next class," Heathe said as he came to a stop where I assume he thought it was safe enough to be away from everyone else.

"So for now, we're going to work on your physical responses, not your magical ones. I think it's necessary you learn how to protect yourself without the use of your gifts," Heathe said, placing his gloves on.

"So, how do I do that?

"Like this, follow me."

Heathe approached and I backed up a little. He smirked and brought his hands up in fists to his shoulder area. He had one hand higher, up by his cheekbone while the other was down by his chin.

"Hold your hands like this. Your strong hand should be higher than your weak. You guard your face with the weak one."

"Strong one?"

"The hand you write with."

I tried to mirror his stance and his hand position but failed miserably.

"Here, like this…" he said, coming around behind me. He placed his hands on my hips and pulled them lower to the ground. From behind, he put his leg between mine and spread my legs further apart and pushed the right one a little bit forward. He grabbed my elbows and brought them up to my sides, which in effect brought my hands up with them.

"Like that. I know it doesn't seem too comfortable right now, but with practice, it will be," he said a little too close to my ear.

I turned my head slightly and we came nose to nose. He smelled like fresh linen and chocolate. Our eyes locked and for a second my entire body tingled. Not with the anticipation of learning how to fight… but with a tingle which went from the top of my head all the way down to the tip of my toes. I literally shivered. I tried to say something intelligent but a movement from my right caught my eye. It was Jen and her partner along with Hudson and his.

They'd moved from their previous position in the field to get closer to Heathe and I. The look on Hudson's face was unmistakable—he wasn't impressed with the 'closeness' Heathe and I were displaying. Suddenly, I realized they might not be the only ones looking at us this way. I grabbed Heathe's shoulder and pulled him over the top of my shoulder and he landed flat on his back, staring up at me with an impossibly proud smile on his face.

"So, you do have some moves." He jumped up to his feet, brushed his suit off, and set himself back up in front of me. If anyone thought there was anything other than two people sparring earlier, I'd have to say after flipping him over my shoulder, they weren't thinking anything now.

"Yeah, yeah I do," I said, bringing my hands up to my face and trying to mimic his stance. Thanks to Hudson. When we were young, he went through a Jackie Chan phase... every single movie ever made with him in it, Hudson made me watch with him.

My kung fu moment stopped Jen, Hudson, and their companions in their tracks. They were all only a few feet from us, but continued on with their own training. We sparred for the next couple of hours. Punches, kicks, and flips were exchanged back and forth as we became comfortable maneuvering with and around one another. Heathe was a great teacher.

I was able to get a few shots and a few flips in, which gave me a smidge of confidence.

It felt good to finally have control over what I was doing. I knew when it came to my gifts, I wasn't in total control. My body—its physical actions at least—I was in control of.

"Class change," Thor announced as he stood in the middle of the field with Ms. Hullen by his side.

Jen and Hudson said goodbye to their partners in the traditional Nemelite way and made their way over to Heathe and I.

"Good work, Jacey. Maybe next class we can work on your gifts," Heathe said.

"Thanks, you weren't so bad yourself," I said, hitting him in the shoulder.

"Hey, you two. Ready for the next class?" Jen asked.

"I am. It's supposed to be the one where we learn about all nineteen Nations," I said, wiping the sweat off my forehead with the back of my hand.

"We need to go shower first. We'll meet you guys in the Great Hall as soon as we're done," Jen said, grabbing hold of my hand and pulling me off into the direction of the door we had initially used to enter the center concourse.

"See you there," Hudson called out.

Ms. Hullen came over to us as we were leaving. "I'll escort you to the nearest showers. There are outfits there for the two of you," she said while walking past us to open the door.

"We don't have any clothes there," I said.

"There are uniforms there for you to wear. While here in the Origin and taking classes, all wear an Origin uniform."

"Are they like the ones I saw Mom, Dad, Aunt Grace, and Gideon wearing in the picture in Celeste's office back at St. Nemele?" I asked.

"They are."

Great. They weren't too bad, if memory served me correctly. They looked comfortable: black pants with white shirts.

We entered a change room area off of the Great Hall. Positioned at the far back corner were showers.

"All the toiletries and your clothes are in the last two stalls. I'll wait here for the two of you," Ms. Hullen said, ushering Jen and I to the showers.

I looked over at Jen and raised my eyebrows in a gesture of 'all right then.' She returned the look and we both entered our respective shower stalls.

Everything I needed was there for me to get ready. Hanging on a hook behind the door was my uniform.

I showered quick and got dressed. The pants were more like the skinny jeans which felt like joggers and the shirt was a short sleeved white polo shirt with a symbol embroidered over the right chest pocket. It was the same symbol which was over the door of our dormitory.

I exited into the common area of the change room and began to braid my hair. I heard a commotion on the other side of the shower stalls. There were two people talking. Ms. Hullen was nowhere to be seen.

"They think a Genapiene from Earth of all places is going to help save anyone here? What are the Elders thinking?"

"Obviously they aren't. Did you see me lay her out?"

"I did. Did Thor get all up on you for doing it?"

"No, he didn't. If she thinks she can just walk in here all *'I'm so important, look at me'*, then I don't mind teaching her a few Rifeaian lessons."

No doubting who one of the girls in the conversation was—Yellesh. I had no idea who she was talking to, but I tried to slink my way back to the shower stall. What was it with me and washrooms? If they came around the corner, I didn't want them to know I was there.

"What a joke! We should be the ones working with Heathe. Verbeyna was right, this girl is..." Before they could finish their conversation, Ms. Hullen called out.

"Jacey, Jen time to move."

Jen came out of her stall ready to go. She looked at me and instantly knew there was something up. I put my finger to my mouth in a hush gesture. She looked at me inquisitively but didn't say a word. I knew she was going to bombard me with questions later.

Yellesh and her partner came around the corner. They knew I'd overheard them. I glanced their way quickly and just as quickly turned my back to them and continued braiding my hair.

"Yellesh, Adiena, what are you doing in here?" Ms. Hullen asked.

"We were just cleaning up a little," Yellesh said, not looking at Ms. Hullen. She was staring holes into my back. I could see her reflection in the mirror I was standing in front of.

"Get going or you two will be late for your next instruction."

They didn't hesitate. Yellesh turned to leave but not before I made eye contact with her. I was tired of being the one who always looked away first. I wanted her to know I knew what she said and I wasn't impressed. I looked her straight in the eye and cocked my head to the side shaking it ever so slightly.

She blushed slightly but covered it up quickly with a seething look my way. She and Adiena turned and left the area.

Adiena was a fairy. Her tanned skin made her jade eyes stand out like gems. Her hair was long and braided and was a mix between blue and green. Her wings were folded onto her back and were a rainbow of colors. At least she looked a little ashamed when we made eye contact.

"I will escort the two of you to Heathe and Hudson, and then to your instruction on the Nations," Ms. Hullen said as we left the change rooms.

"What was that all about?" Jen asked as we followed a few feet behind Ms. Hullen.

"I don't think Yellesh likes me very much, and I don't think she has any problem letting others know it."

"What did she say?"

"Something about a Genapiene from Earth thinking she's all that… thinking the Elders made a huge mistake putting any trust in her and Verbeyna having some opinion about me, too."

Jen stopped and grabbed both of my shoulders. She placed me directly in front of her.

"Seriously, Jacey, that girl is clueless. She has a huge chip on her shoulder. Don't let haters like her get under your skin."

"She's not under my skin. As a *Genapiene from Earth*, I'm not the most educated in the use of my gifts or Nemele and everything and everyone who's a part of it, but I am one with a hell of a stubborn streak. If that girl thinks she's going to take me on… get in line," I said with a little more bravado than necessary. It caught Ms. Hullen's attention. She stopped and turned to look at Jen and I.

"Girls, we need to get going."

I hugged Jen quick. We then caught up to Ms. Hullen.

"Jacey, there are always going to be people, species, and beings who believe they're better than others. Nemele is many things, but it's far from perfect. You'll learn and you will succeed. Know through those accomplishments, that's the best way to silence any cynic," Ms. Hullen said.

She obviously had heard what Jen and I were talking about. She was right and I knew it. I should have known there were going to be some Nemelites who saw me as a threat, or saw me as a joke. I honestly didn't need to be focusing any of my time, energy, or thoughts on any of them right now. Vincent was the one I needed to concentrate on. He wasn't here with me where he should be. His safe return to Nemele and to me was the only thing I cared about right now.

I needed to give myself a little credit for what I'd been accomplishing lately. From being summoned to summoning on my own. When I thought about it, I'd never even known about this world, these beings—Nemele—until a short time ago.

I was bothered by some of what Yellesh had been saying, who wouldn't be? No one likes to be spoken about in a negative way. Especially by someone you really didn't do anything to. Sure, she didn't like me, yeah, okay I'll get over it… but… what was with Verbeyna? What had she said to Yellesh and possibly others that gave them the impression I wasn't someone you wanted to support?

Verbeyna changed things drastically. As a Hinderer, she had created my amulet. She was entrusted with placing a binding spell on me which stopped me from being summoned and now summoning on my own. If she was out talking a bunch of crap about me, how trustworthy would her magic be?

Not to mention, the way Chanary reacted to the fact Verbeyna had been brought back into Heathe's life because of me. She must have known about Heathe being from Draco and a Dragon along with his history involving the Archangels. If he had broken things off with her way before me, then what was the reason for her not liking me? It wasn't like Heathe and I were any more than just friends.

There was so much I needed to wrap my mind around and so much I still needed to figure out. The one and only thing I knew for sure I had to do was re-focus. All of my attention and concentration needed to be on the one thing I wanted above all else—Vincent. He was all I should be caring about right now…

"Hey, everything good?" Heathe's voice called out, bringing me back to the realization there may be one other being I cared a little too much for.

CHAPTER FIFTEEN

Introductions
21 Nations
A melting pot of nationalities
Misconceptions all around

"Yeah, everything's fine. Are we ready to go to Nation's class?" I asked, avoiding eye contact with Hudson.

"We're a little early. We can take our time heading there," Heathe said, coming over to stand beside me.

He was wearing a similar outfit to mine. His shirt was the same polo style but the symbol above the breast pocket was different. It looked like a box with circles on each of its four corners, '⌘'.

"What does the symbol on your shirt stand for?" I asked.

"Gabriel convinced Jordan. The Dracos are now officially a part of the Guild," Heathe answered.

"That's good news," I started to say but stopped once I saw the look on his face. He looked anything but happy about it.

"Why do you look like it's not good news for the Draco to rejoin?" I asked.

"The Elders know we're a race of beings who originally were born to serve the Nephilim. A lot has changed over the last couple of millennia. Jordan has decided his clan of Draco shall rejoin, but there are still a number of others who aren't so happy to be part of the Guild. They believe we're a nation unto itself. In other words, we've been making our decisions for so long, a number of us are not so keen on having to go through anyone else to have any of our decisions okayed. The Nephilim, who we still are part of, are the only ones we've ever taken direction from. The fundamentalists of our kind are still of that mind," Heathe answered as we started off down a corridor within the Origin's frame.

"Have you or the others ever thought *that* may be the reason a number of us have gone out on our own?" a familiar voice asked from behind us.

I stopped and turned to face Chanary as she approached us. She wore the same outfit we all did, except her shirt had a different symbol on it. It looked like two large letter 'C's' facing one another with an apostrophe above the center of the two, 'C͡'.

An angry look crossed Heathe's features for a brief second as he looked at his sister. "No, I didn't... and now is neither the time nor the place to discuss *it* or the reason you're wearing a changeling emblem. We'll discuss it another time. Alone," Heathe answered, leaving no room for Chanary to ask any more questions.

"Are you attending the Nations instruction, too?" I asked her.

"Yeah, I am," she answered. For a brief second I felt sorry for her. It was obvious Chanary loved her brother and she was bothered by the fact they were at odds about the topic of which nation she aligned herself to. It was pretty clear the issue was over the Draco world's customs and possibly their decision to join the Guild.

"Here we are," Ms. Hullen announced. We approached a door with the same markings the main entrance to the Origin had on it. An infinity symbol with a large 'N' in each loop.

She held her clawed hand up to it. Instantly it glowed and opened. All six of us entered the room. Its interior was like nothing I'd ever seen before. It was octagonal in shape. Each of the walls was a visionary from ceiling to floor.

Depicted within each were scenes you'd expect from pictures published by NASA of places like the Milky Way. The difference between NASA's photos and the Origin Nations class *photos*... there was movement within each frame.

"Wow, where are all of these places?" I asked, taking a seat in the center of the room.

There were about thirty chairs set up in the middle of the room. Jen and Hudson sat beside one another. I sat beside Jen and Heathe sat on the other side of me. Chanary took the last seat beside Heathe. Ms. Hullen stood by the doorway.

"The Visionaries depict all of the Nations within Nemele," a female voice from behind me answered.

I turned and saw Bella. I was surprised at how happy I felt about her being present. I liked her even though I didn't really know her well. I think it was because she didn't let Chanary get under her skin at the Great Hall earlier.

"Thanks, Bella," I said, turning my attention to all of the others in the room. A number of them were from the Defensive Tactics class we had earlier—including Yellesh. Great... I was actually irritated she was in the same room with me. I didn't waste any time looking at her or letting her know I knew she was in the room. Instead, I turned and looked at the other beings.

"Hey, you okay?" Heathe asked, placing his hand on mine, which was on my lap.

There was an instant tingling in my belly accompanying his touch. I pulled my hand away and folded it around my waist as I crossed my arms around my belly.

"Yeah, I'm fine. Just a little overwhelmed," I answered, hating that my body was having any reaction at all to him.

The door to the class opened, drawing his attention away from me. In walked a man wearing a pair of beige loose fitting pants and a button down white shirt. Embroidered over the breast pocket of his shirt was a circle with a cross in the center of it.

Without a word, the male drew every single being's attention as he entered. There an aura around him. It was brilliant white. I didn't know if anyone else could see it, but I was mesmerized by it. He was beautiful, almost breathtaking. Not the same take my breath away feeling I felt when I saw Vincent. His was more akin to when you witness something you believe isn't possible… like witnessing a miracle.

A movement from my left interrupted my attention. Heathe got up and made his way towards the man. The man held out his hand and they greeted each other in the traditional Nemelite fashion.

"Would you like for me to introduce you?" Heathe asked.

"No, I can manage. It's been a long time since I've been able to talk freely and I'm looking forward to it," the man said.

His voice was beautiful… if that's even possible. His intonation was captivating. I looked around the room to see if everyone else was being affected in the same way I was. All eyes were literally stuck on the man. Even though I turned away from him, I still felt a pull to turn and look at him. I ignored it and continued to take everyone else in. It was as though they were all under a spell.

I elbowed Jen. "Hey, are you seeing this?"

She didn't answer. I turned to look at her and she was as taken in by the man as everyone else. I elbowed her again and she didn't budge. What the heck was wrong with everyone? Heathe came back over to me and took a seat.

"What's with everyone?" I asked as he came to sit down beside me.

Before he could answer, the man up front spoke. I looked at him and he was staring directly at me. I looked to my right and left, ensuring he wasn't looking at someone else. Nope, he was looking at me. A blush rose into my cheeks.

"Hello, everyone. This isn't going to be your average every cycle instruction today. I was asked by Herecerti to come and do the introduction to you specifically. I understand this will be part of the group which shall traverse the Bulwarks within each Nation to the Charta Zone in an attempt to assist with the recovery of a number of Nemelites who have been trapped there for quite some time. I also understand we are going to assist with the return of Vincent and the team which traveled with him to return Daichi."

At the mention of Vincent's name, my heart jumped and a tear escaped my left eye. A feathery touch broke the stare the man and I had been sharing. Heathe reached up and brushed the tear away with his hand.

"Gabriel will help," he said, squeezing my hand.

My breath caught. "Gabriel... as in the archangel... as in the guy you've been protecting for like ever?" I asked.

"Yes. He," Heathe pointed to the guy in front of the class, the guy I had been staring at—"is *the* Gabriel."

That explained a lot. It was probably why every being in the place couldn't take their eyes off him and why I found him so captivating.

"I am Gabriel. We have not been part of the Guild for eons. Recently, as new revelations came to light, it was decided it was time for us to rejoin. Two of those specific reasons for our reconnection are the Charta Zone information and the resurgence of Necroseek.

"All five of the original creators, the Armers, the Amazarak, the Barkayals, the Akibeels and the Asaradels all exist. We are of Arcadia, however we lost our home a long time ago. It was destroyed along with Ryu, the home world of the Songards, during the Age of Reckoning."

Gabriel paused for a second. I looked around the room, expecting someone to ask something of him, considering he just dropped a huge amount of information on them. Not one being shifted in their seat. They were all still mesmerized by him.

"Is there a reason no one is questioning you or anything you've revealed here?" I asked. I was feeling on edge. I was compelled to him, who wouldn't have been? But I found it disturbing how no one in the entire room seemed to have a mind of their own. They all just sat there… in a stupefied silence.

Heathe held my hand and squeezed it gently. He got my attention so I turned to look at him. He had a look of awe in his eyes. One I hadn't seen on him before.

"What?" I asked, pulling my hand away and giving him a questioning stare.

"You are the one. I never doubt it, but I must say seeing it in action is amazing," Heathe answered.

"I have no idea what you're talking about," I answered, slightly irritated.

"Jacey," Gabriel said, coming towards me. His aura glowed an even brighter white as he spoke.

I lifted my hand, shielding my eyes. "Can you turn it down a little bit? Your aura is pretty blinding," I said.

"Your gifts are extremely strong," he replied.

When he answered, his aura dimmed to almost nothing. The second it did, everyone in the room appeared to come back to normal.

"You, Jacey, have just passed *my* test. I needed to see it for myself to believe in everything I've been told lately," Gabriel said.

"And what's that?" I asked.

Jen and Hudson looked at me like I had cursed or said something out of line. I returned their look. "You guys decided to come back, did ya?" I asked under my breath, loud enough for only them to hear me.

"What are you talking about? What's wrong?" Jen asked.

"I can help with answering that," Gabriel said, returning to the center of the room.

"If any of you are wondering what is happening, I can reveal to you now, each and every one of you were enchanted by my aura. When I entered the room, I magnified it. How many of you witnessed it?"

No one spoke up. "Jacey," Gabriel said, pausing for me to answer.

"Everyone saw it. The second you walked in, everyone in here seemed under a trance. Not one of them took their eyes off of you," I answered.

"Close," he replied, cocking his head to the right. "Every being was transfixed by my aura... not one witnessed it. Only you witnessed my essence. What color did you see?"

"White."

"You are the only Nemelite throughout the cosmos, outside of my guardians, that has seen my aura. An Archangel's aura is used for complicity. It is a way we can explain, reveal, and educate without the worries of conflict. Our auras have never been denied before... that is, until today. You were able to break away from my aura and my intonation.

"You were affected, but only slightly. Where others were completely enamored without desire to question or confront, you became annoyed. You questioned and you were able to block me."

"How is that even possible? I thought every Nemelite could see others' auras," I asked.

"You are correct, however, only partially. The auras of every being within Nemele are visible. However, the auras of the Archangels are not. It is how we have been able to hide in plain sight for so many eons within each of the remaining nineteen Nations. Since we were the originators of all Nations, we were gifted with our auras. The difference, each being here was born into their aura upon their Awakening.

"Every Nemelite and Yietimpi was created by the original five. The worlds they come from, the air they breathe, the blood flowing through their bodies. In their creation, each being's aura was predetermined. As the guides and creators of every society, it is of the natural order for all beings to be bound to comply to any Archangel's aura. Each of us has a different purpose to share with all. When we do so, we use our aura. In all of history there has been no one... Nemelite or Yietimpi, who has been able to block us."

"Block you? By me not paying as much attention to you as the others, is that blocking you?" I asked.

"It is. You shouldn't have been able to think outside of what I was telling you. You should have only been able to take in what I was saying and to see the truth in my words. Because you were able to look around and think of other things, it confirms you are the anomaly. Well, half of it," Gabriel said.

I sat for a minute, taking in everything he said. Everyone in the room had their eyes on me. Talk about being the center of attention, a place I've never been comfortable with. As I tried to ignore the stares and the heat rising up in my ears, a thought hit me.

"Does that mean Necroseek has the same ability?" I asked.

"Yes, he does. That's one of the reasons why we must be diligent in your training and the training of those who will accompany you to the Charta Zone. He may have lost some of his abilities when he turned his back on the purity of his soul. So, his essence should be clouded, murky, almost black. Those faithful to him will also have a darkened aura. His powers are more effective on those who are true to the Yietimpi ways, but he still has the ability to turn Nemelites," Gabriel said.

"How do they stop it? Will I be able to block him?" I asked.

"With the proper training, the others should be able to learn how to repel his calling. For you, when you accepted your destiny, I believe something inside you changed. Changed to empower you and make you unaffected by both virtuous and corrupt auras. Working together, we will be able to defeat him and those loyal to him." Gabriel paused and turned his attention back to the others in the class.

"You will all need to entrench yourselves in the history of the original twenty-one Nations and all of their inhabitants. Along with learning about them, you all will need to study the five Nephilim societies, the Amazarak, Armers, Barkayals, Akibeels and Asaradels. With that knowledge and the studying of the Barkayal's charts, we will all be successful in rescuing your families who are being held by Necroseek and his legions. Today we learn of the original twenty-one Nations. For each of the other areas of training you all will need, the other six Archangels will be addressing those needs."

There was a small bit of conversation throughout the room. Each being seemed pumped to be a part of this group. I, on the other hand, was feeling anxious and a bit nauseous. Was everyone here excited and a truly *willing* participant? Or, were they all under Gabriel's spell? I knew there were at least four beings here who were a part of this for their own reasons outside of the Archangels' influence—Jen, Hudson, Heathe, and Chanary. But why were the others here? What were their reasons?

"So, instead of wasting any more time, let's list the Nations and their creation in a timeline," Gabriel said, going over to the furthest visionary.

195

"This is where Acadia once was." He pointed to a beautiful array of colored constellations. They looked like what you'd expect to see if you were standing in the middle of a tornado looking up inside of it. The swirls of stars and rock seemed to go on forever.

"This, is where Ryu used to be." He pointed to a pathway of rocks and stars. The colors ranged from red and yellow to burnt orange.

"They were the original two Nations. In order of creation, here are the remaining nineteen." Gabriel went from right to left and named each Nation. As he did, the visionary enlarged and the planet of each Nation filled it.

The list was impressive and quite surprising. In order of appearance within the Visionaries, Gabriel listed the Nations:

1) Acadia: Archangels' planet (Kawaneing).
2) Ryu: Songards – Dragon planet (Fire).
3) Hypoboria: Hyperborean planet – air, wind, snow, sun (Air – wind).
4) Rifeas: Fairy, troll world (Closest to Earth – both in geography and make up) (Earth).
5) Remaidus: Mostly water – creatures of the seas, mermaids, mermen (Water).

These were the originating Nations. Each Nation was developed based on one of the five universal elements. From their success, the remaining fifteen Nations were born.

6) Olympus: Zeus – "Greek God" planet.

7) Telnom: A world of fire and volcanic terrain. The inhabitants are formed of the terrain – rock, sand, lava.

8) Nemele: world where all come to train and learn in the ways of the Nemelites and Yietimpi. A world where all of the Archives of the Nations are held.

9) Earth: Mornal Genapienes and the one and only world where all beings from every world can survive and have visited.

10) Daulcron: Witches and warlocks – manipulate all of the elements.

11) Hangcling: World where creatures have the ability to change their body composition – changelings.

12) Cyres: World of banshees and mystic fates.

13) Sagint: A world of giants.

14) Nefzor: A world of ice and crystal.

15) Dullstoob: Vampire, shadow world.

16) Aphaea: World of growth – green fields and every imaginable fruit, vegetable – Genapiene world – power of growth from earth.

17) Shaoc: A world of upheaval – horrific wind storms, hurricanes, fires and brimstone. A warriors planet. Mostly used by Yietimpi contingents.

18) Taurpre: A world of peace and harmony. A melting pot of beings who have interbred and chosen to live their lives out of their natural habitats.

19) Gunjel: A world primarily made up of any and all humanoid, animal creatures. There are many different types of Genapiene on the world.

Its makeup is close to Earth's, however it is more jungle-like than urbanized.

20) Yemirs: A world of turbulent elemental forces. A world where both Nemelite and Yietimpi try to survive together.

21) Kradsens: A planet of shadows. There is little Nemelites know of the planet. There are mystical forces on it but of unknown origins.

I could tell by the reaction of most in the room they were surprised to hear which were the first worlds created. I was curious as to why everyone seemed so taken aback by Gabriel's introduction of the Nations.

"Doesn't everyone learn about the Nations from the beginning of their training?" I asked.

"Yes, everyone does. However, not everyone has been to the other Nations within the Guild. The exact locations of each and their placements within the universe have not been mapped out in this forum before. Not everyone is aware of their creation dates and not everyone knew about Acadia and Ryu and that they'd been destroyed. The reason I am sharing this information with all of you," Gabriel paused and walked to the center of the room where Ms. Hullen met up with him, "is because we have received information that Necroseek is at the furthest point in our universe. He is in the Darkened zone where we believe the true Seeker Lands are located."

"If Necroseek is there, and the Seekers are there, does that mean Vincent is as well?" I asked.

"We're unsure at this point, but our intelligence in the areas has indicated the Fundamentalist Seekers who have aligned themselves with Necroseek have taken all of the Nemelites which were past the Charta Zone and brought them to a new world which was created by Necroseek and his followers," Ms. Hullen said.

"How is that possible? They created a world by themselves?" Heathe asked.

"Necroseek has had eons to prepare for this. He has accumulated an enormous number of legions who have powers and abilities which none here have ever seen," Gabriel answered.

"Hold up a second. Did you just say they brought *all* of the Nemelites to the furthest part of the Universe? Does that include Vincent?"

"We believe Necroseek moved Vincent there in an attempt to draw Faith out. She and the others had asylum with the group of Seekers they'd been staying with, but with the energy signature which had been released from Daichi's return to the Charta Zone, it brought some of the Fundamentalist Seekers down upon their colony. The only information we have is Faith was able to escape with Daichi and a few others, but it appears that Vincent and his team were taken by Necroseek."

My head was spinning. I felt like I was going to puke. I wasn't going to allow myself to faint yet again… my pulse was racing and there was a whistling in my ears that reminded me of the incident I had with Chanary in the hallways of St. Nemele before we came here to the Origin. I could see people's lips moving but I couldn't hear them.

Everyone in the room got up and moved away from me except for Heathe, Jen, and Hudson. Gabriel and Ms. Hullen approached me from the center of the room. Ms. Hullen was staring down at my amulet and saying something.

I looked down and saw the amulet glowing grey-black and floating directly out from my neck and parallel to the ground. I turned and looked over at Heathe, who was talking to Gabriel. I was able to make out 'Necro'—right before a flash of black flew forth out from the visionary Kradsens was in.

As it flew at me, Gabriel transported himself from the center of the room to directly in front of me. He became a buffer of sorts. My senses came back as I felt two pulsing sensations in both my palms. I looked down to my left hand. Floating there was a pulsing energy ball of pure white light vibrating with an intensity so bright it was almost blinding. In my right hand, the seeker symbol blazed and a blood red ball of energy with coal black tendrils pulsed within my palm.

Gabriel turned to me. With one hand outstretched towards the visionary, he was holding the blackness at bay. With his other hand, he tried reaching out to me. Before he could come in contact with me, I started to levitate.

Before my head hit the ceiling, I stopped. With arms outstretched and the amulet parallel to the ground, the black feather I had been holding onto since the not so pleasant dream the night before came up out of my pocket and floated there right in front of me. The smell of brimstone and fire filled my senses.

Everyone in the room had been ushered to the door wall by Ms. Hullen. The only ones left with me were Heathe and Gabriel. I looked down at Heathe. He had grabbed onto my leg, in effect stopping me from floating off any higher or away. Gabriel was chanting in a language I didn't understand and Heathe was yelling out to me.

I could hardly make out what he was saying. There was an unseen source of wind and a loud screeching noise like metal on pavement filling the room. My arms were still shot out from my sides, palms up, with the white and red energies floating around them. Each was gaining ground on my body and moving up my arms towards my chest. Before either touched my chest, my head shot back and a loud howling noise came from deep within me. My head shot back up and the voice coming from me gave me chills. I was trapped within my body. Unable to speak or control any part of myself—I was an onlooker like everyone else in the room. I shuddered as a voice spoke from my mouth—one which wasn't mine, "Gabriel, my brother, it has been so long."

"Necroseek."

"You are wasting your time. We both know she will be mine in the end."

I was infuriated watching the battle going on. I was stuck inside my body but Necroseek had control over it.

"Your soul is rotted and your powers are weak, brother. It's time you return to the bowels of hell." Gabriel reached over and grabbed my other leg. The instant he came into contact with me, I felt my body come back to me... slightly. Necroseek was not giving up that easily.

"She is pure and she is mine!" he hissed. "There is nothing you or any of your 'dogs' here will be able to do to save her soul. From birth it was marked and I will not be denied."

I watched as Heathe's face began to turn from smoothly tanned to rippled and dark.

"Heathe, control! Not here. Not now!" Gabriel called out. I could see the pain and bloodlust in Heathe's eyes. He was incensed.

Internally, I began to scream out to Necroseek. I wasn't going to allow him to take me from this place. I wasn't going to allow him to possess me. "Come and get me!" I yelled out inside myself. "So tough and pompous with a crowd watching. Come to me as you should have the first time we were introduced," I called out.

The wind in the room shifted slightly. I had gotten his attention. "You want me? I'm here! There's no reason you should be involving everyone else. It's me you want, isn't it?" I shouted even louder.

I could sense his confusion. Gabriel had been right. Necroseek had the same abilities to lull one's senses and he wasn't used to someone fighting back—especially a Genapiene. I took hold of my chance at his uncertainty and envisioned the purity of my soul. The bright white aura of the Archangels and every single person in this world and every other one I held dear. I thought of Vincent and the need to rescue him from this evil which was attempting to possess me.

I screamed. I screamed at the top of my lungs! My back arched in an almost impossible arch and my arms bent back with it. The voice coming from my body was both mine and Necroseek's. I was in a battle within myself. My body fell—Heathe was holding me upright from behind. I flung my head back and looked directly into Gabriel's eyes. Reflected in his I saw my own—one filled with the chocolate brown coloring I had been looking through for sixteen years and the other black with red sparks flying around within it.

"I will not underestimate you next time… and there will be one—you will be mine," Necroseek howled as his essence was ripped from body.

"I've got you," Gabriel said as two enormous white wings encompassed me from behind his back—I was embraced within his wings and instantly I was at peace.

CHAPTER SIXTEEN

Blurred lines
The hands of comfort which have been your
guide
Now, take on a more determined role
Can you see someone's soul
through their eyes

I opened my eyes and was lulled for a second into serenity. I was sitting in an open field outlined with huge oak, maple, and blue spruce trees. A warm wind danced around my face, whispering across my cheeks. They were flushed but I was calm. A hand reached out to me, catching my attention as it placed a stray ringlet of hair behind my ear. I looked up.

Backlit from the brilliant overhead sky was a man. At first I thought it was Vincent and I reached up for him. The instant our hands intertwined, I knew it wasn't.

"Gabriel. Where are we?"

"We are at the boundary to the zone you visit your parents in. I brought you to a place on the edge of that one and ours. I figured we could use a less 'being' filled area to discuss what happened back there." He smiled as he came to sit beside me on the grass.

"Is everyone all right? Did he hurt anyone? Are Jen, Hudson, and Heathe okay?" I asked starting to stand.

"They're all fine. They've now witnessed a small taste of what we are up against in the coming cycles. I took you here to talk," Gabriel replied, holding my hand at his side, in effect stopping my attempt to stand. "To talk to you about what happened back there. I was astonished to see the power within you, Jacey. You surprise even me."

I sat crossed legged beside him, blushing. "I can't even begin to wrap my mind around what happened. How did he know to come through the visionary at that exact time? I thought the Guild made arrangements with all of the Visionaries to keep track on any kinds of Yietimpi signatures."

"The Barkayals are aware of the limitations which were set out. They did impose them on the Visionaries. This shows how much Necroseek has grown, how much he has developed. We know he still has some of the charts he stole when he left so long ago. My only guess as to how he managed the attack today, he is utilizing those charts and the legions who follow him to manipulate and corrupt the guardians of some of the Visionaries. He will use whatever is necessary to get to you, Jacey. Can you tell me what occurred while he was trying to possess you?"

"Trying? I'd say he pretty much did. It was like I was a bystander in my own body. He had control over it... over me—completely."

"No, not entirely. You were able to break through to him."

"I was, but it wasn't until I envisioned your aura and everyone I love in my life. When I did, I screamed at the top of lungs to try and get his attention. He ignored me at first, but I think you were right. He was shocked to see I was able to call out to him."

"You're right. He, as all of us, uses his aura to his advantage, which I now know for certain doesn't have the same effect on you as it does with every other being within the twenty-one Nations." He smiled.

"No, it doesn't. But thinking of my loved ones and your aura wasn't the only thing which empowered me. Heathe holding onto me and the instant you came into contact with me seemed to drive him from my body. I'm not so sure I would have been able to do that by myself."

"You would have been able to hold him off for some time. I believe with the proper training, you won't need anyone else's help in the future. You, Jacey, are extremely talented. I have to admit I did doubt the scripts. I was unsure until today about the prophecy."

"Is there more I can read up on it? We tried to find the scripts in the Archives but couldn't."

"They are within the Archives. With the training regimen you will be exposed to over the next couple of cycles, there will be a point when the scripts are explained to you."

"Cycles?"

"Yes, Jacey." Gabriel stood, pulling me into a standing position with him. "I do believe it will take more than one cycle to have not only you, but all the others prepared for the battle we are about to face."

"A cycle is like 20 Earth days... right?" I asked.

"It's close to 20. The rotation of the suns and moons differ from cycle to cycle."

"So, how many 'cycles' are we looking at?" I asked, trying to hide the irritation in my voice and failing.

"I would say five at least—the other Archangels need to come and explain the divisions—there are five houses to explain and within each a cycle will be needed to explore, understand, and utilize the talents within each."

"We can't wait that long! What do you think will happen to Vincent and the others who are being subjected to Necroseek and his followers?" I was starting to hyperventilate a little. I promised myself I wouldn't let Vincent wait any longer than one cycle and I was going to stick to that promise... no matter what.

"Jacey, we need to be prepared. The longest and most trying part of the journey will not be finding Vincent—"

"What do you mean finding Vincent won't be the hardest part? I thought that was what was keeping us back."

"The harshest and most volatile will be travelling through the Nations and finally finding him on Kradsens. The battle we can *prepare* for, it is the unknown that we need to *train* for. If we take the most direct route there, they will be expecting us. They will conquer us. Because of the diverse assemblage of beings we've gathered to be part of this delegation, it would be of benefit to travel safely through each Nation. Necroseek will ensure that our travels are met with blockades at every opportunity. Why do you think he chose the last Nation within our Guild to hide in?"

"I thought he did because it was the darkest planet—easy to hide in."

"No, if it were only that simple. He chose the last Nation because he knows we will travel safely. We will not rush into anything. He knows we have to travel through each Nation to get to him. There are no short cuts. There are no Bulwarks which we can take to bring us directly to Kradsens. He knows we as a group will utilize the Barkayals' systems to travel between the Nations."

"Why... why aren't there any direct Bulwarks? And how did Necroseek get here then? Didn't he travel directly from one visionary to the next?"

"He did travel through the Visionaries. To travel through them is to risk losing yourself. The images are not permanent and they change at the desire of its proprietor. If the image changes as you travel through it, your essence is lost along with your physical being. You would in effect be floating around forever in… nothingness."

"But Vincent traveled through the Bulwarks to bring Daichi back to the Seekers' lands outside of the Charta Zone. Are the lands on Nemele or within another Nation?"

"Seekers' lands are dispersed throughout the Nations. I believe Daichi's world is on Cyres. He chose to use as many Bulwarks as possible to hide their signatures from any Yietimpi who may have been following them or who would use their signatures to travel back and find you."

"So, Vincent knew he'd be gone longer than a few days…"

"He did. He didn't want to worry you and he didn't have the time to explain the traveling system here. Not to mention he knew you'd have refused to let him go without you if you were aware of how long it was going to take him to travel the Bulwarks. He believed he was keeping you as safe as possible."

I was upset with the knowledge of Vincent not being completely truthful with me. Gabriel must have been able to read my body language or the thoughts which were twirling around inside my mind, because he began to explain the Bulwark system to me.

"Jacey, he truly didn't have the time to explain all to you within the Inception Chamber… but I have the time now if you want to listen," he said, as he sat patiently awaiting my response.

"Of course… I want… no, I need to know."

"In the beginning there were Bulwarks, which allowed for direct travel from any of the Nations within the Guild. However, they were all destroyed when wars and inquisitions began to dominate and threaten the very existence of Nemelite and Yietimpi alike. Direct travel allowed for too many to go unnoticed and cause havoc among the Nations. The leaders of the Nemelite and Yietimpi Societies decided direct travel was a system best used by the Elders alone. This is the only stand alone system allowing for transport directly to any planet. It is the Bulwark in the center of Nemele— the mirrored version of Nevaeh on Earth. Each Nation has one, so it can send its students and its Elders to Nemele. For all other business, beings have to travel the Bulwarks, which were allotted for their use by the Guild." Gabriel paused for a second, waiting to see if I had any questions. I didn't, so he continued.

"Of course there were some within the Yietimpi Society who tried to possess the direct Bulwarks for their own uses. They relished in the delights of famine and discord among all beings. But the Elders within each Guild were able to banish the Yietimpi groups who were in possession of the remaining direct routes to their originating dimensions. We believe each and everyone has been sealed."

"So, what you're saying is there are still some direct routes… so, why can't we use those?"

"We cannot use them because Necroseek will have each one watched by some of his closest cohorts. Another reason which became apparent today, Necroseek could not have known to come through the visionary at the exact moment and place unless he had someone working with him. It seems there are some Nemelites who are deceiving the Guild. They have been swayed to the Yietimpi side of our world yet pretend to serve the Nemelite segment."

"You mean someone on the inside? Someone here at the Origin... with us?"

"Yes. There was no way Necroseek could have known the area, the visionary, and the time we would be present. Someone here told him."

"How are we going to find out who?"

"In time their deception will come to light, but until then we must train. We must learn and prepare. You will be no help to Vincent if you are not educated in the ways of our lives. In the ways of both Nemelite and Yietimpi. Jacey, you are the key. I know you are going to ask me the key to what... The only answer I have for you right now is the key to lead us to Necroseek and hopefully to his defeat."

"I only want to get Vincent back and help get Uncle Gideon and Faith returned to Aunt Grace. I don't see what everyone else sees in me. I wasn't raised in this world and I understand you all think I have some crazy powers that are going to help you get Necroseek. But if he's as old as I think he is, like from the beginning of time like the rest of you, how in this world or any other one am I supposed stop him? I'm a 16 year old Genapiene girl from Earth who has never experienced any kind of magic in her life until the last month. He's a fallen angel who has more power and more followers than time has minutes to count." I paused for a second to catch my breath.

Gabriel reached over and placed his hand to my right temple.

"Watch…"

Instantly my vision was filled with my dream colors. When they subsided, I was standing with Gabriel in the backyard of Aunt Grace's house.

"Why are we here?"

"You said you have never experienced magic before. I am bringing you to a place and time in your life which will show you the exact opposite."

Gabriel walked towards the back entrance of the house and waited for me to follow. I did and we entered through the back door.

There was no one in the sunroom. The room looked the same except for a couple of extra pieces of furniture. We ventured further into the house into the kitchen area. I heard a male's voice from the front entrance and looked up into the face of my father as he entered the house.

"Joe, Vi, are you here?" he asked as he walked right through me and into the sunroom.

"Whoa… what was that?" I asked Gabriel.

"We are only observing here. This is your past. This is where you are from and who you are."

"So, no one can see us here? How far in the past are we?"

"No one can see us. I've returned you to your first year of birth."

I was speechless. My father's voice brought my attention back to him and my aunt's house.

"We're upstairs, Hearte," a female's voice called from upstairs.

Dad took the stairs two at a time. We followed. He went into Aunt Grace's old room, the one Jen had been staying in.

The room was set up the way it had been in my dream. With a crib and bright beautiful collages painted on the walls.

"How's my girl?" Dad asked as he walked into Mom's old room through the adjoining door. He bent over the crib and picked up a little girl about a year old—me.

"She and Faith had a pretty interesting day," an old man said, coming around the corner out of Mom's room and heading directly over to the crib in Aunt Grace's old room. He reached into the crib and took out another little girl and held her close.

"How so, Joe?"

"Is that my grandfather?" I asked.

"It is…"

"Where's Violet?" Dad asked.

"She's coming, she went to the washroom to clean up. "

"Hi, Hearte. How was training? Are Ria and Grace with you?" a lady, my grandmother, asked as she walked in from Mom's old room.

"Hi, Vi. Training was productive. Gideon has us all doing extra rounds since Christina warned us of Necroseek's interest in the children. Ria and Grace are still trying to master the Bulwark configuration."

"I'm sure we can start without them," Dad said.

My grandparents and father left the room holding the two children, me and Faith. As they went to pass Gabriel and I, I moved out of the way. I really didn't want anyone walking through me again. As they passed me, the child version of me looked over my dad's shoulder and reached out for me.

I made eye contact with my younger self and the child version of me smiled at me. My heart skipped a beat. Gabriel stood observing us with a curious look.

"Did she just see me?"

"Yes, I think she did," Gabriel answered.

My grandfather exited next with Faith in his arms and she mimicked what the child version of me had just done.

"That is amazing. The two of you were more powerful than we even knew," Gabriel commented.

"They weren't supposed to be able to do that, were they?" I asked.

"No, they shouldn't have been able to. But like I have been saying, the two of you are the anomaly to our species. The gifts you both have are astonishing."

We followed my grandparents and father down the stairs and out to the backyard. Once there, the children were placed in the grass and crawled towards one another. With everyone watching, I reached Faith and held onto her hand. The second we came into contact, a bright white light engulfed the two of us. We then sat facing one another, still holding hands.

No one in the yard seemed surprised or worried in any way with the display before us.

"They've been communicating with each other again using physical contact. It's the most amazing sight," my grandmother said as she went over to where the two little girls were sitting. She sat off the side and watched.

"Have you or Joe been able to understand any of the communications?" Dad asked.

"Nothing verbal, but the sense coming from the two is unmistakable. When they aren't in contact with each other, there is a sense of want, better yet, need you can feel between the two. The second they are touching, it's like they're complete. They seem to thrive off of each other," my grandfather said as he and my father watched Faith and I.

I looked over to Gabriel and he too was watching the spectacle before us.

A movement from the side caught all of our attention. Aunt Grace, Gideon, and Mom had arrived.

"Hello, my little one," Mom said as she came over to me on the grass and picked me up into an embrace.

"Hello, beautiful," Aunt Grace said as she picked up Faith.

Dad walked over to Mom and they kissed hello.

"Mom, Dad, how was the girls' day?" Aunt Grace asked as Gideon came to stand just behind her with his hand on her shoulder, caressing Faith's cheek.

"We think the girls are communicating through physical touch. It's pretty amazing to witness," Grandpa answered.

"Really? That is amazing," Gideon said.

"How about we see what else our little ones have in store for us today," Mom said as she kissed my cheek and placed me back on the soft grass.

Aunt Grace followed suit and placed Faith beside me. Again, the instant we came into physical contact, the white light returned, engulfing the two of us. Watching the two children, it became quite clear they were communicating in some way. The expressions on both of their faces made me think they were way beyond a year and a bit in age.

Faith nodded and I let go of her hand. She pointed up into the sky and all eyes followed. Hovering above was a Seeker.

"Gabriel! You have to do something," I called out.

He reached over and stopped me from moving. "Watch."

"Yes, beautiful, the skies are brilliant today," my grandmother said, standing and walking over to my grandfather.

"Do they not see the Seeker?" I asked.

"No, they do not," Gabriel answered.

I turned my attention back to my younger self and watched as I raised my hand and a brilliant green light shot out from its palm. Instantly the Seeker became visible to everyone else standing in the backyard.

"Christina," Gideon said with obvious irritation to his voice.

"They are getting more observant and stronger," she replied as she floated down from the sky, landing beside Faith. She reached over and caressed

216

Faith's cheek. She then made her way over to me but I had moved over to my mother.

"I was using a very strong invisibility enchantment. Jacey, my, you're getting quite talented," Christina said, coming over to my mother and I.

Mom reached down to scoop me up into her embrace. Faith hadn't moved, Aunt Grace walked over and pulled her up into a hug.

"She is, isn't she?" Mom cooed as she nuzzled my neck.

"I wanted to test them and see if they could detect other beings. I'd have to say they did an amazing job of it," Christina added.

"Yes, they are getting stronger. I believe we need to start teaching them through example in a more secure place. Their energy signals are strong and the guard has been able to keep the signature within our realm, but I fear they're growing and mastering their gifts to the point where we may not be able to continue here. Possibly we could go to the Origin and continue there," Gideon said.

"I'm not comfortable with putting our girls on display. We'll have to come up with a better cloak to keep them home. There are too many that are still fearful of them," Aunt Grace said.

"They don't understand them, therefore they fear them," Dad said.

"I believe as long as we have our family and the guard casting a blanket over the activities here, we should be fine. We need to sit and discuss this with Eve, Bronson, and some of the guard who are trusted," Aunt Grace said.

"I agree with Hearte and Grace. I think our children are much safer here, with us. With Christina helping out and keeping tabs on the Yietimpi contingents, I think we have the upper hand here," Mom said.

"For now then we'll discuss the possibility of keeping the children here—*for now*. But, I seriously think we need to be prepared to move the children when the time comes," Gideon answered.

"We have the ability to move them at a second's notice. We have the portal upstairs and we are trained in its usage," my grandmother offered.

"For the time being then," Gideon acquiesced.

I watched as Christina positioned herself close enough to my mom so she could touch me. As she attempted to stroke my cheek, I became fussy and squirmed in my mother's embrace.

"Shhh, it's okay. You won't be going anywhere," Mom said, rocking me in her arms.

It was obvious she thought I was being fussy because of the conversation—better yet the feel or sense I must have been getting from the tension within the conversation. But as I looked on watching my younger self, it was obvious to me that wasn't the reason.

Christina made her way over to Faith and caressed her cheek. Faith didn't move. Didn't make a sound.

"I don't think I'm uncomfortable because of the conversation," I said to Gabriel.

"No, I don't think you were, either."

"I think it's because of her." I pointed to Christina. "Every time she comes near me I try to get away from her."

"Because even as a child you knew. Your perception of beings was and is acute."

"Why didn't my parents or anyone else in my family know then?"

"Not all were taken in by Christina's charm. Gideon always held her at arm's length and so did—" Before he could finish a flash of red landed in the backyard.

"Sentry Prime." The familiar voice rang out and goose pimples raised on my body.

"Heathe, why are you presenting?" Gideon asked.

"I wanted to inform you that I will be taking the shift for this evening. I also wanted to inform you that the Seeker did not announce herself as she arrived. If it happens again, I cannot guarantee her safety." He looked over to my parents and the child version of me.

He smiled and then shifted his attention to Faith and Aunt Grace.

"We will ensure there are no more *unwanted* visitors." He glared over at Christina and flashed out as fast as he had flashed in.

"Heathe was my guard as a child?"

"He was…"

"It's just about dinner time. How about we all go in and settle by the fire. Vi and Grace made a delicious dinner for this evening," my grandfather said, taking my grandmother's hand and turning to enter the house. Everyone else followed except Gabriel and I.

The scene changed before us. It was dusk and we were standing just outside my mom's room at Aunt Grace's house.

"This is another time I needed for you to witness. You are not much older but your powers are stronger and more refined," Gabriel said as he and I passed through the doorway.

We were in Aunt Grace's old room and Faith was in the crib. The doorway to Mom's old room was closed and the symbol joining the doors was ablaze like they were when Faith summoned me back at the Origin.

Standing in the room off to the side was Christina. Faith was awake and staring at the symbols.

"Shhhh, it's okay little one," Christina said as she held onto Faith and approached the symbol. The instant Christina touched it, her hand sparked and she cursed under her breath. Faith reached up to Christina's injured hand and a pink light encompassed it. Within seconds it was healed.

"You are powerful. You will be praised and cherished forever," Christina said as she held Faith's hand up to the doorway. The instant she did, the doorway disappeared and floating in the center of the archway, the symbols flowed in bright crimson. I could see through to Mom's old room and I was standing in my crib.

Christina started to chant in a language I couldn't quite understand. The child version of me was looking at her with such contempt and dislike, I was taken aback for an instant.

"This is the night, isn't it?" I asked Gabriel.

"It is."

Faith looked very content and unaffected by the portal and its coloring. The child version of me, however, was anything but still. There was a bright purple light encompassing me and I was yelling towards the portal… "Faith… Faith… Faith…"

My hands were outstretched and the purple light was interfering with the symbols of the portal. Christina looked over at me and her eyes were no longer black… they were fire red. She called out, "Necroseek, I summon you through this child, come to me, master. It is you I serve. It is she I offer…"

The child me yelled out as Necroseek's shape filled the portal.

"You have done well, you will be rewarded. Hand me the child."

"N-o-o-o-o-o-o-o-… FAITH!" The child me yelled out. As I did, the purple light encompassing me turned every shade of my dream colors and blasted the portal closed.

"You little brat—" Christina yelled out as she rushed towards me. She was cut off by a flash of red in front of my crib. Heathe had appeared, on guard and blazing.

"Give me the child!" he yelled.

"Faith!" Uncle Gideon yelled as he entered the room.

"She's ours now!" Christina yelled back as she flashed out and landed on the windowsill. The light, which had been coming in from the window, was blackened. The night seemed to move at first glance. When I looked through the unoccupied sill in Aunt Grace's room, I realized the house had been covered in Seekers.

"Gideon, I will get Faith. Bring Jacey to safety," Heathe called out as he flashed after Christina.

Uncle Gideon flashed to the child me and the portal opened between the rooms again. This time the coloring was a golden color and standing within the portal were Mom and Dad.

"Hearte, grab Jacey," Uncle Gideon said as he thrust me through the portal and into the arms of my parents. The second our contact was broken, the portal closed and Gideon rushed off after Heathe and Christina.

"You know the rest of the story, Jacey. Your Uncle Gideon was lost to us and Heathe to this day, still blames himself," Gabriel said as the scene before me faded from the room I shared with Jen to the field Gabriel and I had been sitting in when we first came here.

"Why didn't Heathe grab Faith instead of me? Why did he let Christina take her?" I asked as tears flowed down my cheeks.

"Heathe knew he would not have been able to open the portal to get the two of you to safety. The only ones able to open it were the bloodline to you and Faith. The portal was geared to allow for them and only them to open it. Heathe would have been successful in getting Faith back except for the hundreds of Seekers awaiting him outside of the home." Gabriel paused for a minute and then continued.

"My reasoning for showing you these times in your life was not to garner a sad reaction. My motive was to show you, Jacey, who you truly are. The gifts you possess are formidable. When you said you were a Genapiene girl from Earth who'd never experienced any kind of magic in her life until the last month, I wanted to show you different. When you said Necroseek was a fallen angel who had more power and followers than time has minutes to count, I wanted you to see into your own soul—through your own eyes... Jacey, you faced him as a child and you won. You faced him without the help of the five houses or anyone else. You, YOU defeated him and his minions when they attempted to kidnap both you and Faith. You, Jacey, have more gifts locked away within you. All I want is to be able to help you discover them, and hopefully, finally be rid of Necroseek."

I was stunned silent. He was right. As I played the events over in my mind, I finally realized I truly was the key—*be it only partially*—the means of unleashing the Nemelites who had been lost to the Yietimpi. The source to either vanquishing the darkness which Necroseek fostered in all or on the other hand, the foundation for Necroseek to unite all of his followers under a power so dark, so severe that the worlds as everyone knew them would change forever.

"Gabriel, I'm only part of the answer. I need to tell you, the feelings I have when Faith is around are really confusing. On one hand I want to protect her and love her, and on the other... I watch her expressions and her actions and I'm scared. She isn't who or what we were as children anymore. Watching us as children has only made me trust my gut feelings about her. I have to agree with you now when you say I am the key. But I also have to warn you—Faith is also a huge part of everything. Until we can say without a doubt she's trying to come home to *escape* the Seekers and Necroseek, I think we really need to be on guard with her. I'll do anything and everything I need to get Vincent and the others home. If that means I need to train to learn more about who I am and what I can do, then I will."

Gabriel looked down at me and smiled. He was obviously happy with my newfound direction in thoughts. I seriously wanted to go as soon as I could to save Vincent and the others, but from what I'd witnessed, there were more reasons I needed to take it slow and be cautious. If Necroseek was able to have both Faith and I, life as every single being in the universe knew it, magic ones or not, would be filled with endless darkness and unimaginable suffering.

I looked back up at Gabriel. "I'm ready now."

We returned to the classroom we'd been in when Necroseek made his earlier appearance. As we became visible to everyone present, my eyes locked with Heathe's. From the expression on his face I knew he could tell Gabriel had shown me our past. I found myself wanting to reach out and comfort him. The anguish and guilt were so evident in his eyes I was surprised I hadn't seen it there before.

"Jacey, are you okay?" Hudson said as he and Jen rushed towards me.

Before I could answer, I was taken into a huge bear hug of an embrace. Hudson whispered in my ear, "Don't ever disappear on me again. I thought I'd lost you." His voice cracked and I hugged him back as hard as he was hugging me.

"Sorry," I whispered back. "It won't happen again."

Standing in the room were four other beings I hadn't met before. They all had the same aura as Gabriel.

"Jacey, I'd like to be the first to introduce you to…

CHAPTER SEVENTEEN

Through the eyes of others
You find yourself
Whether you want to or not...

I was petrified she'd see the sweat taking form on my brow. She had always been so much more than an 'anomaly' to me. I'd always known there was something between the two of us. I'd never touched her before yesterday... but when I did, I was more than ready to allow the connection I knew we would have.

I loved Vincent like a brother and never had I ever allowed for anyone or anything to interfere with our connection. I'd promised him I would watch out for Jacey, initially thinking it wouldn't be such a big deal... until I touched her.

What were the gods thinking? How could I feel this way about her knowing she was bequeathed to my dearest and best friend? Wirposhes were hard to find and here she had both Vincent and I. How was I going to deal with my newfound emotions? I knew deep down we could never be together. I was the protector of Armers... I was Gabriel's guard and had been since the beginning. My needs didn't matter.

I would deal with Jacey like I did with all who came close... not that any of them came close to the reaction I experienced with her... I would ignore them. The more pressing matter at hand—How was I going to deal with today?

Her innocent eyes looked up at me and my heart leapt. Instead of doing what I wanted to do, grab her and hold her tight to me, I took deep, even breaths. This was something I needed to be in control of, something at this point in time I didn't need. I was going to have to be extra careful with my physical reactions to her. I knew the draw I had to her. I'd been around long enough and have had enough experiences to be able to disguise my feelings, to make myself look completely disinterested to those on the outside. She, on the other hand, was like a newborn. She would have desires and impulses which I needed to make sure she didn't act on and I didn't, either. I was going to have to envision Jacey as a poison—good or bad, she was one I didn't need.

"I want to introduce you to four of the other Archangels who will be guiding us in our training," I said, breaking eye contact with her and moving over to them as I introduced each one.

"This is Raphael, he will be working with us under the Barkayal's Guild. This is Remiel, of the Akibeel Guild. This is Zerachiel of the Asaradel's

Guild, and this is Uriel of the Armers." I watched as her eyes followed me from archangel to archangel.

"Hi. Thank you all for coming," Jacey said, walking up to each instructor and greeting each one in the traditional Nemelite way. Her cheeks blushed as she came into contact with each angel.

I needed to concentrate on the matters at hand and not the way her ears lit up every time she blushed. Or the tell-tale pulse which presented itself at the base of her neck, telling me she was nervous.

"Each of them will be presenting over the next twenty cycles," I said, moving over to stand beside Gabriel.

Gabriel hadn't taken his eyes off me since he and Jacey had returned from wherever he had taken her to. He looked at me through knowing eyes. I tried to ignore him, but of course I couldn't.

"She will be the key to destroying Necroseek. She needs to concentrate on learning and training. She cannot have any other distractions. Will you be able to be her guard, or do you want me to make up an excuse to have you return to Jordan?" Gabriel asked without moving his lips.

There was a connection a guard had with his arch. We could communicate from anywhere with our minds. Very handy at times, not always convenient though, especially when your thoughts were not… pure. Archs were not always in our mind. They would only communicate this way when there was a physical distance between them and their guardian, or when privacy was needed and there were others around.

"Thank you, but no. I have watched her since the beginning and I wouldn't miss the opportunity to redeem myself and keep her safe," I answered back in my mind.

A nod of his head in my direction indicated our conversation had come to an end.

"I see the signature brought all of the archs here. Raguel and Michael, I am glad to see you came," Gabriel said as he extended his hand out to both archs.

"Uriel felt the transcendence of Necroseek within our realm. He acted immediately," Raguel said.

"Members of the Barkayals believe he had assistance," Michael stated.

"We are of the same mind," Gabriel said.

"We shall all be on guard with the Songards. Jordan is aware and is in agreement with the lockdown of the Origin. Until we can ensure the allegiance of all who have been chosen to come along on our quest, it appears twenty cycles will be the minimum time we are to spend training all," Uriel said.

"Then learn they shall," Gabriel said ushering all six archs to the front of the room.

"Nemelites, please, sit."

I walked over to Jacey and placed my hand over hers. The instant I did the connection we had was amplified. I slowly moved my hand but not before I saw the flash of red re-ignite her cheeks and in the same instant the look of uncertainty in her eyes. I tried not to react because I didn't want to draw attention to us. All I had really wanted to do was to direct her to her seat.

"We should sit," I said, moving more cautiously this time as to not come into contact with her.

"With the information we have just shared, you now know to which of the five houses of Nephilim five of the Archangels belong. Michael and Raguel are the eldest of our kind and take on the role of moderator and overseers to all of us. Each of the five archs belonging to a specific house will be in charge of the training you will receive over the next while. We must train and become aware of dangers we are all about to face." Gabriel paused for a second. "It has come to our attention a being within the Origin is not who they are portraying themselves to be. We know Necroseek could not have done what he did without the aid from a Nemelite within these walls." Without moving my head, I snuck a look over at Jacey.

She didn't budge. She didn't flinch. Her hands rested in her lap and her eyes were pointed straight ahead. I wasn't sure if she was listening to Gabriel or if she was lost in her own thoughts. Through her short life she had suffered so much already, I found all I wanted to do was protect her. Stop anyone else from hurting her.

"The Origin shall be locked down. The beings who are here at this moment throughout the structure shall stay, but no others will enter, none within will leave," Uriel said as he came to stand beside Gabriel.

"Through the Visionaries we learned the information Necroseek had been garnering was transferred through what most here believed was an obsolete mode of communication—sirroms. There were an intricate set of communication devices between the Nations prior to the Visionaries being gifted to us. They functioned similarly to what we have now, except they were unmonitored and utilized within both private and public areas," Raphael said.

"Until we can find the one or ones responsible for the breaches, all will be monitored. We will not intrude upon private areas such as your sleeping quarters, but take notice, from today on, all other areas will be monitored," Uriel stated.

"It is time to return to your dormitories until we contact you again. Jacey, Jen, Hudson and Heathe you will stay behind," Gabriel said.

Everyone else in the room got up and left. I stayed beside Jacey, not moving until she decided to.

Hudson and Jen came over to us, prompting Jacey to stand.

"I won't be letting you out of my sight," Hudson said to her.

"I figured as much," she replied, smiling, but the smile never reached her eyes.

I stood and made my way over to the group of archs in the center of the room.

"I believe we should take her to Earth. Take her to the cities we have been concealing ourselves in since the end of Acadia," Raphael said.

"That would be a mistake. Necroseek realizes most of us stayed on Earth as it is a center point to the other remaining nineteen Nations. He would

231

know to look for her there. We cannot operate openly there. Here we can take complete control," Uriel answered.

"I agree and disagree with the both of you," Gabriel said. "To hide her in plain sight would be ideal on Earth. However, her powers have been re-ignited by her return to our world and her signature would be a beacon to not only Necroseek but each and every one of his followers. I am of the mind, keeping her here with the protection of us seven—being able to openly use our talents, is a much wiser decision," Gabriel finished.

"I agree," I said, coming forth from the rear of the group.

"Heathe, you are too close to this situation to make an unemotional decision," Raguel said as he placed his hand upon my shoulder.

I noticed Gabriel looked at me and nodded slightly, as though telling me to stand up for myself, something I had no issue doing before I had reunited with Jacey. I took his motion as a show of support.

"I'm the best choice of guards to ensure she stays safe… here. I don't believe she should return to Earth. It's too much of a risk. Here, we are now aware of the transference of information and the mode used. We have stopped it. Here, I can watch from my essence and not have to cover my signature, and here is where I will ensure she trains and learns in our ways. On Earth we could not do so," I offered.

"You have been with us since the beginning, Heathe, and I for one trust in your insight. As the previous protector of Necroseek, I see you as our most significant pawn in destroying him," Uriel said.

"I also support my friend," Gabriel said.

"Are all in agreement?" Michael asked.

"Do I get a say?" Jacey asked as she came up to us. I watched as the six archs who had not had the pleasure of meeting her like Gabriel did, looked at her in surprise. For a being to approach and have an opinion in matters which were believed to be an Arch issue had never been before. She had bowled over the archs with her candor.

"Of course," Gabriel said, opening his arms and allowing Jacey to become part of the Archs' circle of conversation.

"I'm more comfortable here. I realized through Gabriel's eyes, that I may be more unpredictable than I even knew. I don't want to put the people I love in any more danger and I think returning to Earth would do exactly that. Hudson and Jen wouldn't stay back, and neither would Heathe. I would worry more for their safety than my own, and I want to train and learn. I want to train where my parents did and where I can still communicate with them." She finished and took a deep breath. Her hands had never left her midsection, where she had been rubbing them together in continuous circular motions.

"If it is where you believe you should be, then it is decided," Raphael stated, moving forward and placing his hands over hers. Instantly she relaxed and smiled up at him.

A twinge of jealously hit me. It was something I'd never experienced before. It was almost unnerving. I knew Raphael had a mate and was devoted to her. However, the mere thought of someone other than myself being able to comfort Jacey was bothersome.

Gabriel's thoughts intruded in my mind. "You will risk losing her with those thoughts. She is not ready for you or for anyone else. She is not yours. Check yourself, Heathe."

I nodded to him and crossed my hands in front of me. I would be here for her in whatever form, friendship or otherwise, that she would have me.

There was no other conversation between the archs. It had been settled, Jacey would stay here under the protection of the seven and myself.

As we were all leaving, she came up to me and placed her hand on my forearm.

"Can I talk to you for a minute?"

"You can talk to me at anytime," I answered.

"In private," she said.

"There is no more 'private' here within the Origin," I said.

"Yes, there is. Can you meet me in my room later? I have a whole bunch of questions only you can answer for me," she asked, looking up into my eyes with a need so great I knew there was no way I would be able to deny her.

"Yes. I'll come by later," I said, watching as Hudson and Jen closed in on us.

"You ready to go?" Jen asked.

"Yep," Jacey replied, looking up at me one more time and making sure I would hold to my promise of coming and seeing her later. I smiled—one which reached my eyes and she visibly relaxed.

Gabriel and the others had already left the room and headed off to where they would be staying within the Origin. Hudson and I walked slowly behind Jacey and Jen.

"You know she has no idea you're interested... right?" Hudson said.

"What?" I responded.

"She is so lost right now, between you and Vincent trying to get her attention, I'm afraid you're going to lose sight on what's really at stake here. Not to mention, she's my sister, and if you hurt her in any way..."

"Whoa...I only have your sister's best interests at heart. She's more special than anyone here realizes. I would never put her in danger and I would never hurt her," I answered.

"Now you sound like him."

"Who?"

"Vincent. He pretty much said the same thing when I confronted him. I get that you guys are both interested in my sister. But she isn't ready for either one of you."

"Pardon? I'm only interested in her because I promised Vincent I'd keep her safe. If you're reading something else into it, then that's all on you," I answered, hoping he'd believe my lies.

"I know you and Vincent are best friends, but I can also tell when someone's interested in my sister. I have no idea why you're trying to deny it. It's written all over your face every time you look at her. I'm not the only one who has noticed, either.

235

Remember Verbeyna, your ex? When she sees you and Jacey together, it's like she wants to rip Jacey's head off... and trust me, man, that will never happen—because I'll be making sure it doesn't," Hudson finished.

I looked at him and knew I'd now be holding him in a higher regard. He was an entry level Nemelite who had no qualms about telling off and putting on notice a Songuard—one who, by the way, had been around since the beginning of time and who was known for not having the nicest of temperaments.

"Hudson, I only have her best interests at heart. I won't hurt her. I won't confuse her. I only want to protect her," I said with as much heartfelt truth in my words as possible.

"I'll hold you to it," was all he said as we continued on in silence to Jacey and Jen's dormitory.

We'll be around in shifts watching," I said.

"I'll be back after I grab something to eat. Mom and Dad probably want to catch up with us, too. How about we get some rest and when it's my turn to come back, we go talk with them at the Infinite Waters?" Hudson asked.

"I'd like that. How about Aunt Grace? Do we even know where she is?" Jacey asked.

"I think she's been with Eve and the other Elders. I know she's been keeping in contact with Gabriel to ensure you were okay," I said. "Hudson, if you want to get going, I can take the first shift. I'll send for you when it's time to change up."

He looked at me through slanted eyes. I knew he still wasn't comfortable with me watching Jacey, but I thought he had finally realized all I wanted to do was keep her safe.

"I'll come back as soon as you need me," Hudson said, holding his hand out to me.

I took it and we parted in the traditional Nemelite way, "Until we meet again may the five elements keep you eternal." I envisioned Jacey being safe the entire time I had Hudson's hand in mine. He visibly relaxed the second our hands came into contact.

"See you soon," Hudson said, hugging Jacey.

"Not going anywhere without you," she answered. He turned to Jen and took her into an embrace which made it obvious to anyone watching that this man was completely taken with this woman.

"Keep her safe. See you soon," Hudson whispered into Jen's ear and kissed her lips as he left in his pure form.

"Still trying to get used to that," Jacey said, holding her hand up to the dormitory entrance door.

"I'll follow in essence. I don't want everyone here to know you're being guarded. Plus having a male in the dorms sometimes makes others uncomfortable," I said. As I turned from her to change into my essence, she grabbed onto my arm.

"Remember."

"Yes." I flashed into my essence but not before I saw the rush of color in her cheeks.

I was comfortable in this form. I knew no others could see me unless I wanted them to. But I also knew Jacey had the ability see me whether I wanted her to or not. She'd proven that to me in our second encounter as she made her way to St. Nemele two days ago. It seemed like a lifetime ago with everything that had gone on since.

I had been so taken back by the fact she could see me I'd reacted before thinking that day. No one had ever been able to see me... really see me as she had, unless I wanted them to.

I flowed above her and Jen as they entered the main area of the dorms. A cursory search of the area showed all of the Visionaries had been sealed. I watched as being after being stared at her as she walked by them. She was oblivious to the effect she had on those around her. For someone who wanted to go unnoticed through life, she was going to have to learn here she would not be able to. She may have been able to do it on Earth under the guise of 'human,' however here she was known as the anomaly.

From the history of the remaining nineteen planets, I was hoping we as a society had evolved into beings who would be more understanding of those who were not the 'norm.' We should learn from our mistakes and our successes in life. What I feared, what I knew to be true, was there were beings who were deeply rooted in the 'norm.' Their ignorance would cause others to fear Jacey and her history. That would breed fear in the hearts and minds of those who were easily swayed by others. I feared Jacey finally realizing who she truly was; it put her in more danger, not only from Necroseek but from others here as well.

I watched as they spoke in hushed tones to one another as they made their way to their room. A Songard's hearing was acute. I could listen in on pretty much anything or anyone I focused on. I wanted Jacey to have some semblance of privacy so I chose to only watch and not listen in.

As they entered, she turned and looked directly at me. She lifted her hand slightly in a small waving motion, then entered her room. I stayed outside for some time, going over the events of today and the promise I made to come and see her in her private room. I knew the questions she would have. I saw them in her eyes when she and Gabriel returned to us after Necroseek's attempt.

I knew she deserved answers and I wanted to give them to her, but was I prepared to open my soul to her? The events over my lifetime were ones I held close. There had been no other I felt the need to share with, until now.

CHAPTER EIGHTEEN

Promises made
Promises kept
The truth
Whose version do you reveal?

I went into her room expecting her to be waiting for me. I was surprised and somewhat relieved when I saw Jacey asleep on her bed. For the first time in a long time, she looked at peace. She was wrapped up in a blanket on top of her bed. It was obvious she had been waiting for me to come and see her. She was still dressed in her clothing from earlier. As she laid on her side, her long brown hair had fallen over her face. I reached down and swept her hair behind her ear. She moaned and moved onto her back, shifting to her other side.

I decided to sit and watch as she slept. I sat back in the chair in the corner of her room and waited. I knew she'd be awake in a while and I didn't want to lose the opportunity to share everything with her. Not to mention if I left, I really didn't know if I was going to be able to come back with the conviction I had now—to tell her everything. She was the only being in this entire universe I'd ever felt this pull to. Strange, considering all Songards are supposed to only have Wirposhes from their own kind.

When she shifted to her side, the amulet Verbeyna had given her revealed itself. I wanted to reach out and grab it off her neck. I knew Verbeyna had been summoned by Herecerti to 'help' with Jacey's control over her powers. However, I also knew Herecerti had no idea how truly powerful Verbeyna was.

I sat thinking of all the time I had spent with her, not knowing from the beginning who she really was. It wasn't until I had decided to break things off with her that she finally came clean and told me. She was a direct descendant of the Archs. She was Gabriel's daughter. It made it more difficult to break up with her, but with some convincing from Gabriel, Verbeyna finally saw we were not meant to be together.

Her mother was a Mornal from Aphaea. She had not lived through Verbeyna's birth. Gabriel was the only parent she had from the beginning. However, her mother's sister Rose raised Verbeyna as though she were her own. Rose was a very powerful Hinderer and with Verbeyna's gifts of half Arch, half Mornal, Rose worked with her to make her a powerful Hinderer... if not *the* most powerful. Not many knew she was the daughter of Gabriel.

Throughout history, the Archs were known for finding Mornal wives throughout the cosmos. Most of them didn't survive childbirth, however it didn't stop the Archs from falling in love with them. I could not recall one single Mornal to date who had lived to parent their offspring with an arch.

Verbeyna was the closest to a mate I had ever come. Don't get me wrong, I had a number of beings within my lifetime who I shared time with, however none had gotten as close as she had.

I chose to break things off when she tried to use me as one of her potions. She and I had researched all there was about Ryu and the Songards. I knew enough about my history, but Verbeyna was entranced anytime she discussed it. She believed all Songards were gifted with the ability to bring life into the world, not through the carnal way—through our blood.

I never discussed it with Gabriel, but I started to believe Verbeyna had begun to dabble in the Yietimpi side of potions and magic. That, ultimately, was what had caused me to break things off with her. Initially she was very hard to leave. She refused to leave me alone. She believed all I needed to see was how 'good' we were together.

It took me leaving Nemele for nearly a century for her to finally come to terms with me not wanting to be with her. Upon my return, I'd been assigned to Jacey and her family. Verbeyna tried to re-connect, but I was steadfast in my decision.

She knew I would put all my time and effort into my assignment—Jacey. Even then, when Jacey was a child, Verbeyna would show up unannounced and show a side of herself I had never seen in the past. She was jealous of Jacey. Anytime she could, she would try and steal my attention away from my guard.

I hate to admit it, but there were a few times even I couldn't resist her. She was not merely beautiful, she was someone I had entrusted my thoughts, dreams, and beliefs to. I thought she was a friend. I found out quickly I had misjudged her.

The night Faith had been taken from Nemele, I believe Verbeyna had helped Christina in summoning Necroseek. To this day I can't prove it. It was a gut feeling, but nonetheless, I believe she had a hand in it. I knew she hated Jacey. At first I thought it was because I was spending so much time protecting the family. However, in time I came to realize she was jealous of Jacey herself. Unfounded as it was, she had come to believe Jacey and I had a bond that she knew she and I would never share.

Funny, as I think of it now, she was right. Even though I had never bonded with Jacey as a child, I had always felt a pull to her. It wasn't until we had finally greeted traditionally, did I even know that she was my Wirposh. Someone I thought I would never meet.

A light from Jacey's amulet caught my attention and drew me out of my thoughts. Instantly I was swirling around Jacey and her room.

"You need to come to me."

I relaxed a bit. It was Verbeyna.

"What do you want?" I asked.

"What I have always wanted… you really need to ask?" she replied with a hint of amusement.

Since Verbeyna had helped Jacey, and in turn helped me keep her here, I felt the need to repay her. Chanary had been right to be upset with me. She knew I would do anything to keep Jacey safe and if that meant keeping Verbeyna 'happy' on the side, I would do it.

"I'll be there soon. How did you know I was here?"

"The amulet, of course. I knew you wouldn't be able to control yourself around *her.* I can sense any others around her. Especially you. Finish what you need to there. I need you," Verbeyna replied.

"I'll be there once I'm relieved by Hudson," I replied, leaving no room for her to demand my attention again.

The amulet dulled until it finally had no light left within it.

"Damn it," I seethed between my teeth.

Jacey stirred and awoke. "Heathe? Are you here?" she asked in a sleepy voice.

I turned into my corporeal self and sat on the edge of her bed. I reached over and placed her wayward hair behind her ear again.

"I'm right here," I answered.

"I know what you did for me. I know it's been you since the beginning," she said, waking fully and coming to a seated position directly in front of me.

We were so close I could feel her warm breath against my cheek.

"In a way, yes. But I have missed a lot," I said, breathing in deeply.

Our eyes met and all I wanted to do was grab onto her and hold her. I wanted to feel her body against mine and her breath against my skin. I wanted to take her scent in and relish in the upsurge of emotion it brought to my entire self, heart and soul. I could see the confusion in her eyes.

"I know you want answers, Jacey. I'm here to give them to you," I said, reaching out to take her hand in mine.

She pulled her hands in to her stomach and slid back on the bed until her back hit the wall. I had felt the same pull she had when our eyes met. I was weak, she was strong. I was willing to dive head first into whatever she was willing to give me. Yet, she was mindful enough to put space between us. That in itself made me want her more.

"I know you were there. I know you were there when Faith was taken. That's *all* Gabriel showed me. But I need to know, have you always been there? Did I... confuse you and Vincent?" she asked.

I wanted to lie. It was a feeling I wasn't used to having. My honesty and forthrightness was something I had always held onto as my anchor. My moral center.

"No, you didn't confuse me with Vincent. Initially, I was your guardian. I was the one there with you in the beginning. But when your parents left Nemele, none of us could find you. They were very good at hiding you in plain sight." I paused for a second, took a deep breath to steady myself, and brushed both of my hands through my hair. I stood up and made my way over to the chair I had been sitting in earlier. Space seemed to help clear my thoughts.

"When Hudson came into his Kawanening, he came to Nemele looking for answers. It wasn't until then that I was able to re-connect with you. I was surprised to see Vincent had found you. He was the one who tried coaching you through your dreams. I watched in the background. I didn't want to confuse you. I knew time would give me a chance to explain everything to you," I said, letting out a deep breath I hadn't realized I was holding until I let it go.

"So, you were there. You were there for all of the moments I had with Vincent?" she asked.

"I was," I admitted.

"Did Vincent know you were there?"

"He had no idea I was there and I have never told him about our history, Jacey. I never told him."

"Why?"

"I never told him because it was obvious he was enamored with you. It was clear there was a connection between the two of you. I didn't want to interfere," I confessed.

She sat back looking at her hands, they were twining together over and over as though she were outside in a snowstorm and was trying to warm them. It took everything in me to not get up and hold her hands close to me for warmth. I knew she was nervous. I knew it was a lot to take in.

"I care for Vincent as though he were my brother. I would never want to hurt him," I added.

She looked up at me then. I could see the uncertainty in her eyes. I knew she felt torn inside. With everything going on in her life right now, this was something she didn't need.

"I don't know what this is," she said in a small voice. "I don't know how I'm supposed to be feeling." A single tear escaped her eye and streaked her cheek.

I wanted so bad to reach over and wipe it away while I held her and told her it was all right. I wanted to tell her she wasn't the first Nemelite to have found two Wirposhes. I wanted to tell her I would be here for her no matter how or who she chose. I wanted to be her happy.

"Jacey, I only—" Before I could finish, her amulet began to shine again. I knew it wasn't anyone but Verbeyna summoning me. It was the same light she had used to speak to me earlier. Jacey looked down at it, confused by its sudden burst of light.

"What's going on?" she asked, jumping up onto her knees, grabbing the amulet in her hands.

I wanted to tell her all about Verbeyna, but I knew now wasn't the time. I also didn't want to cause her any more concern than she was already dealing with.

"I'm not sure, but I know it's nothing to worry about. I'll go to Verbeyna and find out what it means," I said, turning to leave her room.

A hand on my arm stopped me instantly. The warmth and electric feel my stomach and heart rate felt was exhilarating. I chose not to stop… not to wait. I was so in the moment I didn't want her to think or believe I was confused by our connection… I knew what I wanted.

I turned and pulled her in to me. Our eyes met and I threw caution to the wind. I was tired of waiting for everyone else to be okay with what we had.

"I have never felt this way about anyone… ever… I am so… so tuned into you that I can't control myself. I want you, Jacey. Like nothing I have ever wanted before. I don't know what the right answers are. I only know what I feel." I leaned in and kissed her.

I pressed my lips to hers and felt the connection instantly. It was like I had come home. She tasted like raspberries and vanilla. She responded to me. She grabbed onto me and pulled me in to her. I felt her body against mine and lost any kind of control I thought I had over my own body.

I leaned in to her and we fell onto the bed. I pressed my body against hers and instantly I was on fire. I had never wanted anything so bad before in my entire life.

"Heathe… Heathe… Heathe, I can't…" intruded my thoughts.

"Why?" I responded as I kissed her neck, making my way to her breasts.

"I—I can't. I need to make sure he's okay. I can't forget him. He left everything for me."

I stopped as I approached her collar bone. I breathed in her scent and laid my head down on her shoulder.

"Jacey, I would never want you to do what you aren't ready for." I took a deep breath in, hoping I could control myself. Her scent, her being made me crazy. I wanted her more than I wanted air, more than I wanted to be alive.

I rolled onto my back and took in two deep cleansing breaths. My heart and soul would be hers… forever. Whether she knew it or not.

"I'm confused. I have feelings for Vincent. But when I'm with you, it's like I've never felt this way about anyone. I get lost in you," she said, curling against my side.

"Jacey, I've... I've never felt like this for anyone. You have got me..." As I was trying to find the words, her amulet began to shine.

I knew Verbeyna was summoning me. I resented her for it.

"Is it safe for you to go to her?" Jacey asked.

"Of course," I said, rolling onto my side and watching her as she grabbed onto her amulet and rolled it between her fingers.

"You know," she said, turning onto her side and facing me. "I'm feeling so split in two. In my life I've never been interested in anyone—ever. Now, I find out who I am and where I'm supposed to be and bang—there are two totally amazing guys I'm so completely into, but confused by also," she said, looking down to my chest as she laid her hand against my heart—as it beat in unison with hers.

"Jacey, I promise you," I took her chin in my hand and lifted her head so she was looking me directly in the eye. "I promise you, I will never make you choose. I only want you to be happy, complete. If it is with me, then I am blessed. If it is with Vincent, then I will accept it." I looked into her eyes and saw me—saw who I am—saw the man I had always known had been there—the man who loved without condition, without compromise. The man who would be hers—forever.

I leaned in and kissed her gently on the lips, expecting nothing in return. She latched onto me and pulled me in tight.

"Heathe, I'm so confused..." she said between kisses.

I positioned myself above her and stopped kissing her.

"No pressure, no expectations," I said, leaning in to her and taking in her kiss one last time. I nuzzled her neck and slowly moved my lips up her neck to her lips. I paused right before I came into contact with them.

"I never want to be the reason you are hurt. I never want to be the reason you feel lost. But more than anything, I never want to be the reason you want to run away from everything. I won't make you choose. I only want to make sure you know I'm an option," I said, breathing heavily down upon her. I wanted to consume every inch of her. I wanted her to consume me. I leaned in to her and pressed my lips against her forehead.

Instantly, she relaxed. She let out a deep breath she'd been holding and nuzzled into my neck. I rolled off of her and laid beside her. She cuddled into my side with one arm over my stomach.

"Thank you," she whispered in my ear.

I hugged her and breathed in the scent of her once again.

"It's close to Hudson's time to come and sit with you. I'll find out what's up with your amulet," I said, trying to sit up.

She held me down. "Can you stay until I fall asleep?"

"Of course I can," I said, lying back down and holding her in my arms.

Staring up at the visionary on the ceiling, I let my mind wander. How was I going to keep Jacey safe? How was I going to make sure she wasn't torn between Vincent and I? How was I going to tell Vincent? Could I finally be happy? Could I find it with Jacey even though she wasn't a Songard?

I was going against everything I'd been taught from the beginning. Songards were allowed to venture out and dabble in relationships with other nationalities, but I'd always believed a Wirposh would be another Songard—as I'd been taught. How was this possible? Could I go to Gabriel and ask him?

As I laid back lost in my thoughts, the most unbelievable thing happened. I fell asleep. I knew I had when my dream color, crimson red, flashed before my eyes. Within my dream I sat up and found myself in a very familiar place—Verbeyna's cottage outside the Origin. I was in the living room—alone. I walked through to the kitchen and then into the backyard.

Verbeyna was sitting on one of the wooden chairs outside. It was dusk. Her back was turned to me.

"If I couldn't get you to come here of your own free will, I figured meeting you here would remind you of our arrangement." She stood up and turned to face me.

Looking at her now, I was reminded of the times we had spent together as a couple. She was breathtaking. Her long blonde hair was loose around her shoulders and hung just below her breasts. She was wearing a peacock blue camisole which left little to the imagination. As she moved around the chair, the wrap around white sheer skirt she was wearing opened to her mid-thigh and stayed that way as she approached me .

She stopped directly in front of me and took her left hand and caressed my right cheek. She then pointed her finger and trailed it along my jaw line, neck, and then to my chest, where she stopped.

Our eyes met. "Verbeyna, what is it you want?" I asked, stepping back and putting space between us.

Without warning, she was on me. Swirling around me. "You, of course…" she whispered in my ear. As she did, she grabbed onto me and we were transported to a stone walled room. Two of the four walls were lined with bottles and plants of all sorts. She let go of me and stepped back.

"I've tried to be *nice,* I've tried to be *patient,"* she said between her teeth as she walked towards a large wood burning fireplace on the far wall.

"All right, Verbeyna. Enough!" I roared. My patience was waning and I wanted to return to bed, to Jacey.

"Never… Never has it been enough. *You* of all beings should know that!" She chanted a few words and walked over to a cot that was pushed up against the only wall which didn't have any potions or herbs on it.

As she chanted, she raised her hands above her head and a light began to appear. The color was the same one which she had used to summon me through Jacey's amulet. I took a step over to her and she turned and looked at me.

Her eyes were a dark violet and her face was a mix of fury and sadness.

"Stay," she said, holding one of her hands out to me, stopping me instantly.

"What is this, Verbeyna? Come on." A feeling of dread as well as some bile had risen to my throat.

"She will not be what you think. She isn't going to come between us."

As she said it, an apparition of Jacey appeared. She was floating over the cot, encompassed in the same light Verbeyna had summoned me through. I tried to move to her, I tried to call out, but my throat was dry and my voice was lost. My limbs felt like cement and I couldn't move. This dream had suddenly turned into a nightmare.

"I will squish her soul if you continue to play your games. No more, Heathe. She will be lost to you and everyone else if you don't follow through with our deal. I made her safe from everyone—as you asked. Safe from everyone but me."

Jacey appeared to be unconscious. She floated there, oblivious to the danger she was truly in. We may be in a 'dream,' but within our world anything that occurred here could have the same affect or worse in our conscious state. From Jacey's appearance, it was obvious her 'body' wasn't here, it was her essence.

"J-just," my voice was back, "just leave her out of this. I already told you I would stay with you. She has nothing to do with you and I," I said, moving slowly towards her.

"She has everything to do with you and I! She is the reason we aren't together anymore! She is the reason you don't want to be with me, with who you truly belong." She ended her tirade in a whisper.

"I'm coming to you now. You have to let her essence go back to her. I promise you, Verbeyna," I said, reaching out to touch her face. "I promise myself to you. My blood, my life." I held her face now in both my hands, looking her directly in the eyes. Her eyes turned back to her true coloring and as they did, Jacey's essence dissipated until there was nothing left of her.

I took Verbeyna in my arms and hugged her. Now, not only did I have to worry about Necroseek, and trust me he was someone to be reckoned with—but I also had to deal with Verbeyna and her jealousy, something which may prove as dangerous if not more than Necroseek.

I woke with a jolt and Jacey stirred in my arms but didn't wake up. I looked down into her face and my heart skipped a beat. I knew I would do everything and anything I could to keep her safe. I wouldn't let anyone, including myself, put her in danger.

I decided then and there she would never know about Verbeyna and the additional spells she had put on the amulet. The talisman, which was supposed to keep others from putting her in danger, was in fact the one thing which had put her in more danger than anyone would ever know.

I knew there would be an enchantment on it so it couldn't be removed. I needed to out-think her. If I was right, she had been watching everything Jacey had been doing. The amulet was like a open visionary. Verbeyna would be and had been watching… everything.

CHAPTER NINETEEN

Decisions made
Putting your own needs second
Feeling as though your heart will never be the
same
Hurting the ones you love
Because you love them

I shifted to get off the bed and Jacey woke.

"Is everything okay?" she asked, looking up into my eyes.

"Yeah. Hudson should be here soon and you still need to get some sleep. I don't think it's a smart idea for him to find me in here. The last time he and I had a 'talk' about you he was pretty straight forward about what he thought," I said, pulling my arm out from behind her and sitting on the edge of the bed.

"He's all bark and no bite, you know. He's worried I'll get hurt..." she said, cocking her head to the side and looking at me through inquisitive eyes.

256

"I won't hurt you, Jacey." I began to reach out to her and the amulet glowed the summoning color Verbeyna had used earlier. I stopped dead in my tracks and pulled my hand back onto my lap.

"So, did you find out what that is?" she asked, grabbing onto the amulet and pulling it out from her chest so she could see it. The color faded the second she grabbed onto it.

"I didn't leave when you fell asleep." I smiled at her. The look on her face was one of mixed emotion. She blushed and smiled a little at the same time.

"I fell asleep with you, but now I should go. I'll let you know what I find out once I talk to Verbeyna," I said, standing up and backing towards the door.

"Are you sure everything's okay? I mean, before we fell asleep, you seemed, well, you seemed more—" Before she could finish, I cut her off.

"Everything's fine, Jacey." I felt the lie cut deep into my soul. It was nearly as bad as the look on her face. She knew I wasn't being truthful with her, but I knew I couldn't tell her anything. I couldn't tell her about Verbeyna, I couldn't tell her the true way I felt, I couldn't be the reason she was put in danger. I wanted to make sure I was going to be by her side when we ventured to Kradsens to rescue everyone.

"We need to concentrate on your training. It's going to be intense and I don't want anything to add any pressure on you. I want to train you and train with you." I hoped she read into my ramblings that we needed to cool down. I hoped it was enough of an excuse so she wouldn't question me. I really wasn't sure if I could keep up the lie.

With the hurt and anger which had taken over the look in her eyes, I had to physically restrain myself from holding her in my arms.

"Yeah, you're right. Training *is* my priority." She rolled over onto her side away from me. I watched as her shoulders raised and fell in rapid movements. I couldn't tell if she was crying or breathing heavy to avoid jumping up off the bed and smacking me.

"I'll see you at training in the morning," I said as I turned into my pure essence and left her room.

Hudson was waiting for me outside the dorm room.

"Where were you?" he asked.

"I was doing a circuit around the dorm to make sure no unwanted visitors were hanging around," I said, looking down at my feet.

"Sure," he said, staring at me.

"I'll be back in a while to check in on you. If you need me, call," I said, disappearing before he could ask me anything else.

I flashed through the Origin and went into my dorm. I went into my room and flopped down on my bed. The range of emotions I was feeling today were all over the map. I was exhausted, considering I was so used to hiding them. As I laid back with my arm over my head, my visionary over my bed came to life. Chanary's face filled it.

"Hey. I think we need to talk," she said.

"Seriously, Chanary, now is not a good time.

"Seriously, Heathe. Now *is* the *only* time. If you won't come here, then I'll see you in your dorm." She didn't leave any room for me to argue with her.

"Wait. I'll meet you out in the West field. You know you can't come here," I said, getting up off the bed and waving my hand in front of the visionary to shut it off.

Great! Now I had to deal with an overprotective sister on top of everything else. She wouldn't be as easy to lie to as Jacey was. I knew I'd have to tell her what went on. At least she'd be able to help me think this mess out. She was the one who helped last time with Verbeyna.

I got up and flashed into my essence. I left my room and headed to the West field. On my way there, I passed the Infinite Waters. Grace and Herecerti were standing there with Ria and Hearte floating above the waters. I slowed and listened in on their conversation.

"Ria, she's fine now. We've done everything here to ensure he won't get another chance at her," Grace said.

"That's not good enough! How on Nemele did he know when and where to even get a first chance?" Ria yelled.

"We're looking into it," Herecerti calmly replied.

"Looking into it. It's obvious, isn't it?" Hearte asked.

"What's obvious?" Grace asked.

"There's someone here working for him, just like last time. What are you going to do about it, Herecerti? What are the Elders doing?" Hearte asked.

Like last time… what was he talking about? This was something I wasn't aware of .

"The Archs have come back to us. The Songards have to. We're training the most elite within these walls to venture with her to Kradsens in approximately twenty cycles," Herecerti answered.

"The Archs *and* the Songards, that's almost unbelievable. But what will they have that he doesn't to keep her safe? Who decided she was going to venture off to Kradsens?" Grace asked.

"Do you really think she'd stay here, Gracie?" Ria said.

"No, but I don't think it's a wise decision for her to travel there. Why am I only hearing of this now?" Grace asked, looking quite disturbed.

"You've been with Eve since she learned of Vincent. No one wanted to interrupt the time you were spending with her. Jacey is a strong-minded young Genapiene. There was no way you or anyone else would or will be able to talk her out of going to get Vincent," Herecerti stated, moving over to place his hand on Grace's shoulder. "She will endure the training of the five houses of the Archs like everyone else. However, what she has that no other does is Heathe. He'll be by her side through it all. He won't let anything happen to her," he said gently, squeezing her shoulder for an extra added bit of reassurance.

"With him by her side, I can say I'm more at ease. He is a Songard of his word. He's the best choice, considering he used to serve as Necroseek's guard," Hearte said.

"I'm still bothered with the idea of her not being near. Should I go on the mission with them?" Grace offered.

"At this point in time, I do believe all assistance would be appreciated. Training starts in a quad," Herecerti said.

"Since Jacey's had the amulet on from the Hinderer, I haven't been able to talk with her. I realize she has a number of things going on, but I want to speak with her before she begins training. Can you arrange that, Gracie?" Ria asked.

"Of course I can. I'm heading back to our dorm now. When she wakes, I'll have her and Hudson come here," Grace said.

"Until then. May the Elements keep you eternal," Herecerti said as he turned to leave.

"And you," Ria, Hearte and Grace replied.

Everyone left the area and headed in opposite directions. Ria and Hearte...well, they disappeared, and Grace headed towards her dorm. I watched from a distance until she was completely gone. I moved through the chamber and came essence to face with Herecerti.

"Why didn't you join in on the conversation?" he asked me.

I formed in front of him. "I didn't want to intrude. When I heard Jacey's name, I knew I had to listen in."

"The next time, if there is one, I will not allow the others to believe they're alone in conversation. If you have a question or concern, you must show yourself, not lurk in the background." Herecerti turned and floated away.

Great, now I had the headmaster irritated with me. I made a mental note to never eavesdrop on him ever again. It was obvious he could see my essence even when I tried to cover it. Herecerti was powerful, more powerful than I even knew.

I hustled my way to the West field where Chanary was waiting for me. I didn't take any other detours.

"Where were you?" she asked.

"I had to take care of a few things. I'm here now," I answered, more snarly than I meant to.

"Hey, relax. I'm not the enemy, remember?" she said, raising her hands up in front of her in a gesture of surrender.

"I'm sorry, Chanary. It's been one hell of a night," I responded, running my hands through my hair.

"I know. We need to talk about Verbeyna and what you *paid* her for her to be *soooo* helpful with Jacey. I remember how much she hated her when she was a child. So, having Jacey being all grown up and the center of your attention… I can't see Verbeyna taking that very well."

"She didn't. I need to find out how Herecerti came across her as the best solution for Jacey. I think she's put some kind of reverse summoning potion in the amulet," I said.

"Reverse summoning? What do you mean?"

"I think she's made the amulet around Jacey's neck a kind of visionary. When I was with her tonight—" Chanary cut me off.

"With who?"

"With Jacey. When I was with her tonight, the amulet started to glow and I heard Verbeyna tell me to come to her."

"So, two questions. One, where were you and Jacey when this happened? And two, what did Verbeyna want?"

"We were in Jacey's dorm," I wasn't going to get into it with my sister about being in Jacey's room, "and Verbeyna wanted more," I answered.

"You know you can't give her more. You know if she thinks the two of you are a couple again you're never ever going to get rid of her again. The last time it took both Gabriel and I to convince her she needed to move one. Now I can see that she never really did." Chanary paced back and forth in front of me.

"Did she ask for more blood?" Chanary asked, coming to stop in front of me.

"Not this time," I answered, looking away from her for a second. "This time she dream walked and brought both Jacey and I to a place I've never seen before. This time she brought Jacey's essence into this room and threatened to crush her soul." I looked back up into Chanary's eyes to gauge her reaction.

"How did Jacey react to all of this?"

"She didn't, she doesn't have a clue what happened. She was unconscious throughout it. I didn't tell her and I don't want anyone else to, either. You're the only one I've told. I don't know if I'll include Gabriel in this, either," I said, running my hands through my hair again.

"Why not tell her? She needs to know that 'psycho' is watching everything she does."

"She's already got so much to deal with, Chanary. I want to think this through before I come up with a plan to get the amulet off of her. I'm pretty sure Verbeyna put an enchantment on it making it impossible for anyone other than her to remove it," I said, walking over to a makeshift bench on the edge of the field which was created by an enormous fallen down tree.

Chanary followed and sat down beside me.

"You are my main priority in life… you know that, right?" she asked as she sat.

"Of course I know that. We're all we have left," I answered.

"I want you to be safe. As for Jacey, I get all the hype about her, I really do," she said, holding her hand to the middle of her chest over her hearts.

"Don't think I missed the point where you said Verbeyna dream walked while you were in her room. I don't know what game she's playing with you—" I cut her off before she could go on.

"She isn't playing anything with me. She was upset. I sat down in the room with her and we both fell asleep. That's it… that's all. Vincent is my best friend and I promised him I would keep her safe. I don't plan on going back on that promise," I said with a little more force than necessary.

"O-okay. All I'm saying is if Verbeyna can see everything Jacey is doing… you on that list would push her over the edge." She reached over, putting her arm around my waist. "I love you, Heathe. I would do anything for you," she said, looking me directly in the eye.

"I know that, Chanary. I just need a little time to figure out what I need to do and who I need to bring in on everything," I replied.

"When's the last time you flew?" she asked.

"Seriously, I don't remember," I answered.

"How about now?" she asked.

I thought for a minute before I answered. I always loved being in my natural form. I loved the feel of wind all over my body. I loved the warmth of my fire within my chest. It would be the perfect opportunity to go over things before I needed to go see Verbeyna.

"Let's go," I said, standing up.

As I did, Chanary grabbed onto my arm and turned me towards her.

"Heathe, you know you can't give her any more... right?" she asked.

"I need to do what I have to, to keep everyone safe." I answered.

"Heathe, with our blood she could become invincible. She could bring back beings we haven't had to deal with in eons. With our blood, she could kill Jacey," Chanary said.

"Tell me something I haven't already thought of," I said as I ran out into the middle of the field and willed my transformation into my natural form.

As I ran I felt my legs transform first, then my body, then my head. As my wings formed, I galloped and then, I was free... I was airborne.

I soared higher and higher, losing myself in the rhythm of the air swirling around my massive frame. As I made my way towards the moons of this world, a flash of red made me slow. Chanary had changed along with me and she was flying figure eights around me. She came to steady rhythm beside me and we flew off towards the Krocy mountain range, which was the back drop of the Origin.

"You know, I've always loved the way we looked like this," she said through our connected telepathy.

"I know. You look, you look regal, Chan. I hope you know how much we need you," I said, willing her to understand how very rare she was to our species.

"Yeah, yeah, I know. Hard for us females to ignore the fact that we're almost extinct," she replied as her wings grazed my side in a gesture akin to a finger prod as she took off in front of me.

"Catch me if you can!" she called back.

"You're on," I replied, taking the challenge and losing myself in this almost perfect moment— Verbeyna wouldn't let up and I needed to figure all of this out. Me, Jacey—Jacey, Vincent, Verbeyna and Necroseek. For a quarter of a quad, I would allow myself to forget and revel in my true nature— flight and fire.

CHAPTER TWENTY

Reality…
Bites.

I couldn't believe I had allowed myself to open up to Heathe. What a jerk. I knew I was going to have to train with him over the next twenty cycles, which in my time is like four hundred days. I just didn't know how I was going to deal with him. Maybe if I went to Verbeyna and asked for a—I stopped myself mid thought—*come on, Jacey, you should know better. Follow your gut. That girl was nothing but trouble,* my inner me was yelling.

Yeah, I know she's trouble, but the hole in my stomach and the yuckiness I was feeling since Heathe gave me the cold shoulder earlier was yelling a little louder at this point. I rolled over onto my back and thought of ways I could summon her and ways I could work this out on my own. There was a sharp pain in my gut which I'd never felt before.

I closed my eyes and visualized Verbeyna. As I was about to call out her name, there was a knock on my door. It totally interrupted my attempt at summoning her. I pounded both hands down by my sides and got up off my bed. I answered the door—Jen was standing there in her pajamas.

"Hey, I couldn't sleep. Major nightmares. Mind if I join you in here?" she asked.

"I couldn't sleep either, come on in," I said, moving to the side so she could enter.

We both flopped down onto my bed.

"What was going on in your dream?" I asked.

"I can't even totally explain them." She blew out the remaining air in her lungs and crossed her arms over her head.

"Have you ever had one like it before?" I asked, rolling onto my side and looking at her.

"No, I haven't. That's what's bugging me so much."

"Well, why not try telling me the parts you do remember? Maybe that'll help," I offered.

"I guess I could try." She didn't move from the position she was in. She started to recount what she could remember.

"It started off with you and me at the maze in Nemele. We were all alone. Then it flashed to the center of the maze. Everything was hazy. The symbols seemed to be in slow motion and when you were talking to me, I couldn't hear you. That wasn't the part that freaked me out. The part that made me wake up sweating was Kawanening opened when you were standing on it but all of its colors were black. It swirled up and around you. Not down so you could step into it. I tried to grab you but it was like sticking my hand in the middle of a tornado," Jen stopped and rolled over onto her side to look at me.

"There was screaming coming from inside the tornado. It sounded like a thousand beings being burned to death, yelling for their lives. I could even smell the fire from within the tunnel. I turned into my pure essence and burst through the wall. That's when everything went black." She stopped to take a deep breath. "When I came to, there were swirling bursts of purple and blue above me. I was lying on my back looking up at you floating over a cot in a stone house. You were wearing a long white gown and Heathe was there. He was angry and yelling... but it wasn't at you. From the way you looked, it was obvious you had no idea where you were. Then everything turned red, you disappeared, Heathe took off, and I heard you screaming... it wasn't a yell like you were in danger. It was more like, more like you were hurt. I woke up and came here." She rolled onto her back, placing her arms over her head.

From what Jen said, I could relate to the screaming/Heathe thing. But I didn't have a clue about everything else.

"Jen, I'm fine." I stopped for a second, wondering if I should tell her about tonight... nope. I wasn't going to. "I haven't got a clue why you had the dream you did, but I'm glad you're here."

"We only have a few more hours before we have to start training and I could really use some sleep. How about you?" I asked, hoping she would stay. I seriously felt like someone had punched me in the gut and I didn't want to be alone tonight.

"Still freakin' a little over the dream. I haven't told Hudson about it... yet. But I agree, we need to get some rest. It's going to be pretty intense at training. You okay if I stay here?" she asked, as if I was going to say no.

"Sure. Like I said, I could use the company." I rolled over and turned off the bedside lamp.

I was glad Jen had come. I was worried she'd felt what I was feeling right now. My emotions felt like they were in a huge black hole—I knew I had very strong feelings for Vincent. I knew he felt the same for me. I knew I needed to get to him and the others to make everything all right in my world again. What I wasn't sure of... how I was going to react to Heathe at training. I was torn. He hurt me. At the same time I wanted to walk up to him and slap him in the face. I found I also wanted to go up to him and lose myself in his embrace. How screwed up is that?

The last thing I remembered before my dream colors came was Jen saying we had been in a stone walled cabin.

A buzzing overhead woke me with a start. Damn, another dreamless sleep. I so wanted to see Vincent, I knew it would only be in my dreams. Damn this flippin' amulet, I thought as I grabbed it, wanting to pull it off my neck.

"I wouldn't do that if I were you," Jen said in a sleepy voice. "Herecerti had it made to keep you safe and if you take it off... he'll probably be pretty pi—" before she could finish, Ms. Hullen's voice filled my room.

"Girls, it's time to get ready—Gabriel won't wait for us to begin."

I rolled out of bed and headed to my closet. "Do we wear our uniforms?" I asked Jen.

"Yep," she replied as she rolled off the bed on the other side. "I better get to my room and get ready, too. I'll see you in the main area." She left my room and I began to get ready.

After showering and getting dressed, I sat in the living room waiting for Jen. Aunt Grace came out of her room and seemed surprised to see me.

"Jacey."

"Hi, Aunt Grace. How are Eve and Bronson?" I asked, getting up to give her a hug.

"They're doing as expected. They're anxious for everyone's training to begin so they can leave and find Vincent," she replied, hugging me back.

My belly jumped at the mention of Vincent's name. "I miss him, too. We'll find him and bring him back," I paused for a second then added, "along with Faith and Uncle Gideon."

Aunt Grace became a little stiff and patted me on the back. "I know, Jacey, I know you'll try and find all of them," she said, walking over to the kitchen and making herself a coffee.

"I spoke with your parents last night. I didn't know you had planned on going with the team venturing to Kradsens," she said as her coffee poured out of the machine on the counter.

"How are they? I haven't been able to get to the Infinite Waters to see them."

"They are concerned, as I am. Why do you feel the need to go along with everyone else? Why not stay here, where it's safe?" she asked, grabbing her coffee cup and heading over the kitchen island to take a seat next to me.

"As if I was going to stay here. There's no way I'd let everyone else go and find Vincent and the others without me," I said.

"It's just, it's just so—" I cut her off before she could finish.

"I know, dangerous. I am so sick of everyone saying that! How many beings had to lose their lives for me the last time Necroseek was here?" I asked, but didn't wait for an answer. "I know how many, Gabriel showed me. I'm not going to sit here and wait for everyone else to do what I need to do—find Vincent and get rid of Necroseek."

"Gabriel showed you? How?" Aunt Grace asked.

"I don't know how he did it, I just know he did."

"Getting rid of Necroseek isn't as easy as you make it sound," she said, going back into the kitchen to pour the remainder of her coffee down the sink.

"I know. But, with the Archs and the Songards back with the Guild, I know we have a fighting chance," I answered.

"Fighting, something I was hoping we—" before she could finish, Jen came out of her room and interrupted us.

"You ready—oh, hi, Grace," she said, coming into the kitchen and grabbing some juice from the fridge. "You ready, Jacey?"

"Hi, Jen," Aunt Grace replied.

"Yeah, I'm ready," I replied, getting up from the kitchen island.

"Where are you two off to?" Aunt Grace asked.

"We're heading to the first day of the next twenty cycles—training," Jen replied.

"Be safe. I may see the two of you there later," Aunt Grace said as she left the kitchen and headed back to her room.

"Hmmm, she's obviously got a lot on her mind," I said to Jen as we left the dorm.

"What makes you think that?" Jen asked.

"I don't know. She just seems… distant," I said.

Hudson appeared before us as we exited the female dorm.

"Hey," he said as he approached Jen and took her into a tight embrace. Before the two of them kissed, they both looked at me—like I was going to deny them the happiness they obviously had when they were together.

"Go ahead," I said, walking out in front of the two of them so I didn't see the kiss I knew they were going to share. Not because it would gross me out. Of course it was going to do that—but because there was a knot in my stomach the size of a bowling ball. I knew Heathe was around and even though he was a total ass last night, I still wanted to see him—kind of.

The second I thought it, he appeared beside me.

"How was the rest of your night?" he asked, falling into step beside me.

"Seriously?" I answered, leaving no room for him to talk to me again. I tried to quicken my step so he was a little behind me and I didn't have to walk beside him.

He grabbed my elbow and made me slow to walk beside him. I pulled my arm away.

"Don't—touch me again," I said through my teeth.

"We need to work together, Jacey. I'm not going anywhere. Giving me the cold shoulder is fine here, but when we start to train, you can't," he said, not making eye contact with me whatsoever. He walked on, making sure I was by his side the entire time.

As Jen, Hudson, Heathe, and I made our way to the room which had been allocated for the academic portion of our training, I noticed a number of essence signatures along the way, more than normal.

"Why are there so many Sentry here?" I asked Heathe.

"Since we believe the information Necroseek is getting is coming from someone here within the Origin, we felt the need to ensure you are safe wherever you travel within its walls. How many do you see?" Heathe asked.

"They're a lot of them. Some look blended," I answered, looking at him.

He looked tired, something I had never seen in him before. He actually had black circles under his eyes.

"Did you get any rest last night?" I asked.

"A little."

"Did you go see Verbeyna?" I asked, feeling a twinge of jealousy in my gut.

"I did."

"A-n-n-n-d…" I said, waiting for his reply.

"And nothing."

"Seriously, you think I'm going to be okay with that as an answer?"

"You're going to have to take that as an ans—"

"But—" I cut him off. Before I could get my question out, he pointed in front of us.

"For now. You're going to have to take it as an answer for now. We're here," he said, raising his hand to a doorway with a symbol which resembled a key engraved on it. The second he did, the door dissolved and we entered what I assumed was the room we would be training in.

I stumbled for a brief second as we entered. There were at least double the amount of beings here compared to the last couple of training sessions, one which caught my eye, Chanary. She made her way up to Heathe and I and stopped right in front of us.

I expected the same snarky attitude I'd been accustomed to from her, but I didn't get any attitude at all. She completely over looked me and went straight to Heathe.

"You look tired. You okay?" she said, placing a hand on his lower arm.

"I'm fine," he replied, pulling his arm away and putting it behind me to urge me forward. I jumped a little before his hand was able to come into contact with my back. I knew no one else noticed, but Heathe did.

"I've got some seats in the back," Chanary said, leading Jen, Hudson, Heathe and I to the back of the room.

As we made our way there, I took in my surroundings. This was no ordinary room—not that anything here was 'ordinary,' but this room was huge. It was the size of like eight football fields put together and along each of the walls were a number of doorways. Each one had a different symbol engraved into it.

There was only one visionary and it was at the front of the room. To date, it was the largest one I'd seen—taking up the entire front of the room from floor to ce… I looked up and realized there was no ceiling in the room. Above were blue/purple skies and swirls of clouds.

"Wow," I muttered under my breath.

"This room is usually saved for first ranked elemental training. Only those who have been here for years usually get to train in here," Heathe said, taking a seat to my right. I sat and so did everyone else who had come along with us.

I tried to keep my eyes straight ahead and not pay attention to the unseen heat accumulating between both mine and Heathe's seat. If he thought for one minute I was going to let what happened last night between the two of us cause me to lose perspective, he was totally wrong. My brother may be the king of one liners, but I was going to become the queen of denial. I wouldn't have an issue acting like nothing happened. If he thought so little of our connection, then so would I.

From his obvious lack of interest once he had time to think about things, I would need to apologize to Vincent. This Wirposh thing was way overrated… Heathe proved to me last night that I needed more training and education than I initially thought. I knew the connection between Vincent and I was pure... right. Yet I felt a heat, a want when I was with Heathe that I couldn't stop myself from trying... last night. But never again. He proved I should have stuck with my initial gut feeling about him—dangerous—stay away.

An elbow to my left rib caught my attention.

"What are you thinking about?" Jen whispered.

"No one, I mean nothing... important, anyway," I said loud enough for her and Heathe to hear.

"You could have fooled me. You okay?" Jen asked.

"Yeah. I will be," I answered, again loud enough for Heathe to hear.

I could tell he was getting uncomfortable. He shifted in his seat. I felt like a total fool for letting my guard down last night. I promised myself the tears I cried when he left would be the only ones I ever shed because of him. I needed a change of topic. I could feel a well of tears fighting to break loose in my throat.

"What area are we training in first?" I asked, coughing as I tried to hide the higher octave my voice took on the last word.

"I'm not sure, Heathe, do you know?" Jen asked, still looking between the two us with more than a little curiosity.

Heathe turned to look at the two of us and we both sat a little straighter. The hurt and anger in his face was so evident it took our reactions to his look for him to shake it off.

Good, I thought to myself, now he knows how I felt… reality—right now it bites.

CHAPTER TWENTY-ONE

Lessons

Amazarak
The key to knowledge is education

Armers
Protection for all... overseeing ourselves

Barkayal's
The cosmos will be our salvation... our future

Asaradels
To balance the elements is to balance the universe

Ariel
Markings will guide the way to absolution or ...

GABRIEL

Before he could answer, Gabriel appeared at the front of the room.

"May the elements be present with you always," he greeted everyone.

The intensity of his aura was minimal compared to the first time we had met.

"Today we start our training within my own house—The Amazaraks. How many of you have been to the Archives and attempted to research the original five house of the Archs?"

No one replied.

"I thought so. As a society, we have ventured so far from our roots, I sometimes worry, thinking, how are we to progress? Without knowing where we originated or what our elemental gifts were meant for, how are we to guarantee our existence?"

No one replied. His aura dimmed to almost invisible and I could swear I saw a fog lift from everyone in the room.

"I'll ask it again in different terms this time. Who here believes we need to understand where we came from so we can better know where we are going?" Gabriel asked.

"I do. My parents were Makara and Siren. A mixture I am sure most have not seen. However, I have been gifted with both elements through them, Ria and Tower. I have not gone to the archives to see the history of both elements but, I am curious to know why I have been gifted with both and how my parents found one another," Bella said in her sing song voice.

There were a few curious looks from others in the room. One which caught my attention was Yellesh. She wasn't looking at Bella in a curious way. She was looking at her as though she were a freak.

"There are those who believe because I am not pure, I shouldn't be gifted with anything," Bella continued on.

"Sorry, what does that mean? Pure?" I asked, interrupting her.

"Because my parents were of different houses, of different ethnicities, most frowned upon them when they announced their Wirposh for one another. My mother use to tell me stories of beings who would go out of their way to make her and my father uncomfortable," Bella said.

"Here, now, those attitudes are no longer acceptable. Yes, there are still fundamental communities who believe in the purity of the society by bonding with those of direct descent. However, I can tell you the thought of the past is not the belief in the future. All are accepted. I am here to teach you of our beliefs from the beginning and how they have evolved. How all of us have evolved. Knowledge is key—The house of Amazarak holds all of the information for each of the gifts and all of the nineteen Nations within our societies. Here and now is where we are all going to learn of our differences and our likeness," Gabriel said, drawing everyone's attention back to the front of the room.

"All of the five Archs will be coming to this room to conduct training, except the Armers. We will need to enter the doorway with the crossed swords to train within that house." Gabriel pointed to a doorway off to the far right.

"So, let us begin... In the beginning there were..."

I sat and listened as Gabriel went over the five houses:

1) Amazarak—the educator
2) Armers—the guards of Nemelite, Yietimpi and Archs
3) Barkayal—creators of the cosmic structures and pathways
4) Asaradels—the chosen who bequeath each with one of the five elements and oversee the sixth,
5) Akibeel—creators of markings, deciphers of code—guardians of purgatory.

We learned which Arch belonged to which house and that some belonged to more than one. We learned over the next twenty cycles we would immerse ourselves in the history of Nemele and the prophecies during our time with Gabriel.

"Let us begin at the beginning...

The Amazaraks were the Keepers when Acadia was the only planet within Nemele. They were gifted with each of the five elements—Ria, Tawer, Nidw, Rife, and Hearte. The Amazaraks could create and control each within Acadia. They learned how all were fundamental for a planet to exist.

In the beginning there was only the Nemelite portion of the Archs. All was good. There were no wars, no death, no strife between them. Through evolution, they realized there were so many more aspects of their universe. From prophecies, written and uttered, it was apparent there would be more houses formed to support the information and education throughout the generations of Archs to come.

The Armers came second. They were the guards and overseers of the Amazaraks. There had been conversations between the Original and their offspring about which was stronger and who should be the leader. With the Armers ever present, the balance of principal power was even among all five elements, all Original Archs. They also started to allow beings to be blessed with more than one elemental gift. This led to the creation of the Asaradels.

The Asaradels were the first fundamentalists within Nemele. They believed allowing the mixture of gifts would skew the balance of power and in effect cause one nation within Acadia to become more powerful than the Archs as a whole. They oversaw each nation as it was born and attempted to ensure all were blessed equally with fundamental and combined elemental gifts.

As time progressed, Acadia became populated with more beings than Archs. As this occurred, strife reared its ugly head. This lead to the creation of the Barkayal. They were the scientists of the times. They looked to the cosmos and believed they could go out into them and create new 'Acadia's' throughout.

With the evolution of travel, the Akibeel were created as the architects of symbology to keep track of where we were headed and where we had been.

With the evolution of Nations within Acadia, the first of the Yietimpi had also been created. He sat in wait, watching as all of creation came together. He thrived off of creating chaos between Archs and beings alike. Not one of the Original Archs had seen it coming until it was almost too late. He was the first of the Original Archs to suggest the creation of the Songards. He was the first to create Ryu. He believed he would be able to take complete control over all of the Nations with the aid of the Songards. What he didn't foresee was within each society there is righteousness. The Songards were born to be moral and just. He over estimated his influence upon them. He would not possess them or rule them. The would be the defenders of Acadia and each was assigned to protect an Arch. He had convinced all that Acadia had been too small to encompass its progress. They had achieved so much as a society, they needed to spread it throughout space. In combination with all five Archs, they began to explore the cosmos and create world after world within it. The Songards were assigned to each of the Original Archs and they were kept as a fundamentally pure society. Their bloodlines were kept within their world and only the Archs were allowed to visit or speak with them.

They were the guards of the Archs. They were regal and loyal to a fault.

It wasn't until the one who sat in waiting for eons came forth in a coup to overturn all of the others to take on the main leadership within the societies that anyone ever questioned ... Necroseek.

As you are now all aware, it was the internal discord of the Archs which led to Necroseek being essential in the obliteration of Acadia and Ryu." Gabriel took in a deep breath and turned his aura up a little.

"The next training will be with Uriel. This session is at a close, however, be prepared, my friends. We have much to learn over the next twenty cycles. It will be intense and it will be educational." He turned and looked directly at Heathe and I. "The mistakes of the past should not constitute the path of the future. Remember, sometimes all is not as it seems. Until we meet again, may the elements keep you eternal."

In a flash of light, Gabriel was gone. I sat still for a few minutes, taking in the massive amount of information he had just shared with everyone.

"If that's day one of info, I'm pretty sure we're going to need more than twenty cycles to get everything we're going to need to travel to Kradsens," A male fairy said to another as they passed me, leaving the room.

I was starting to feel a little overwhelmed when Aunt Grace's voice broke into my thoughts. "Jacey, how was your first session?"

I turned and she was standing with Jen, Hudson, and Heathe. Everyone else in the room had exited. I had been oblivious to them.

"It was..." I stood and went to stand beside Jen. "It was really intense."

"Just wait. That was only the introduction. When Gabriel decides, he'll go through each of the evolutions of the nineteen remaining Nations. It's that information which will be imperative during the travels to Kradsens," Heathe said.

Aunt Grace came over and put her arm around me, pulling me into a semi-hug.

"Well, I've made a decision." She stopped for a brief second, ensuring she had all of our attentions. "I'm coming with you."

From the look on Hudson's face, he wasn't expecting her to say what she had. The looks on Jen and Heathe's face mirrored Hudson's.

"Are the Elders in support of that?" Heathe asked, taking a step towards me.

"Of course they are. I approached them this morning and proposed I travel with you. They thought it was a fantastic idea," she said.

"Me too," I replied, hugging her back.

"It's time to go to the Great Hall and get some lunch. We have a full day ahead of us," Heathe said.

"I'd love to join you all but I have to go see Eve. She and I have been working at getting some healing charms perfected. Nemele knows, on the trip we're all about to face, I'm going to need as many chants as I can summon," Aunt Grace said, leaning in and kissing the top of my head. She turned to leave and semi-hugged Hudson on the way out.

"Is it just me or are you guys not too happy about Aunt Grace joining us?" I asked as soon as she had left the room.

"Jacey, you weren't conscious when Heathe brought you to the infirmary. I love our aunt, but I'm not too sure she has our backs," Hudson said.

"Seriously, Hudson. She's been there for every good, great, and horrible moment in our lives. I think she has the right to come with us. Remember, it's her family as well as our own we're going to try and return," I said with a little more attitude than I meant to.

"One will be virtuous while the other shall—bear a resemblance in attempt to deceive but with sureness ought to befall the core of depravity— Don't think we have forgotten, Jacey. We love you. We won't let Grace or anyone else, for that matter, get in the way of your safety. I'm not trying to say Grace doesn't have your best interests at heart, but you seriously have to think about the fact she now has a line on how to get her daughter and her husband back. Would she choose you over the two of them... I really don't know. Maybe this is a conversation Ria and Hearte would be better to give advice on," Jen said. She put her arm around Hudson's waist and hugged him to her.

"I haven't forgotten, but she's still family, and until she does something that puts her loyalties into question, I don't think any of us should be questioning her," I said, not leaving any room for anyone else to question me or her.

I turned to leave the room when Heathe caught my arm. The heat of his touch went right to my gut. I stopped and turned to him.

"What?"

287

"I second Jen and Hudson. I won't let anything or *anyone*—" he emphasized anyone—"hurt you or try to take you away from…" He trailed off, his face was void of emotion but his eyes couldn't lie. Heathe had a huge secret he was keeping from me. He could try and hide it in his actions, he could try and hide it in his words, but I could tell by his touch, his eyes, his soul—he was only holding on by a very thin string. He wanted me like he had last night.

"What's going on in there? " I asked, pointing to his heart." You're confusing the crap out of me." I almost let my guard down.

The instant I looked away and back up at him, the shield he'd placed over his emotions was back up.

"I made Vincent a promise and I plan on keeping it, Jacey." He prodded me forward towards the exit.

"We need to get some food. I think it's training with Uriel next," Heathe said as we all exited the room and headed to the Great Hall.

I didn't know what to think or say. There was definitely something up with Heathe. He was being so guarded. I wanted to talk with Jen and see if she would be able to help me come up with a reason why he was acting the way he was.

I tried to slow up and let Jen and Hudson catch up to us but Heathe continued on with me in tow. We didn't speak at all until we entered the Great Hall.

"I need to use the washroom. Jen?" I asked, waiting for her to catch on.

"Ummm, yeah. Me too," she said, wrapping her arm through mine and pulling me in the opposite direction of Hudson and Heathe.

"Can you grab us some food, please?" Jen called back as we made our way to the restroom.

We went into the bathroom. Jen checked every square inch of the place before she spoke.

"Spill. What's going on?" she asked.

"I think I may have two Wirposhes."

"What?" Jen asked, leaning back onto the wall.

"You heard me. I think I have two. Vincent and... Heathe. What do I do?"

"Do they know?" Jen asked.

"Vincent doesn't know about Heathe. Heathe and I, we just, we just happened. I can't even tell you how confused I am."

"You just happened? As in you bonded? Or you did something else..." Jen asked.

"No, we bonded. When we greeted, I felt a pull to him, but it wasn't until the last training session where Necroseek came at me that I saw who Heathe really was."

"Seriously, now I am confused," Jen said, rubbing her temples.

"When Gabriel brought me back to when Faith was taken, I saw Heathe. He's always been a guard of mine. From the beginning. He's even been in my dreams."

"No way."

"Yes way. But last night, something happened. We talked and he seemed really into me, until we fell asleep. I woke up and he was totally cold to me.

Telling me the both of us needed to concentrate on our training and that's it. Nothing else."

"Jacey, I don't know. I've never heard of it before. Having two. Are you sure?"

"Yes and no. I don't know. Remember," I paused and pointed at myself, "New to all of this stuff."

"I know, I know. I, well, maybe we could," Jen paused. "I don't know what to say. Do you feel the same way about him as you do for Vincent?"

"No. I have completely different feelings for both. Vincent, when I think of him, every inch of my body tingles. Kind of like you get when you're really excited about something and waiting for it to happen. With Heathe, it's more like, in my gut." I wrapped my arms around my stomach. "It's like my gut is all twisted up and then I start to overheat. My cheeks, my hands, everything." Just thinking of him made my palms sweat. I wiped them against my pants.

"How are we going to deal with this?" Jen asked.

"I don't know. I figured last night he had a shot of reality after we talked and he realized I wasn't the one for him. Is it possible that I may feel a certain way about someone but they may not feel the same way about me?" I asked.

"Yeah, it is. Look at Chanary and Vincent."

"Umm, I'd rather not," I replied.

"Sorry. I've just never heard of this before. Are you sure he's a Wirposh?"

"You know what, Jen? I'm not sure of anything anymore—other than I made a mistake with Heathe. Vincent is who I need to put all my energy into. Thanks for listening," I said, giving her a hug.

"I didn't do much," she said, hugging me back. "But if anything like this comes up again, t-a-l-k to me. Don't leave it until you feel like you're losing your mind."

"Okay."

"Promise?" she asked, pulling away from me and looking me directly in the eye.

"Promise," I said, grabbing her hand and giving it a squeeze.

We left the washroom and headed to the Great Hall. When we entered we found Hudson and Heathe bent over the table, almost head to head in a heated conversation.

"Hey, what's going on?" I asked both of them as Jen took a seat beside Hudson and I took a seat beside Heathe, but far away enough to ensure we didn't come into contact with one another.

Hudson looked up at me. " Nothing. Just talking about training strategies."

Heathe didn't stop looking at Hudson. "Yeah, training strategies."

Both Jen and I could feel the tension at the table. Hudson and Heathe were lying through their teeth. Anyone with a brain could have caught onto them.

"We need to eat. Uriel is the next training session and I, for one, am going to need energy for that," Jen said, trying to break up the staring contest Heathe and Hudson were locked in.

It seemed to work. There was food on the table. Porridge, toast, cereal and fresh fruit. Instead of asking anymore questions, I filled my plate with fruit and two pieces of toast and ate in silence. Everyone else did the same.

Once we were done, Chanary came over to the table. "Ready?"

"You have no idea," Heathe said, standing up and turning to leave. He stopped just short of leaving as though there were a tether holding him to the spot. He grunted loud enough for only us at the table to hear him.

"Jacey, we have to go," he said, looking at Hudson the entire time he was talking to me.

"I can meet you there, Heathe." I replied in the most nonchalant voice I could muster.

That seemed to snap him out of testosterone mode. He looked at me and for a brief second he had the look of a man lost. Lost in emotion and thought. He quickly shook it off and made eye contact with me.

"We need to go now. I would app—" he paused as though he was having a hard time saying the next couple of words. "I would *appreciate* it if you'd come with me. I still need to make sure you're safe, whether it's at training or getting there."

A twinge in my gut broke through my own wall of pissed-off-ness. He looked completely sincere even though he'd said everything through clenched teeth.

"Jen, Hudson, are you guys ready to go?" I asked, standing up.

Jen began to stand but Hudson put his hand on her arm.

"Well, meet you there, Jacey," Hudson said.

Jen looked between Hudson and I. She was obviously confused and so was I. At this particular moment in my life, I had a bit too much of my own drama to deal with so I didn't push.

"Okay, we'll see you two there." I walked off with Heathe and Chanary.

"Thank you," Heathe said.

"For what?" I snapped without meaning to.

"For not making a scene. For being who you are and trusting me," he said.

"It wasn't for you, Heathe. It was for me. I need to screw my head on right and pay attention to everything that's going on. I don't want to get involved in anyone else's crap. I need to concentrate so we can go and save Vincent," I replied. When I did, my amulet began to get hot. I pulled it out from under my suit. It was glowing the same color it had last night.

"So, did you figure out what this was yet?" I asked as Chanary came up beside me, staring at it.

"It's a summoning repellant. Verbeyna put it in your amulet to go off in sporadic bursts to ward off anyone attempting to latch onto your signature," he said, not looking at me while he talked.

I knew there was something else going on, but like I said earlier, way too much drama... not interested anymore. I needed to train, learn, and leave—whether it be with or without the group of others who were training with me. The time had come to finally just breath. Eat, sleep, and breath my heritage, my lineage... my true destiny.

***

URIEL

I would train with the best warriors throughout the Nations. I would learn about my body and my mind and how they worked as a unit. Sometimes my body would react without having to think and others my body was like a fine-tuned machine which would only move when I decided or stop when I decided.

These were the words Uriel used to describe how each and every one of us would see ourselves at the end of our twenty cycle training regimen. It took everything I had not to chuckle under my breath. Me a lean mean fighting machine... not. I was in shape. I'd always loved sports, but I seriously couldn't see myself coming anywhere close to where the warriors from folklore, myth, and fairy tale were.

I was happy to see Ms. Hullen had joined us for this training. She stood by Thor and together they were breathtaking. I let my mind wander for a minute, wondering if she and he were Wirposhes. The second it jumped into my mind, I shut it off. There was no way I was going to allow myself to travel down that road—wondering about others—on my own.

"It's time to learn the basics. Partner up," Uriel said as three walls in our room disappeared with a wave of his hand. In their place was huge open field. It was the center court of the Origin.

I walked out with the rest of the class and looked at the turrets of the octagonal walls of the interior of the Origin. The walls which had disappeared had reappeared as stone walls, leaving us no way back in.

Upon the towers along each of the roof tops were lines of sentry guards. They stood stoic, looking down into the yard.

"Why are they all here?" I asked Heathe.

"Because once we start to train, our signatures are going to be able to be traced. With the collective powers of the Sentry Guard, they can control the output." Heathe walked out into the middle of the field. I followed as well as everyone else.

"And we're outside. When we're within the walls of the Origin, we have the added protection of the enchantments which have been present since its beginning. Out here, there's nothing," he added as we came to a stop in the center of the field.

All of the other beings stopped along with us.

"Have we all paired off?" Thor asked.

Crap, I hadn't. I looked around and everyone except for Heathe had a partner. At this point I would have even worked with Yellesh.

"I don't bite, you know. Well, unless—" Heathe whispered in my ear.

"You don't want to finish that comment..." I said, holding an arm around my gut to keep the burning sensation at a minimum.

"Come on," he said, placing his hand behind me and ushering me over to a space no one else had taken.

There was no way of getting out of it. I was going to have to train with him. Note to self: next session tell Jen she was going to be my partner.

"Now that we've all chosen a partner, get comfortable," Thor said, standing in the center of all the beings. Ms. Hullen was standing by his side.

"This will be your partner for the next twenty cycles," Thor announced.

"No, flippin' way," I muttered under my breath.

Heathe chuckled slightly and elbowed me. "Yes, flippin' way."

***

RAPHAEL

I was battered and bruised by the end of the session with Thor, Ms. Hullen, and Uriel. I should've only wanted to crawl into a hot bath and not come out for a few days but… I felt amazing. I was able to move in ways I didn't think I could. I was hit and I hit back.

Heathe and I had been electric together. I thought I was going to be completely uncomfortable with him, but it was the exact opposite. We were actually good together—when we were fighting.

An ear shattering screech had stopped our session. We all looked to the roof of the Origin and floating from its top was the Morrigan who had led me into the Origin on my first day here.

"Zena," Uriel said as he approached her in the center of the field.

"Uriel, may the elements be with you always," she said, holding her hand out to him. He took it and they greeted in the traditional Nemelite way.

"What a sight! I am impressed by the calibre of warriors we have here. I am excited to see their progression over the next twenty cycles," Zena said as she and Uriel separated.

"As am I. The doors have reappeared and it's time to prepare for the next session. Shower up and onto the next session. Raphael will be waiting for you all within the training area," Uriel said as he and all of the instructors left the field.

"How are you?" Heathe asked as we approached Jen and Hudson.

"Good. I'm good," I replied, rubbing my forearms, trying to get my circulation back into them. I was definitely going to be bruised.

"A cooler shower will help to slow the bruising," he said back.

"How was your training?" I asked Jen and Hudson as we caught up to them.

"Aerobic," Jen said, smiling.

"That's a new one," I replied.

We walked over to the doors and entered the Origin.

"How was yours?" Jen asked.

I paused for a minute, thinking of the best way to describe beating the crap out of Heathe... The first word to pop into my head was my answer, "Satisfying."

"See you both outside of the change room by the Great Hall in a couple of minutes. We can grab some water and be back for Raphael's session in time," Hudson said to Jen and I.

"Sounds good," I said.

Heathe was quiet. Chanary had been waiting in the instruction area when we entered.

"I'll walk with you guys to the change room," she said, not waiting to be invited.

We were all in and out of the change rooms within minutes of one another. Heathe was waiting outside the door when I exited.

"You did good today," he said.

"Thanks. So did you."

"Do you want to wait for the others or let them meet us at our next session?" he asked.

"I told Hudson I'd wait. If you want to, go ahead," I started to say but was cut off by Hudson's appearance.

"Yeah, Heathe, I've got it from here," he said.

"I'll wait for everyone else," Heathe replied.

Standing in the hallway waiting for Jen and Chanary was almost excruciating. Neither Hudson or Heathe were talking. It was completely obvious they were peeved at one another.

"So, does anyone want to tell me what's going on?" I asked.

"With what?" Hudson replied.

"With the two of you. You both might think no one can read the two of you, but someone on another planet would be able to see you're both irritated with each other."

"Irritated isn't the—" Before Hudson could finish, Jen and Chanary both came out of the change room.

"Good to go?" Chanary asked as Jen went over to stand beside Hudson.

"Yeah," Heathe said, waiting for me to move along with him.

I looked over at Hudson. Jen had wrapped her arm through his and pulled him off the wall he'd been leaning against. Now wasn't the time to push the conversation about what the heck was going on between Heathe and Hudson, but I wasn't going to let it go. At the end of the day, Hudson and I were going to sit and talk... whether he liked it or not.

"Off to Barkayal then," Heathe said, walking slightly behind and beside me. "I think you're going to find this session pretty amazing," he said while we made our way to the class.

"I'm finding them all amazing so far. I have to say, originally I thought twenty cycles was completely crazy. But only having gone through the first two and seeing what each is made up of, I hope four hundred days is enough," I replied.

"It will be," he replied.

We returned to the group of rooms and engraved in the door was a four pointed star. Hudson raised his hand to it and we entered.

The others had returned and taken their seats. There was a hushed excitement in the room. We all went back to the group of seats we had occupied earlier in the day.

As we did, the rumblings between beings silenced. I turned as I sat and at the front of the room was Raphael. His aura was the same in coloring as Gabriel's except there were streaks of neon blue light flashing through randomly. The aura wasn't at full strength, but needless to say everyone in the room fell silent and Raphael had all of their undivided attention.

"May the elements be present with you always," he said as he raised both of his hands above his head and did a swooping gesture toward all of the walls within the room. As he did, each one turned into a visionary. There were eight in total—seven along the walls and one on the ceiling.

"I want to introduce you all to the Lechann." When he finished waving his hands to all of the Visionaries, they lit up, each a different color from the other.

"The Lechann are sentient beings who discovered us when we began to look outside of Acadia for life. They guided us in the creation of the cosmos and its pathways." Raphael stopped and watched as each of the screens began to fill with beings.

They appeared as clusters of constellations, but all formed within the shape of a Genapiene. Each was made up of every color you could imagine. They sparkled.

"Thank you for inviting us to this momentous occasion," the Lechann directly to my right said.

"No, Andromeda, thank you and your brethren for blessing us with the gifts of travel through the cosmos. Without your guidance, none of us would be where we are today," Raphael replied.

"We are humbled, as always. As one we can travel and explore the universe," Andromeda replied.

"So we shall. Nemelites, I introduce you to your future. Your way of venturing to places you have never been before. Places you have only dreamed of," Raphael said.

For the rest of the session I sat enthralled by the information presented to us. The Archs had been the first of any kind to attempt to venture outside of their homelands. When they did, the Lechann were their guides. They assisted in the development of the Bulwarks and their implementation upon each of the Nations of Nemele.

Neither Raphael or Andromeda told us how long or how old the Lechann had been around, but it was evident they existed before the Archs.

After the session with Raphael, I realized the gift to travel between universes was just that… a privilege, not a right. It was the Lechann who gifted the Archs the Visionaries to oversee and keep watch upon the worlds they created. They were, of course, the first of many gifts to the Archs. Working in conjunction with one another, they realized working together would allow both Nations to explore further into the cosmos.

Each benefited from the other.

"Over the next twenty cycles, we will explore the mapping of the systems from Nation to Nation. We will look at the modes and methods of travel which are to be utilized, and the ones which the Yietimpi have counterfeited. The training will be intense and will include learning how to create a channel or pathway on your own in emergent situations." Raphael turned to the seven Lechann. "Until we meet again, may the five elements keep you eternal, my friends."

"As you," they all replied, and as each one did, their visionary turned black.

"Your next session is here with Zerachiel," Raphael said as he turned and left the room.

"That was pretty intense," Hudson said.

"And that's only day one," Heathe replied.

***

Zerachiel

"Do we have time to get something to drink?" I asked Heathe.

"There are some drinks and snacks in the room over there." He pointed to a doorway behind us.

"Thanks," I said, getting up and going over to the doorway. Jen joined me.

"How are you doing?" she asked.

"I'm good," I said, raising my hand to the doorway. It opened and we entered. There wasn't anyone else in the room.

"Do you know what's going on with Heathe and Hudson?" I asked as I made my way over to a table covered in foods I'd never seen before. It took up the entire back of the room.

"Not yet. But trust me, once we have some alone time, I plan on getting it out of him. Glad to see I wasn't the only one who noticed something going on," she replied.

"Well, when you find out, make sure you let me know. I was going to ask Hudson myself, but he'll probably tell you first," I said as my stomach grumbled loud enough for both of us to hear.

"Let's eat," Jen said, walking over to the table with me.

"I haven't seen more than half of this stuff before. What's safe to eat and drink?" I asked.

"It all is." Jen chuckled as she went over to a mound of yellow flower petal shaped objects. She grabbed a handful and brought one over to me.

"These are my favorite."

"What are they?"

"Trust me, just try one."

I took one from her and nibbled the end of it. Once the flavor hit my taste buds, I was addicted.

"Wow, these are great! They're like a cross between grapes and raspberries."

"I know. Most of the stuff on the table are like fruits from Earth. They're full of protein and will give us a boost of energy. The drinks are the same." Jen pointed to a cooler full of different colored bottles.

"Let's get back. I'm sure Heathe and Hudson are having a great time staring one another down. I'll grab a couple for them," I said, taking three extra drinks out of the room with me.

Heathe and Hudson hadn't moved. They weren't talking to one another but you could almost seriously see the tension between the two.

"Here, guys," I said, handing them both a drink.

"Chanary," I said, handing her the third drink.

"Thank you, Jacey," Heathe and Chanary said.

"May the elements be present with you always," the voice from the front of the room called out.

"Zerachiel," Heathe whispered in my ear.

"I am so pleased to see you all here today. I understand you've had a large amount of information shared with you today. There are, of course, only two houses left to introduce. My own, the Asaradels, and the Akibeels, which will be introduced by Remiel."

"Our instruction today will outline our gifts," Zerachiel said as he raised his hands to the Visionaries on the walls and on the ceiling. Filling each of the Visionaries were the constellations I had been falling asleep to for most of my life.

Along the walls, each visionary held a gift, a talent an element. Ria –Air, Hearte – Earth, Tawer – Water, Rife – Fire and Nidw – wind. The remaining two Visionaries filled with a mix of all five elements. It was like watching an artist paint upon a beautiful tapestry. Each element twisted and combined with the others to make new and stunning combiNations. They appeared as kaleidoscopes of color and symbol.

I watched as they danced within the Visionaries but one was missing.

"Where is Kawanening?" I asked.

The stunned silence which had taken over the room when Zerachiel entered was interrupted for a moment. Some of the other beings turned to look at me like I had said something completely out of line.

"I was, I was just—" I stuttered as Heathe reached over and squeezed my knee.

"It's okay. You asked the right question," he whispered loud enough for only me to hear.

"Jacey, it is a pleasure to finally make your acquaintance. The others were correct in their assessment of you. My aura really has no effect on you?" Zerachiel asked.

"I think it has more effect on others than on me," I answered.

"Diplomatically stated. You are correct, I haven't introduced Kawanening, until now," he said, pointing to the roof visionary.

It was... it was beyond words. Kawaneing took up the entire roof and reached down into each of the seven Visionaries. Its beginning and end were indiscernible. In the center of the visionary, the Kawaneing from the Bulwark I used to enter St. Nemele shone brightly and pulsed out to an unheard tune.

"Kawanening is the central part to all of our gifts. It is through your Awakening you are bound to your talent. Kawanening is Awakening," Zerachiel said, turning his back to the class. He stood with his arms out and his head back. He was chanting something I couldn't quite make out.

As everyone watched, the symbols which represented each of the five elements began to swirl and move within the visionary. A part of each reached out from the Visionaries and flowed over to Zerachiel's finger tips. His aura took on the colors of each one of the elements. He turned and began to speak.

"Each of the elements is alive within us. In the beginning, Acadia was created with each of them. Without all five, our world would not have been. As the house of Asaradel was chosen to bequeath other Archs and beings with one of the gifts, it is our responsibility to ensure no nation was in control of the elements more than another.

"So from the onset of our world, it was always known the elements were essential to our survival. As the Barkayal began to explore, the first Universe created was Ryu—the Songard Nation. With their creation, it was of no issue for Archs to travel to Ryu to gift the Songards with their talent. It was apparent their primary element was fire, however through evolution, a number of them began to have the ability to possess more than one element.

"As their world filled and Acadia flourished under their protection, we began to create new worlds. As each was created and time passed, we came to find beings who were not birthed or brought up on Ryu or Acadia needed a conduit to initiate their talent. Thus Kawanening was introduced to the Nations," Zerachiel informed us.

For the remainder of our time learning about the Asaradels was fascinating. Zerachiel went on to explain over the next twenty cycles we would be learning how Nemele became the Origin when Acadia and Ryu were destroyed. How each of the Nations were gifted talents directly in relation to their survival within their Nation. He made mention about how initially it was outlawed for beings of other species to mix with beings not of their Nation for fear of offspring being born with more than two talents. In the opinion of the Archs, a being having the ability to manipulate more than two elements led to the possibility of a Nation overtaking others who were not as blessed with talents.

He concluded by indicating each of the talents were predetermined for the being it was bequeathed upon. The Asaradels are the Sentry of sorts when it comes to the elements and who is gifted with which one and how many.

"I shall now leave you with one question: do you believe the talents should be evenly distributed throughout the cosmos or," he paused for a brief second and we made eye contact, "do you believe it is possible for any one of us or any other being to be able to garner them all and not be tempted by their power? Until we meet again, may the five elements keep you eternal."

Zerachiel then held his hands up to the Visionaries. Each of the five elements left his body and re-entered the visionary they had come from, rejoining the symbols which represented each. He peered over at me for a brief moment, smiled, and looked up into Kawanening. As he did, Kawanening opened and he entered it in a flash of multi-colored light.

"Now that's a way to make an exit," I said under my breath.

"Wait until you meet Remiel. They saved the best for last," Heathe said with a hint of sarcasm to his voice.

***

Remiel

307

My stomach was in knots. I hadn't been nervous about any of the other Archs. There was something about Remiel I couldn't quit put my finger on— and—I hadn't even met him yet. Jen and Hudson must have been able to tell I was nervous. Both of them reached over to me.

"Jacey, you okay?" Jen asked.

"Yeah, just a little—" Before I could finish, a familiar smell caught my attention. Brimstone. A lump came up into my throat and I started to sweat. It was like the dream I had with Necroseek in it. I looked at all of the Visionaries and then to Heathe.

"Do you smell that?" I asked.

"Smell what?" he asked, concern evident in his eyes.

"Jacey, you look pale. Do you need—" before Hudson could finish, a voice boomed from the front of the room, catching all of our attentions.

"May the elements be present with you always."

I looked at the front of the room and standing there in perfect fitting black jeans and a white v-neck t-shirt was one of the most beautiful men I'd ever seen. I was stunned for a second, jaw open and all.

"I am Zerachiel. Arch of the house of Akibeel."

No one replied, not even me this time.

"I understand I am the last to present today. I know it's been an overload of information so far, however, this is why you were all chosen for this quest. You are the best of the best and we know you can handle what we are entrusting to each of you. I shall be presenting my house." He swept his hands out to his sides towards the Visionaries.

Filling each of the seven along the walls were a number of symbols differing in color and size.

"We are the decipherers of code and symbol. Throughout the Nations, symbols range in significance." Remiel moved from the front of the room and began to walk around to each of the Visionaries.

I had finally snapped my jaw shut and began to take in who I saw before me. All of the Archs were cute, some more than others. They all appeared to be in their late 20's to early 30's. Each of them had an intensity to them which differed slightly from any other being I had met to date. Their auras were unique to them and were used to ensure beings were compliant. Remiel didn't have an aura like the others. He was different.

There was a luster to his being I could barely make out. The others could intensify or wane their auras at will. With Remiel, I strained as I tried to see his. It was there, however it was masked. In an ever so thinly lined silhouette, there it was.

I sat back, somewhat alarmed by what I saw. Remiel's aura wasn't only not like any of the other Archs. His had a trace of grey throughout .

"Has he always been an Arch?" I whispered to Heathe.

"Yeah, why?" he answered.

"Just wondering. He isn't like the others... is he?"

"As always, Jacey, you see what others cannot," Remiel answered instead of Heathe.

I blushed so bright I was pretty sure people in other Nations could see me.

"You are right. I am not like the other Archs. During our time together you will see what I have. You will understand how very close the lines of Nemelite and Yietimpi are. Not everything in life is black and white…" He came over to stand nearest the visionary to my right.

He touched it and we were shown Nations covered in fire, smoke, and haze.

He moved from the visionary and made his way to stand behind me. He bent over my shoulder from behind and whispered in my ear. "You *s-e-e* me. I have been waiting for this. Welcome to our joint dream or nightmare, whichever you prefer." He placed his hand on my shoulder.

Instantly, I felt a heat move from my shoulder throughout my body. It was as though I had been freezing and stepped into a boiling hot shower. Comforting yet painful.

He backed away and returned to the front of the class. Heathe had tried to move when Remiel had touched my shoulder but it seemed he was frozen in his seat. The second Remiel moved, Heathe let out a breath which he'd been holding.

"Are you okay?" he asked in a breathy tone.

"I'm fine," I replied.

No one else in the room seemed to have noticed the exchange between Remiel and I.

Heathe, on the other hand, had moved his chair closer to me and seemed to overshadow me.

"Are you okay?" I asked, trying to move my chair a little away from him, realizing that I couldn't, I decided to sit and go with the flow.

"Yes. We need to talk… later."

For the remainder of our session, Remiel explained how the house of the Akibeel created all of the symbols throughout Nemele. They were also the Archs', who were able to decipher any symbols which were created outside of themselves.

"Over the next twenty cycles, we will explore each of the Nations and the symbols which were bestowed upon them. We will also explore the symbols which they created on their own.

"I have a question for those who have wondered how close are the lines between Yietimpi and Nemelite." He paused for what I think was effect and when no one bit, he continued.

"If there is one within this room who has not felt the pull of jealousy, anger, hatred, or envy, please come forward." His aura intensified with his question. He waited for a prolonged period of time before he spoke again. When no one answered, he did.

"I am placated by the decisions made to include all here. For if one of you had attempted to communicate they had never felt in any of these ways, I would have asked for your discharge. None of us are perfect, none of us are chaste. Those who attempt to masquerade as a being of purity are the ones we all need to be heedful of. To understand the ones we must overcome, we must first rise above ourselves." He raised his hands above his head to the last visionary on the ceiling. Swirling above was a symbol colored in greys and whites. It was shaped like the Barkayal's, however there were two four pointed stars superimposed upon one another.

"Until we meet again, may the elements keep you eternal," Remiel said as he turned into a twisting cone of essence, grey, white, blue, brown and yellow, and entered the symbol overhead.

I sat staring at the symbol as it stopped turning and then disappeared. I was unsure of how much time had passed until Hudson put his hand on my shoulder.

"Are you ready to go?" he asked.

"Yeah, give me a second. I have to ask Heathe something. I'll meet you and Jen by our dorm."

"You sure?" he asked.

"Of course. I'll see you guys there."

At the same time I saw Heathe having a somewhat heated conversation with Chanary. She looked over at me once and then nodded at Heathe. She left with Jen and Hudson.

Heathe came over to me and sat beside me.

"Did you smell it?" I asked.

I expected him to act as if I was crazy or ask me a question in return. Imagine my surprise when he actually answered me.

"Yes."

"Why? Why does he smell like Necroseek?" I asked.

"Remiel is the only Arch which Necroseek allows to enter and exit his worlds without a fight."

"Again, why?"

"Because they're brothers."

I was speechless. I knew Necroseek had been an Arch. I knew he had a history with them. But what I didn't expect was for him to have family. For him to be... tied to anyone else but himself.

312

"It's been a long day, Jacey. Tomorrow and the next 399 days are going to be even more demanding. I'll bring you to your dorm so you can get some rest," Heathe said as he stood and brought me to a standing position with him.

"How can we trust him?" I asked.

"We trust him because he is the gate keeper," Heathe answered.

"The what?"

"The gate keeper."

"So, now I feel a little more lost. The gate keeper of what?" I asked.

"Perdition."

I had to think about it for a minute before the word actually made sense to me.

"You mean, purgatory? Like in Angels and Demons kinda purgatory?" I asked.

"Yeah, he's the only Arch who can travel between the Universes without question or bother. He's the one who's supposed to be the guide for all of us, Yietimpi and Nemelite alike."

"Why does that make me nervous?"

"I'd be worried if you weren't," Heathe said as we left the training area and headed to my dorm.

***

Revelations

My walk back to my dorm was silent. I had a million and one questions running through my mind. I was exhilarated and exhausted all at the same time. Today I'd received a breakdown of each of the five houses of the Archs, something which I found comforting yet terrifying at the same time.

"We're here," Heathe said, bringing me back to the present.

"Oh, thanks," I said, raising my hand to the symbol in front of me.

Heathe reached up and grabbed my hand before the door opened. With his other hand, he grabbed onto my amulet and covered it completely within his grasp.

"I'll be here tonight watching. Call me if you need me." He looked down into my eyes, and for an instant he was the Heathe from last night. The want and care in his eyes was almost overwhelming. The burning in my gut told me I was going to have a much harder time keeping my feelings for him under wraps than I initially thought. I was tired and didn't have the energy to have a heart to heart with him right now.

"When you're ready to talk, I'm here to listen," I said as I pulled my hand from his and opened the door to my dorm area. I turned and left him standing at the entrance.

I didn't look back.

I made my way to my room and entered. It was late into the night. There was no one around outside in the common areas and there was no one in my dorm. Jen and Aunt Grace were either in their rooms or out with friends.

I welcomed the silence. For the first time in a long time I was able to be... alone.

I went to the refrigerator in the kitchen and grabbed a turkey sandwich and a drink and went into my room. I showered and got ready for bed.

I pulled out the pink fluffy monkey covered pj's Aunt Grace had bought me so long ago. With them came the memory of Mom and Dad. I would go to the Infinite Waters tomorrow and talk to the two of them to let them know everything that was going on.

I laid back on my bed and ate a few fruits and took a couple of sips from my bottle of water. I was pooped. I turned out the lights and reached up towards the visionary on my ceiling. Instantly, reflected in it were the symbols which I'd been finding comfort in ever since Mom introduced me to them.

As they flashed across the screen in a multi-colored ballet above me, I fell asleep. For the first time in what seemed like months, my dream colors rushed at me. I was taken aback at first, wondering how they were able to find me. Verbeyna's amulet was powerful and I thought it was able to stop any kind of communication through the dream world, from anyone.

I watched as a grey fog encompassed me. I wasn't fearful. It was as though I were watching from afar. As the fog began to recede, standing in front of me was Faith.

"Long time no see. Where have you been?" she asked.

"Herecerti had a hinderer make me an amulet which repels summons," I replied as I reached up to my amulet and spun it around in my hand.

Faith reached out to the amulet and tried to take it from my hand. The second she came into contact with it, it spun and began to glow in blues, reds, and purples.

"Whoever she is, she's quite strong," Faith said. She raised her hands out to her sides and the rest of the fog dissipated.

We were in the field I had seen her and Vincent in the last time I'd dreamed about the two of them.

"But not as strong as me," Faith said, backing away from me.

Out of the forest surrounding us came Seekers. They floated above the trees and walked out from the shrubbery to encompass the field.

"What are you trying to prove, Faith?" I asked with way more bravado than I felt.

"That *I* should have been the one Heathe saved," she said through gritted teeth.

Appearing in the center of the field, a woman about my mother's age turned and faced me. She was the same one Gabriel had shown me when we returned to the nursery the day Necroseek took Faith.

"Jacey," the woman said as she approached Faith and placed an arm around her shoulder.

"Christina," I replied.

"It's time for fate to come to fruition," she said in a sing song voice.

A loud applause and cheer erupted from the hundreds of Seekers present.

"No longer are we to hide in the bowels of darkness. We *are* the stronger of the species," Christina called out.

I took in a few deep breaths. I knew I was dreaming but I also knew in some dreams the reality of them could have an effect on me in my corporeal body. I had to handle this situation… diplomatically.

As I was trying to come up with a plan, Faith suddenly attacked. She ran at me from Christina's side and hit me on the right side of my face. I was stunned for only a moment.

"What the hell?" I called out as my knees hit the ground.

"I was the stronger one. I was the one who taught you! I was the one who should have been…" Before she could finish, I got up and smacked her right back. Heathe was right. I did have a good right hook.

Faith was only stunned for a second. She looked at me as she wiped the blood from her lips.

"You… have no… idea…" she said before she ran at me.

As she approached, she held her hands out in front of her, palm facing me. Two red/black energy balls the size of baseballs formed in her palms. She chanted something incoherent as she ran at me.

"Teadh, teadh, ahhhhh," the orbs in her hands flew at me.

I jumped to the right and rolled on the ground. They narrowly missed me and struck two trees behind me. The trees burst into flames.

My heart was beating so hard it felt like it was going to burst out of my chest. Before I could get up off the ground, Faith was on me.

"Poor little *Jacey*, we have to protect her," she said through her teeth. She raised her hand to strike me again and I kicked her off me. She rolled over onto her back and sprung back up onto her feet.

I was up and put some distance between the two of us. "What the hell are you doing, Faith?" I yelled at her.

"Because of you, he thinks it's you he's supposed to be with! It's not! You've taken everything from me, but I won't let you take him, too!" she yelled as she ran at me again.

My brain was in overdrive. I wasn't sure how to react. I thought back to what Uriel had said in training today. My body should react without me having to think about it... Yeah, that wasn't happening!

Just as she was about to reach me, a huge fireball landed between the two of us. It had come from above. The impact of it sent me flying backwards. I didn't see where Faith landed.

I ended up on my back with the wind knocked out of me. I saw stars—not the constellation kind, the kind when someone almost knocks you out. I blinked like a hundred times trying to get my vision to focus.

My breathing started to sound a little more normal and after a minute it didn't feel like an elephant was sitting on my chest. There was an eerie silence all around me. The only noise was my labored breathing.

I propped myself up on my elbows and tried to focus again. This time, through squinted eyes, I made out a figure coming towards me through the grey fog which had returned to my dream. It was huge! I knew I should have been frightened, but I wasn't. I watched as the large figure turned into a smaller one as it made its way towards me.

A hand reached out and pulled me up. I stood and was face to face with Heathe.

"Are you okay?"

"Yeah. I'm okay. Where'd you come from?" I asked, wiping my hands over my legs and straightening my hair.

"I've never left, Jacey. I've always been in the background of your dreams," he answered.

"Am I dreaming?"

"You are."

"How? I thought Verbeyna made it so I couldn't."

"I guess she not only underestimated *you* but also the strength of those looking for you," Heathe said, taking hold of the amulet.

There was no reaction from it as he held it in his hand.

"I haven't learned about dream walking yet. Is everything that happened here… true?"

"In a sense it is. There are people looking for you—the ones represented here may not be the ones who attacked you. They may be using the forms of others to hide behind."

"Seriously, I don't get it."

"You're not supposed to yet."

"So when am I, then?"

"In—" Before he could finish, I cut him off.

"Don't you dare say in time."

"In Asaradel's training," he answered, letting go of the amulet. He reached up to my face and brushed a strand of hair off my cheek, tucking it behind my ear. He was looking down at me like he had the night we fell asleep together.

"No time for that, remember?" I said, backing up a bit.

He cocked his head to the right and brought his hand down to his side. He smiled, one which reached his eyes.

"Do you want to stay here, or go somewhere else?" he asked with a mischievous look.

"Are there going to be beings there that want to blow me up?"

"Not while I'm around."

"Let's go."

He looked nervous for a second. "I trust you. Stay here for a second."

The fog returned and Heathe backed into it. I could still make out the outline of his body. He crouched down and then the fog filled with the same huge form I'd seen right before Heathe had appeared.

I stared in awe as the form emerged from the fog. My breath caught and I stumbled backwards. I fell back onto my butt and watched as the most magnificent creature I'd ever seen approached. It was a dragon, slowly and timidly, it moved towards me.

It looked like the ones depicted in the books I'd read growing up, but was way more majestic. It was brown and gold in color and had large horns on either side of its head. It stopped in front of me and bowed its head so it appeared to be laying down at my feet.

I sat transfixed at the enormity of it. I looked into its large brown eyes and saw Heathe. I stood up and tentatively put my hand out in front of me. I touched its face by its nose. It was warm and soft.

"Heathe?" I asked.

The dragon let out a breath it seemed to be holding and I swear… smiled—one which reached his eyes.

"Wow…"

I walked around to his side and took all of him in. He was massive. His wings were folded into his sides and he had lain down at my feet. His body was splayed on the grass.

"I want to show you something," Heathe said in my mind.

"You're beautiful," I replied out loud.

"Not something a guy really wants to hear." He chuckled.

"Sorry, I'm not too sure what to—" Heathe cut me off.

"Climb up on top of my neck."

"How?" I asked as I walked over to his long slender neck.

Before he answered, I saw the texture of his skin allowed for me to grab ahold and scale his neck. I didn't need to be asked again.

I made my way to the top of his neck and sat.

"How do I hold on?"

"It's your dream, Jacey."

Instantly I thought of a seat with a strap around Heathe's neck and it appeared.

"Wow…"

"Hold on," he said while he stood up and stretched. When he did, he let out his wings. They unfolded from his side.

"I've never done this before, I want to share this with you," he said.

With that said, his wings began to flap and we were in the air within seconds. It was amazing. The sky had turned blue/purple and I couldn't make out the ground. The wind rushed through my hair and the suns warmed my skin. I couldn't remember a time I'd felt more at peace.

"Thank you… thank you for trusting me," I said.

I sat back and closed my eyes, allowing the suns, wind, and Heathe to lull me into a sleep within my dream.

I woke in darkness.

"Heathe?" I tentatively called out.

There was no answer.

I didn't dare call out again. I knew he was there. I didn't need him to respond. I stared out into the darkness of my room and went over my dream.

I definitely needed to talk to Verbeyna about this amulet. The 'fight' I had with Faith had left a couple of sore spots on my body. I didn't want to be surprised again by another not so nice appearance of my cousin. Or… was it my cousin? I wasn't sure. I needed to talk to Uriel about dream walking and what and who are represented within them.

I was still exhausted and needed to get more sleep. I also found I'd missed my dreams. So when I fell asleep this time, I envisioned my dream colors calling out to them—with one thought in mind—Vincent.

My dream colors came and I appeared in my room at my Aunt's house. It was designed in the same way it had been when I left it. No cribs, no baby stuff anywhere.

I sat on my bed and looked up at the symbols on the roof. They began to move and mix together.

I reached up and entered them—like in the Bulwark. I was suspended in mid-air and surrounded by all of the elemental symbols as they swirled around me. I looked down at myself and saw I was in a purple silk spaghetti strapped floor length dress. I held my arms out and ran my fingers through each of the symbols as they passed me.

"I'm still here," a very familiar voice whispered.

My belly reacted first and then every inch of my body began to tingle.

"Vincent?" I called out.

"I'm here, I'm waiting for you," he said.

"I miss you. I'm coming," I replied.

I looked around in the area I was floating and a figure was floating above me. It began to make its way down to me.

As I flowed with the symbols, the form stood in front of me, it formed into Vincent. My heart leapt.

I reached out and stopped just before I came into contact with him.

"Is it really you?" I asked.

"Who else could it be?" he responded.

I reached out and touched him…

"There's so much I have to tell you…" I said as he reached towards me to embrace me.

I could smell him... Cinnamon, saffron...

My body ached to be held by him. There was a connection to him I couldn't deny.

A thunderous noise interrupted us before we could come together. We both looked upwards, and circling down were five cylindrical shapes, spinning and flashing in every color you could imagine.

"Not this time!" Gabriel called out as he entered the top of the Bulwark. It had grown in size. The chasm Vincent and I were suspended in looked as though I was looking up to the top of a tornado from inside the bottom of it.

Spinning down upon us were the five Archs. Each were within one of the spheres. At first I thought they were floating down within them, but a closer look revealed they were riding upon dragons within the spheres.

For a second I was stunned, not really comprehending what was going on.

Then it hit me—brimstone.

I looked over at Vincent. He had moved away from me. He was struggling, his feet were kicking back and forth and both of his hands were grasping at his neck. Curled around it was Necroseek's hand.

"Come to me or he dies," Necroseek called out.

"Jacey, run!" Vincent called out.

"I can't! I can't leave... not again!" I called back as I tried to make my way over to him.

My legs felt like bricks and it took every amount of power I could muster to move—but I did. As if in slow motion, I reached over to Vincent—Just before I grabbed him, Necroseek grabbed onto my upper arm—a searing heat burnt my skin.

I yelled out in pain, "Owwwww."

"Like I told you before, you're mine," Necroseek said as he bent down towards me, eyes full of fire. Vincent was still suspended in his grasp. He was trying to fight him off but it like a mosquito trying to fight off a raven.

I looked up behind Necroseek and his wings had been extended to their full span. As he was about to wrap me within them, the five spherical shapes came down, cutting through Necroseek's grip, causing me to fall to my knees. I watched, helpless, as Necroseek enveloped Vincent and the five Archs gave chase.

Then, there was silence. I sat entombed within the silence of the spinning spheres. A light from above cut through and I grabbed for it. I was pulled into consciousness.

I sat upon my bed back in the Origin and noticed I wasn't alone. My room was filled Archs, Heathe, and a couple of other beings I assumed were Songards. Pushing his way through them was Doctor John—the centaur. In his hands were wrappings and a jar filled with a bright purple fluid.

"What's—what's going on?" I asked.

There was an intense pain in my upper right arm.

I looked down and branded there was a five pointed star with a symbol in the center I hadn't seen before. It looked like four number nines. Two upright and back to back connected to the other two, which were reflected below them.

"What is that?"

"Necroseek's calling card," Gabriel said as John came over and treated my burn.

325

John reached over and smeared the purple fluid on my arm. It stung and was cold at the same time. He wrapped my upper arm in the dressing he'd brought.

"This should minimize the scarring," he said as he backed away from my bed.

I reached up and gently squeezed my arm.

"The Archs have chased Necroseek back towards Kradsens. We tried to get Vincent, but were not successful," Gabriel said, looking down at me.

"Why? How? I thought he couldn't get to me with this around my neck," I said, holding up the amulet.

"Our dreams are sometimes used to play games with our heads and our hearts, Jacey. The parties represented within them may not be who they appeared to be. I fear the person who has been giving information to Necroseek's faithful has found a way to now torment you within your dream state. I will contact the Hinderer and we will work together to strengthen your amulet," Zerachiel said.

I looked over at Heathe and for a second, the fury in his face was evident. He was quick to cover it up when he saw me looking at him.

I watched as the Archs spoke to one another in hushed tones. Each of the Songards stood with one of the Archs.

I stood up and made my way over to my door.

"Can we take this out into the living room?" I asked.

I held my hand to the door and we all flowed out of my room. Aunt Grace, Hudson, and Jen were all waiting in the kitchen area.

"Are you okay?" Jen asked.

Before I could answer, she went on, " You were yelling and floating over your bed. You were screaming and then you were burning. I couldn't stop it, Jacey. None of us could."

"What are you talking about?" I asked, pulling Jen over to the couch and making her sit with me.

"Jacey, you were out. You were out for days! None of us could get to you. We've been sitting by your bedside for nearly a full cycle," Hudson said, coming to stand behind me.

"A full cycle… I've been out for like ten days?" I asked.

Aunt Grace came over and kneeled in front of me. "Jacey. The Archs and everyone here have been trying to get you back to us for days. You've been unconscious in your room for all that time." She held onto my hand.

"I believe it's time to lock down the Origin," Herecerti said, coming out from behind Uriel.

"It's something we haven't done since Necroseek's true intentions came to light eons ago. We'll only allow the Elders, the Archs, and the beings chosen to venture with us to rescue our kin within these walls. We'll shut out everything and everyone else until our training is completed. Until Jacey has experienced the five prophesized ascensions. She'll master each house and then and only then will we allow any movement within these walls," Remiel said.

There were no questions from anyone in the room. Not one being disputed Remiel. For the next

380 days, I would be here, I would learn…I would wait.

The Archs, Herecerti, and the Songards left my dorm room. Heathe, Hudson, Jen, and Aunt Grace remained.

"I don't think we have 380 days," I said, while rubbing my upper arm.

"What do you mean?" Hudson asked.

"I don't think anything the Archs, the Songards… frig… any being here can do anything to stop Necroseek. Especially now…" I trailed off.

"Especially now why?" Jen asked.

I looked over at her and she jumped back a bit.

"Jacey, what's with your eyes?" she asked.

"What do you mean?" I replied as I got up and went over to the mirror in the washroom.

"What the he—" I stopped as I stared into my reflection.

Staring back at me were not the brown eyes I'd been looking through for all of my life—staring back at me was one brown eye and one blue. I covered it and then uncovered it with my hand. It was still there—the blue color but my pupil was fire red.

As I looked into the mirror, my arm began to burn again.

"Damn," I said, reaching over and covering the brand Necroseek had burned onto me.

Heathe came over to the washroom and looked inside.

"Can I come in?" he asked.

"What's wrong with me?" I asked.

He came in and stood behind me in the mirror. He reached around from behind me and lifted my chin so I was staring at him from the mirror.

"There's nothing wrong with you. Necroseek attempted to initiate the Nephilim Prophecy within your dream state. He didn't realize that by doing that, you and Faith would end up sharing in each other's physical beings. Remember within the Archives when it said one may overtake the other?"

"Yeah."

"He underestimated you again. He thought you were too weak to fend off Faith. When the two of you fought, you took a little bit of her and she..." I cut him off.

"She took a little bit of me..."

"Yeah, something like that," Heathe said.

"My parents were right." I turned and looked up at him.

"About what?"

"No one here can protect me... I don't even know if I can protect myself," I said, looking down at my feet.

"I believe in you, Jacey. I believe with all my heart, together we will be able to conquer anything and anyone."

"I'm not so sure..."

I left the washroom and Heathe followed. That night we all sat in the living room going over the dreams I'd had over the last ten days. Nothing jumped out and said, 'Hey, this is what we need to do.'

The only things which revealed themselves over the course of the evening—

Necroseek had branded me—No one knew how or what that implied. The Archs, Songards and Elders were on guard—they were confident they were going to be able to stop any further breaches into the Origin, they were confident I could be trained.

There was definitely someone within the Origin feeding the Yietimpi contingent information on me and what was going on here.

I needed to get rid of this amulet, it had to go. I couldn't get it off and no one was willing to help me get it off, including Verbeyna.

And the most shocking revelation—which no one in the room was going to be made aware of... I wasn't going to be able to wait 380 days... Vincent needed me—now.

ACKNOWLEDGEMENTS

There are so many people who have helped me along my writing journey. First, I need to apologize if I miss anyone—I will try not to.

Of course I need to thank my amazing publisher Limitless Publishing for believing in me and my writing. God, my family and friends...each has had a significant impact on my life.

I need to acknowledge all of those who have believed in my writing and encouraged me to be better.

Of course my husband and children are first and foremost.

Thank you to the following people who read "Revelations" in its unedited—Hally-form.... I know at some points it must have been painful.

Andrea Kleinsteuber—You are an amazing woman with an incredible talent! Continue to write and when you're ready, please put yourself out there to be published.

Stacey...Chippewa Secondary...Thank you for taking my debut novel and soaring with it. Friends for 22 plus years..and at least 100 more.

Christy Hemmer, you are inspirational, your talent is amazing and I thank you for loving my work.

Brenda... Thank you for being my anchor.

For those of you who have been a supporter, a promoter and a friend:

Michele Loranger—your dedication to the students and to my work is inspirational.

The book club at Confederation High School—Thank you guys for choosing "Awakenings". I truly appreciate your support!

Kristina Rivard-Gobbo—thank you for showing me that people over the age of 17 are interested in my work.

Corrine, Diane, Joann, Anna, Victor the CYAC and every other person within the Greater Sudbury Police Service who has support, endorsed and promoted my work...THANK YOU.

The teacher's, Vice Principals and Principals I have had the honor to work with over the last year—thank you for allowing me to share my story.

DROLET Distribution...Rob and Jerry and Kimmie Stewart...Thank you taking an unknown author and making her work available to... Walmart...and a number of more places from Sudbury - North, East, West and South! You guys ROCK.

Tania Renelli...Thank you for taking a chance on me.

Rick Bartolucci, Dawn Noel de Tilly—Your generosity and support has been unwavering.

Rita, Andrew, Rachel—Chapters Sudbury— Thank you for being supportive and encouraging!!

Chico, Melanie and Pete: Kingsports wear—your creativity and support is appreciated.

Stephen and Jennifer—Thank you for your support and 40 + year friendship.

Mom, Dad, Jen, Jason, Lise, Gerry, Liz, Carolyn, Dave, Leah...Love you...

ABOUT THE AUTHOR

Hally was born in Sudbury, Ontario Canada. She is a Police Officer with the Greater Sudbury Police Service. Hally enjoys reading both fiction and non-fiction novels. She is a self proclaimed, writer of all things imaginative (both poetry and novels). She also holds a strong belief in – If you put your mind to it, you can accomplish anything!

She met her forever partner Jerry, thirteen years ago. Together they accomplished the greatest feat anyone can—they were blessed with two gifts from God, their sons Jacob and Jordan.

Hally enjoys spending long summer nights by the camp fire with her husband and boys and cold winter nights snuggled up watching movies in their home.

In 2009, Hally had an idea to write a novel. The idea for Awakenings came to her in a dream and never left.

Between working full time, being a wife and mother, Hally finds the time to write when her kids go to bed, when Jerry's at work or when their new puppy Jersey decides to wake her up every morning around five a.m.

Facebook:
www.facebook.com/hally.willmott

Twitter:
https://twitter.com/HallynJerry

Website and Blog:
www.hallywillmott.com/

Goodreads:
www.goodreads.com/author/show/6982761.Hally
Willmott

Amazon Author Page:
www.amazon.com/Hally-Willmott/e/B00CI383Y2

CPSIA information can be obtained at www.ICGtesting.com
Printed in the USA
LVOW06s1259190814

399874LV00005B/313/P

9 781495 496028